Mending FENCES

LUCY FRANCIS

Mini Gray Moose Publishing

Mending Fences

Contact Information: kissybooks@yahoo.com

Cover Design by Lucy Francis
   Images from:
   © Deklofenak / Bigstock.com
   © Visceral Image / Bigstock.com
   © Mark Bonham / 123rf

ISBN-13: 978-0615603094
ISBN-10: 0615603092
Publishing History
First Edition, February 2012

Mini Gray Moose Publishing
South Jordan, UT

Published in the United States of America

Dedication

To my hero, John, for always encouraging my crazy dreams.

And to my beloved ladies of the Hive, without whom this book would never have been written.

Chapter One

Curran Shaw treasured his anonymity, but maintaining it required solitude. And the damned solitude was killing him.

Sanctuary presented itself on Halloween in the form of a massive party at a local club. The event promised fulfillment of his primary needs at the moment—a mass of humanity surrounding him, buoying him up, plus the nameless, faceless facade provided by costume-only admittance.

He arrived late, saving himself a long wait in line to enter Brindle's. He paid his cover charge in cash. No sense in flashing a card with his name emblazoned on the front. Notable names and faces appeared with some regularity in the Park City area, so staff members, such as the skinny young man cashiering tonight, generally said nothing when they recognized him. Still, being recognized at all bothered him. He'd grown accustomed to no longer seeing his name and photo in the tabloids, but there was always a chance some reporter's curiosity about his disappearing act would set the bloodhounds on his trail.

For tonight, a black, hooded cloak and a leather mask covering his face down to the tip of his nose rendered him unidentifiable.

He stepped through the main doors into the club. Pulsating flashes of color ripped through the dimly lit interior, reflecting off the polished walls and churning through the fog on the floor, cutting through the starlight cast from a mirrored disco ball spinning above the central dance arena. Whiffs of different perfumes, bubblegum from the fog machines, sweat from the bodies crowding the dance floor, and the spicy tang of the club's chicken wings all tangled together in his nostrils, the intensity of each shifting and changing with every step he took through the crowd. The deep, driving beat of music thrummed through the air, pounding against his bones when he crossed the corner of the dance floor. In the table sections, the clever design of speakers and sound walls kept the music controlled, soft enough to allow conversation, should a body be so inclined.

His eyes adjusted to the low lights as he made his way past throngs of vampires, monks, and witches. He edged into a narrow open spot at the black and chrome bar between a Star Trek yeoman and Doctor Who in a tweed jacket, bow tie, and red fez.

The bartender, painted with zombie-grey makeup and fake blood, passed a white wine spritzer to Marie Antoinette and turned to him. "What can I get you?"

Curran glanced over the menu board on the wall behind the bar. "You still stock that honeyed porter from the microbrewery up the street?"

"You bet. Coming right up."

He looked around while he waited for his beer, watching the flow and eddy of the crowd as it moved like water through the club. Brindle's was always busy, but bodies filled it to capacity tonight, for which he was grateful. He missed going out all the time, being surrounded by people. A crowd assimilated him, turning him into a simple cell in a greater entity. The energy generated among a mass of people, the electricity, made him feel alive in a way nothing else matched.

A woman dressed as Red Riding Hood laughed at the end of the bar with her date, the Big Bad Wolf. Yeah, that was another way to feel alive, one he dearly missed. But one didn't troll for women when one was living anonymously. Eleven months now he'd lacked female company, and what a hell of a price to pay for a private life.

The bartender slid his beer across the bar. Curran paid with a generous tip and stepped away from the bar to make room for an intrepid fellow decked out in full Dr. Frank-N-Furter regalia, right down to the fishnet stockings and deep red lipstick.

He raised his glass to the man. "Impressive, mate."

Dr. Frank laughed. "Thanks. My girlfriend bet me I wouldn't dare go out in public. She owes me a hundred bucks."

Curran grinned. Bringing *The Rocky Horror Picture Show* to life in an outfit like that took far more courage than he had. He'd settled for black, from cloak to boots. With the mask over his eyes, he wasn't a character. He wasn't himself. Just an enigma in the dark.

He leaned against a pillar supporting the upper floor of the club and sipped his beer, watching the mass of bodies writhing on the dance floor. He glanced to the left as the crowd near him shifted, and glimpsed a woman sitting alone at a small corner table. The glow from a jack-o-lantern on the table brightened her chin-length curls to a glossy medium brown, glinted off her long-sleeved black dress and the high spiderweb collar rising behind her head. Fine, pale fingers tipped with short, dark nails tapped a rhythm on the tabletop.

A mummy and Cleopatra shifted into his line of sight, so he stepped past them to get a better view of her. She wasn't wearing a mask. Sculpted cheekbones, a narrow, rather pointed nose. Very nice lips, not too full. Attractive, though not a stunning beauty. Tall, given the length of her frame in comparison with the chair. She held herself with a degree of elegance—reserved, almost distant from her surroundings, like royalty thrust into a throng of commoners.

She held the single glass on the table. Perhaps she was waiting for someone. Then again, maybe she was alone, too, fighting off the solitude before she lost her mind.

Her head turned and her gaze sheared directly into his. *Caught staring at the pretty girl, way to go, Shaw.* Narrowed eyes, rimmed with wide, heavy smudges of black, met his evenly. A flood of heat coursed through him, doubling his pulse, tightening his groin. He'd felt instant chemistry before, but never like this—powerful, demanding.

The warmth pulled at him. Where there was heat, there would be fire, and he'd been cold and alone for a long time. Hell, if she had some brains, simply talking to her for a while might be nice. He drained his beer, deposited the glass on the tray of a passing waitress, and headed across the floor. Her wary gaze followed his approach. When he reached her table, he grasped the curved silver back of the extra chair. "May I?"

"It's a free country." She shifted her gaze to the dance floor.

Hmm. Not a welcome, nor exactly a dismissal. Royalty didn't usually appreciate an invasion of personal space, but he was already here, standing at her table. There was no sense in going back. After such a strong initial reaction, the need to follow through compelled him.

He lowered himself into the chair. "Glad I'm not the only one who went for basic black."

She tensed and her eyes snapped back to his, glittering in the lantern light. Amber. She had wolf-eyes. A sense of familiarity tingled at the edge of his mind, weaving through the air between them. He'd seen those eyes before, somewhere.

The barest of smiles crossed her mouth. "When you make last minute decisions, it's difficult to be a character. Black works." Her low, smoky voice toyed with his senses. The tremor of recognition shivered through him again.

He nodded and chuckled softly. What a ridiculous way to start this, she was going to hate it. "I know this is the world's oldest line, but—have we met?"

Her eyes widened and she stared at him for a moment. "Does it matter?"

"No, I suppose not." If she did recognize him somehow, she obviously wasn't going to make a big deal out of it. The idea should make this whole thing a non-starter, but at the moment, she could be anyone other than his ex-girlfriend and he simply wouldn't care. Not with the heat flaring inside him at every glance of those golden brown eyes. What was it about this woman?

She turned her attention back to the dance floor. Her fingers tapped against the empty glass on the table. "You're dry. Can I buy you a drink?" He winced. Damn, that was lame. Surely he hadn't lost all his charisma and social skills in less than a year.

Amber eyes met his and narrowed. The Queen was not amused. "Yes to the drink. No to anything else."

"I wasn't aware I suggested anything else, but I'll take that under advisement." He smiled, searching her hard gaze for fire, or at least humor.

Nothing. Seriously, what the hell? He couldn't remember his approach ever being so flawed. Women he found interesting always responded in kind. That was simply his reality. Now he fumbled the way he had as a scrawny kid of fourteen, trying to ask Sara Myles out for his first date.

He raised a hand to get the waitress's attention. The Queen arched one delicate brow at him before looking away, accepting the refill of sparkling water with two lemon slices from the perky little waitress with 'Miranda' etched on her name tag.

The Queen sipped her drink, then raised her glass in his direction and said, "Nothing for you?"

"Two is my limit when I'm driving, and I had one at the bar already."

"Wise."

"Not really. Wisdom calls for something along the lines of water."

She smiled. Just a partial victory, though. The smile softened her sharp features, but failed to light her eyes. Tension shimmered around her, visible in the way she sat with her back straight and her free hand closed into a fist on the table. She was trying very hard to appear relaxed. He obviously made her nervous. Maybe it was time to chalk this one up to a lost cause. "I apologize. I've intruded on you and I think it's probably time for me to rack off and leave you be."

Her gaze locked onto his and he felt the weight of her full attention for a moment, sending a tendril of heat through him. With a sigh, the tension unwound a bit, and she shook her head. "No, you're fine. I'm just...I haven't done this get-to-know-someone thing in a while."

Hmm. A little encouragement. He leaned forward, crossing his arms on the table. "I'm out of practice myself. Let's see, what's the next line I should try...ah, yes. Do you come here often?"

That got her. She gave a genuine laugh, the rich sound tossing tinder on the flame her gaze had lit inside him. "Occasionally. And you?"

"About that often." Perhaps that's why she seemed familiar. He might have caught sight of her at the club before.

She sipped her drink. "Tell me, do they celebrate Halloween in Australia?"

He jerked back a bit and blinked. After all this time in the States, his accent had mellowed enough that people who noticed it rarely identified it properly. "You have a good ear. But I might be faking the accent. This is a night to pretend, isn't it?"

She brushed her fingers across her forehead, shifting her curls away from her eyes. "Someone pretending would lay it on a whole lot thicker. How long have you lived here?"

"A very long time." The wistfulness in his own voice surprised him.

She laughed softly. "Well, well, a homesick expatriate."

He smiled. Time to turn the conversation around to her. "What about you? Are you from Park City?"

Her expression darkened slightly, an edge of wariness returning to her eyes. "No, just came into town for the party."

"Alone?"

Her brow rose as she leaned back in her chair. "Do I live alone or did I come to the party alone?"

"Yes."

"Both. You?"

With a bit of a chuckle, he nodded. "Both. Are you happy being alone?"

Her eyes narrowed, but a hint of a smile played across her lips. "Is that a pickup line?"

For a moment, he focused on her red-stained lips, on what they might feel like under his. That little contemplation simmered his blood. He flicked his gaze back up to meet hers. It wasn't intended as a pickup line, but maybe it should be. Or not. He hadn't thought this through, he was just pushing ahead full-throttle. "No, it's a legitimate question."

"Living alone has its advantages." She raised her glass and took a long drink. "I can make my own rules. It's quiet or noisy, depending solely on my mood."

Curran nodded. "You don't have to dress if you don't want to. You can eat chili straight out of the can and no one will complain."

She grimaced, wrinkling her distinctive nose. "Chili from the can, at room temperature? Gross. That's such a *guy* thing."

He couldn't help laughing. "Yeah, comes pre-loaded on the Y chromosome, along with belching and scratching ourselves. The same way a love of shopping and shoes is hard-wired into women."

Her eyes widened, but her grin spoiled the look of indignation. "I do not live to shop, thank you."

"How many pairs of shoes are in your closet?"

"I only have what I need."

He leaned a little closer to her. "How many?"

"I don't know…the basics. Pumps in black, navy, neutral, ivory. Running shoes. Flats in brown, black and…" She stopped ticking them off on her fingers and laughed. "Okay, okay. Let me guess, in your closet, you have running shoes and dress shoes."

"Actually, I'm a little more in touch with my feminine side than most. I've a couple pairs of boots, too. And a great pair of fuzzy slippers."

A laugh bubbled out of her, pulling a grin onto his mouth. God, her laugh…talking to this woman lightened his heart and stirred his desire at the same time. He liked it. "What about the disadvantages of living alone?"

Her smile faded. "I find they're a small price to pay for being able to be myself."

"And you can't be yourself without being alone?"

She finished her water. "Not in my experience."

The edge in her voice snagged his curiosity. It sounded like a conclusion she'd come to at some great cost, but he doubted she'd appreciate him probing for details.

The urge to touch her struck him, making his skin itch. He brushed his gloved fingers along the knuckles of her hand where she held her empty glass. Her eyes darkened and he caught the slight tremor that shivered through her. So, the chemistry wasn't one-sided. She felt it.

It had been nearly a year since he walked away from his life. Was that long enough to give him the obscurity he needed to take a chance on this? To pursue the connection pulling him to this woman whose name he didn't even know?

He lifted her hand from the glass and caressed her long, pale fingers. The sound of her breath catching kicked the slow burn in his gut up a notch. Oh, yeah, she definitely felt it, too. "Do you ever get lonely?"

Her gaze left their joined hands and slid into his. "Do you?"

He swallowed hard, his mouth suddenly dry. "Frequently."

She leaned a bit closer, enough for her scent to drift toward him. He breathed her in. Flowery, sweet, with a hint of something deeper, more exotic.

"And how do you deal with your loneliness?" Her smoky voice reached inside him, fed the fire until the sparks soared.

"I find a crowd and become a part of it for a while, until the worst of it passes."

"Funny," she said softly. "I do that, too."

Curran raised his hand, lifting her fingers to his mouth. He watched the fire dance in her golden eyes, his own temperature climbing in response. He held her gaze and turned her hand, exposing her wrist, pressing his lips to her delicate skin.

Her scent clawed through him, reshaping the heat in his body into a distinct ache.

Her pulse leapt beneath his lips and lightning flashed in her eyes. She drew a sharp breath, then slid her hand from his and said, "You're moving fast. I take it we've gone beyond the need for lines?"

Curran couldn't contain the wicked grin that spread across his face. "They get progressively more pathetic from here, and you've likely heard them all before anyway."

"Probably."

"I suppose I could cut to the chase and ask if you have plans for the evening. Want to get out of here?" He tensed the moment the words tumbled from his mouth. He hadn't intended to take their conversation quite that far, but his desire raced ahead of his brain.

Her brows lifted and she laughed. "You get points for being direct. Has anyone ever turned you down?"

Now there was a question he'd never been asked. "Truthfully? Not since I was sixteen."

"Really. Never once, in all that time?" The Queen pushed her chair away from the table. She rose, stepped toward him as he slid his own chair back. She fisted her pale hands in the black satin of her long dress and pulled, hiking the fringed hem up to mid-glorious-thigh, exposing a hint of black lace at the top of her stockings. Without warning, she straddled him, lowering herself onto his lap.

Curran sucked in a harsh breath, his erection instant. She reached her hands into his hood. Grabbed his hair. Covered his mouth with hers.

Rational thought scattered.

She kissed him hard, her tongue thrusting into his mouth, brushing his in a tantalizing stroke. She tasted sweet and sharp. Her scent, her warmth filled his senses. Something deep inside him knotted and a groan escaped him as he slid his hands along her thighs. The whole of his existence focused on the primal need to thrust inside her.

Before he could return the kiss, or even properly respond to it, she dropped her hands to his chest and pushed herself back off his lap.

"Thanks for the drink," She straightened to her full height and smoothed the reflective surface of her dress. A hint of a smile curved the edges of her mouth. "But I turn into a pumpkin at midnight."

Curran's head swam. His skin tingled all over, his blood surged in his veins. What in the hell had she done to him? Never had a woman kissed him in a way that completely short-circuited his brain.

It took a moment before the synapses fired correctly again, and in those few seconds, she had vanished. He leapt to his feet, scanning the club for her.

She was gone.

"No, no, no," he muttered, cursing under his breath. "Not fair."

The waitress came by, gathering glasses and bottles off the neighboring table, then leaned close to talk to him. "I don't know what you said to Victoria to get a kiss like that out of her, but you've made a lot of guys here very jealous."

His spine stiffened. "You know who she is?"

"Just her first name." Miranda threw him a smile and walked away.

He turned the name in his mind. Victoria. Perfect. He'd been thinking of her as a queen already. Elegant name for a cool exterior, belying the heat of her kiss. He made his way back to the bar and downed a second beer in an effort to kill the fire inside him.

It failed. Miserably.

Half an hour later, Curran unlocked his front door. He trudged down the hall into the master suite, flicking on the lights, stripping his clothes as he went. So much for a night of fun on the town, finding rejuvenation in a crowd. God, he needed a cigarette. He'd picked the wrong time to try quitting.

He stepped into the rock-walled shower, turned the faucet to cold, and let it rip. The icy water pounded against his skin, taking his breath away, but it did little to temper the blaze she'd kindled.

Victoria. He still felt her hands in his hair, her tongue in his mouth. Her taste, her scent, those unique eyes stayed sharp, penetrated deep into his thoughts and hardened him all over again.

Curran mentally kicked himself. How had he let this happen? He'd gone and let his hormones come out of dormancy, reminding him precisely how much of a bitch celibacy could be. It was far too easy to picture Victoria beneath him, her creamy skin soft under his fingers, her long legs wrapped around his hips.

He swore. The carnal need was bad enough on its own. To make matters worse, this wasn't just sexual. She'd piqued his interest, and her disappearing act would nag him relentlessly. This wasn't how it worked, damn it. He should have the opportunity to decide if she was worth investing his time before he then chose to walk away or stay.

He'd be damned if he'd end up looking back on Victoria as the proverbial one who got away. Finding her would severely test his resourcefulness. Her first name gave him next to nothing to go on, but he would find her, somehow, to finish what she'd started the moment her lips touched his.

* * * *

She knew he wouldn't follow her. He was her fantasy, not the other way around. Still, Victoria Linden didn't wait around Brindle's to find out.

She drove carefully out of Park City, heading west down the interstate to the Salt Lake valley, focusing hard on the road before her and trying to keep herself from mentally replaying the evening. To keep herself from going back to him.

When she finally turned the beat-up SUV off in her parking spot, she ran her hands through her hair and slumped in the seat. The adrenaline overload had ebbed, leaving her drained.

That was probably—no, it was absolutely, hands down—the brashest, most ballsy thing she'd ever done in her life.

She'd kissed Curran Shaw. Curran multi-millionaire, owner-of-a-huge-corporation, dated-every-supermodel/starlet Shaw. What a rush!

His voice had given him away tonight, the sonorous tones and Down Under inflections revealing his identity under the black hood and half-mask. She'd always liked hearing him speak, liked the way the natural rumble in his voice vibrated in her chest.

She locked the car and hurried up the stairs to her apartment door, shivering in the cold. He hadn't recognized her, of course. She'd attended a couple of his press conferences, and interviewed him—along with over a hundred other journalists—at a massive press junket four years ago, on a freelance assignment from Business Wired magazine. In his memory, she'd be a blonde with wire-rimmed glasses, probably blurred together with all the other interviewers who spoke with him that weekend. If he remembered much from that weekend at all, given the partying that had reportedly gone on.

Inside the apartment, she threw the deadbolt, dropping her purse and coat on the chair near the door. She glanced at Sassy's cage and maze, covering a table along the far wall. The rat scampered through a tunnel and into the feeding area, climbing in and out of her empty food dish. Victoria kicked off her shoes. "I know, Sassafras, hold your horses."

Moving the rat's home next month would be a pain. She'd have to tape numbers to each section in order to put the tunnels back together in the new apartment. Assuming, of course, that she could find a new apartment. She barely afforded this little hole in the wall, and soon her building would be torn down and rebuilt as luxury condos.

She grabbed a handful of kibble and opened the wire roof of the cage, pouring the food into Sassy's dish. The rat turned happy circles, paused to wash her cream and white pinto face, and pounced on the food. "Relax, it's not like you haven't eaten today."

Victoria stripped out of the costume, grabbed a carton of chocolate-cherry ice cream and a spoon, then sat cross-legged on the rug beside Sassy's cage. She couldn't begin to guess how much money an interview with Curran Shaw would bring now, nearly a year after his sudden retirement. He'd dropped off the face of the planet after stepping down as CEO of DCS GlobalTech. Simply disappeared from the public eye.

She looked over and found Sassy staring at her intently. "Are you done eating already?"

Sassy blinked at her and pawed at the clear acrylic cage wall.

"Fine, I'll let you out." She reached into the cage and picked up the pudgy rat, setting Sassy on her shoulder. "So, Miss Sass, what on earth is he doing in Utah?"

Sassy tugged on a lock of her hair and squeaked. "Go easy on the hair, girl. I wonder if he's shopping for a ski condo or something."

Victoria briefly reconsidered returning to Brindle's. If she could somehow convince him to give her an interview…no, wait, back up. He wouldn't give her the time of day if he knew she was a freelance writer. He'd barely masked his dislike of the press when he led a highly visible life. After his vanishing act, he'd like a journalist even less now.

Oh, well. Going back wasn't an option anyway. She'd spent every ounce of courage she had when she kissed him. She had to, though. It wasn't every day a man like that paid attention to a woman like her. And small wonder he managed to keep a succession of starlets and hot young things on his arm. It definitely wasn't just his bank account they liked. Even catching him off-guard, that was one of the better kisses she'd ever had.

She shook her head, nearly dislodging Sassy from her shoulder as she tried to clear the memory of his heat, his taste, from her mind. No sense in reliving something that wouldn't, couldn't, and shouldn't ever happen again. He'd shown an interest in her, and that alone made him off limits. She shivered, a thread of cold winnowing through the lingering heat of that brazen kiss. No, a safe little fantasy moment was all she could handle, and even that pushed the envelope.

Victoria stood and adjusted the rat on her shoulder, then returned the remaining ice cream to the freezer as her cell rang. She glanced at the display. What was Mara calling for at this time of night?

She answered the call. "Hi, cuz, you're up late."

Her cousin snorted. "God, you're getting old. It's *so* not late yet. Sorry, should have called about this earlier, but I just remembered. Stepmom Number Three had dinner guests tonight, the Campbells. Anyway, they're heading out before winter kicks in and their usual house-sitter moved to Ohio. And with you needing to move and stuff, I recommended you!"

All thoughts of Curran Shaw vanished as she gave Mara's voice her complete attention. "Wait, what? They need a house-sitter? For how long?"

"All winter, I think. They don't do snow anymore, so they're leaving on Thanksgiving-ish. I don't know, I was in a hurry to get to the party, so I don't have details, but I'm texting you the number. You have to call them tomorrow or they'll look for someone else."

Mara's text hit her phone as her cousin said goodbye. The girl could be such a flake, but she might owe Mara big time after this.

She cuddled Sassy like a baby in the crook of her arm. Even if the pay for the house-sitting was minimal, with free housing she could make huge strides on paying off the student loans that still sucked the life out of her budget after all this time. And she'd have even more time to hunt for a decent apartment.

Sassy nibbled at her finger and she smiled at her pet. "Don't worry, pretty girl, I won't take the job if they have an aversion to rats. Or, if there are cats in the house." Who was she kidding? She'd take it anyway and just make sure Sassy was well-guarded from kitty claws.

She needed this so badly and any way she looked at it, she couldn't see a downside. This would change everything for the better, she was certain. She felt it in her bones.

Chapter Two

The third day of January dawned bright and clear, with a gorgeous blue sky and a foot of fresh powder transforming the landscape into a classic winter wonderland. The scenery beckoned to Victoria, begging her to come out for a ride in the frosty New Year air. How could she resist such a delightful invitation from Mother Nature?

She slipped the bit into the big bay gelding's mouth and eased the crownpiece over the horse's ears. She pulled on her gloves and lifted the hood of the parka over her head. Sliding a pair of sunglasses on, she led Old Joe out of the stable and into the perfect morning.

Sunlight glittered on the snow like diamonds strewn by last night's storm, coating the surrounding mountainsides and dressing the bare aspen branches in a sparkling blanket. The crisp air tingled in her lungs. She gathered the reins and swung up into the saddle, nudging the bay into a gentle walk across the snowy meadow and onto the trail that meandered through the sparsely populated canyon.

She intended to squeeze every last moment of relaxation out of this day off, or at least the few hours she would likely allow herself to play before her inner taskmaster cracked the whip. Because she really should be writing. She'd made deadline last night on a set of articles for a pets website and she didn't need to start developing help screen text for her software developer client for a couple of days.

Precious days when she should work on her own novel. It had been going so well, words pouring out of her over the last few weeks whenever she had a spare moment for her own work. But she'd slammed into writer's block and now the novel refused to cooperate. Today she'd slept in until after ten, and when she woke up the snow was there, calling to her. Resistance was futile at that point.

She patted Old Joe's neck as he walked along, solid and sure beneath her. Winter birds twittered in the trees and she settled into the saddle, comforted by the rhythmic shushing of the snow as the horse's legs made a trail through the powder.

Another sound caught her attention—snorting and a weak cry, coming from somewhere beyond the slight ridge ahead.

Victoria reined in. The sounds continued. An animal, she was certain, but nothing she recognized. She urged the horse forward and laid the reins against his neck, bringing him to the right. She circled around a thick stand of huge blue spruce trees, up the ridge and across a broad meadow. There, in the middle of a snow drift, was the source of the noise.

It had to be a bison. It was far too big and shaggy to be a cow. The animal shifted a bit. Yes, definitely a bison, the heavy head slung low on a huge humped neck. The bison shook its head and snorted again, then let out a strange bawling sound and lurched forward. When the animal didn't actually move more than a few inches, she recognized the problem. The bison was entangled in a barbed wire fence.

Victoria dug her heels into the big bay, encouraging him into a faster pace through the deeper snow. Near the fence line, Old Joe shied away from the bison. That's all she needed, a spooked horse bolting back to the barn. She slid from the saddle, led Old Joe behind a couple of pines and tied his reins to a low branch. If he couldn't see the bison, maybe he wouldn't get nervous.

Slowly, she pushed through the knee-deep snow until she reached the huge animal. The snow was trampled in a wide swath around the bison. The heavy, earthy smell of damp animal hair reached her nostrils, and steam curling up from the sweat soaking its sides. How long had it struggled? "Hey, big guy," she said softly. "I'm not going to hurt you. I just need to see how badly you're tangled up."

A warning surfaced in her head, one she'd heard as a child in Yellowstone: avoid the bison. Wild bison could prove truly dangerous, but the only wild herd she knew of in Utah lived on Antelope Island in the Great Salt Lake. Several ranchers in the state raised bison, though. This one had to be a domestic animal. Most of the ranchers she knew spoke to their animals, so what could it hurt? Maybe the sound of her voice would calm the poor thing down before it hurt itself worse.

"Easy now, Shaggy." She hesitated a moment, the sheer size of the wild-eyed animal giving her pause. She continued murmuring to the bison. It seemed to settle a bit and focus on her. Seizing a wisp of bravery floating inside her, she rubbed her gloved hand on the bison's head, and it bawled, sending her jumping back a few feet.

It heaved a shuddering breath, too tired to fight any longer. She relaxed slightly, sidling closer to it as she looked down the fence line. The snow, probably driven by the storm last night, had drifted over the wire and concealed it. "Poor thing, I'll bet it just looked like a new hill for you to climb, didn't it?"

The bison's weight had broken one fence post and it hung in the air, suspended by a wire knotted in the wooly hair around the bison's neck. The other two wires had snapped off the post and were hopelessly tangled across its chest and around its forelegs.

Old Joe whinnied a greeting a second after she heard another horse entering the meadow. She looked up to see a man riding a leopard-spotted Appaloosa. He pulled up at the east edge of the meadow, lifted a hand in greeting to her, and dismounted. He closed the remaining distance on foot.

Something about his frame, the way he carried himself, seemed familiar. Even with his pulled-down Stetson and the turned-up collar of his sheepskin coat obscuring most of his face, the sense of recognition tugged at her. But who would she possibly know out here?

As he strode closer, the bison tugged against the wires, and stepped sideways, blocking the man from view behind its hulking body. She heard him on the other side of the animal, seeing only the top of his hat and his gloved hand as he stroked the huge back.

"Don't worry, Peg-leg. I'll have you loose in a jiff."

The words were spoken softly, but the deep resonant voice carried through the thin, cold mountain air without effort. In the sound of his voice, she found the answer.

Curran Shaw.

Memories of Halloween bubbled to the surface, bursting into a flare of heat in her stomach. She pushed away thoughts of her mouth on his, allowing the curious journalist in her to take over. She'd thought he was visiting in town when he'd approached her at Brindle's. He was obviously living here. Why?

Her train of thought derailed when he leaned around the bison's shoulder and gave her a slight smile. "He really did a number on the fence."

Photographs never quite caught the tiny gold flecks in his green eyes. Then again, in still shots, he was merely average-looking. Even video didn't do justice to the innate power, control, and charisma he naturally exuded. In person, he weakened her knees.

Everyone she'd interviewed for the magazine article had described him with the same words. Powerful. Charming. Focused. Brilliant. Captivating. All those characteristics emanated from him in an almost tangible aura, as if his soul were too large to be contained within the frame of his body.

Dear God, what *had* she been thinking when she kissed him?

He showing her the tool he held. "I don't suppose you have wire cutters on hand? A second pair would help."

She found her voice. "I don't normally ride with a pair."

"With fences like these around, you should. But I reckon another set of hands will do. Help me keep Peg-leg calm. I'll cut on this side, you cut on the other, and we'll get him untangled." He didn't ask. He didn't wait for her response. He just gave the order in his low voice and expected her to do her part.

Victoria suppressed a shiver, her concern and desire to help the bison warring with her growing need to beat a hasty retreat back to the house. If she'd known he was living in the area, she'd have brushed him off at the club and left immediately. Instead, she had kissed him.

Rubbing her gloved palm on Peg-leg's forehead, she watched Curran carefully cut the wires holding the bison's legs. What a stupid thing to do, kissing him. She couldn't even chalk it up to impulse. No, she'd kissed him very much on purpose, because it thrilled her to have a man of his stature find her attractive enough to try picking her up.

She'd figured she could lay one good hot kiss on him and vanish before he had a chance to take control of the situation.

Suddenly, it dawned on her how awkward he might have felt afterward. She'd put on such a show in the midst of a crowd. He probably hadn't appreciated that.

"Here, take this piece when I cut through it," he said.

She eased the barbed metal away from the bison's leg, careful not to tug or tighten the wire and cause more damage. Curran searched for another good place to snip. Her stomach quivered. If he recognized her, if he remembered Halloween night, heaven only knew what he might do.

"Your turn," he said, handing the cutters to her, then pointing. "Cut through right there, where the wire is a bit loose."

"Okay." She worked carefully, and just as carefully avoided his gaze. Walking away after kissing him was one of the more difficult things she'd ever done, but she knew better than to risk involvement with a man like him. All her research told her Curran Shaw was accustomed to getting what he wanted, no matter how much pressure he had to apply to get it. He lived large, in a world she very much didn't belong in.

"Damn, Peg, if you weren't such a nosy thing, you wouldn't be in this mess. Always wondering if the grass is greener on the other side." Curran held his hand out for the cutters when she finished snapping the blades through another twisted section of wire.

"Or the snow whiter, in this case." She examined the cuts and scrapes on the bison's right foreleg as he cut wire away from the left leg. The animal was bleeding in places, but only a few of the wounds looked deep. "Do you ranch bison?"

"Nah, he's my one and only. He was going to be put down, but I convinced his owner to hand him over to me instead. He's friendly enough, just physically pathetic." He patted the leg he was working to free. "This leg here is about an inch shorter than the right one, and his right hind leg is turned inward some. He's an ugly bastard, but he has a good nature."

Victoria grabbed the cut sections of wire and pulled them back, away from the bison. She ducked under the remaining wire, then worked her fingers along it, trying to feel whether the barbs were tangled in wool or flesh. She glanced at Curran through her sunglasses. He stood up on the other side of Peg-leg's head, tossing the final piece of wire from the bison's leg onto the pile she'd made.

"Almost done, mate," he said. He cut the wire stretching across the bison's neck.

Peg-leg jumped backwards, and Victoria found herself face down in the snow. The bison bawled and Curran cursed a blue streak as she was pulled by the arm and dragged deeper into the snow. Suddenly, the pulling stopped and she heard the lumbering footfalls and snorting of the bison as Peg-leg walked away. She put her hands in front of her and pushed herself out of the snow, but she could only get to a sitting position. She looked down her arm at the hole in her sleeve, from which barbed wire protruded.

"Peg felt the tension go when I cut that wire and he bolted," Curran said, sinking into the snow beside her. "Your parka's torn to hell back here. Did the barbs cut you?"

"I don't hurt anywhere, so I'd say no. I'm freezing, though. Nothing like a face full of snow." Victoria wiped the snow from her cheek and neck with one hand while he pulled the barbed wire free of her sleeve. Great, a ripped coat. Just what she needed. At least it was January. She should be able to find an affordable one at a clearance sale somewhere.

Curran worked a barb loose from the fake fur edging her parka hood. He tugged, and the hood slipped back onto her shoulders.

The air between them stretched taut as a fence wire. His gloved fingers snagged one of her curls. His other hand grasped her sunglasses, sliding them off her face. His hard gaze caught hers, the recognition in his eyes freezing the blood in her veins.

"Victoria."

Her heart skipped a beat, then began to pound. "How did you know my name?"

"The waitress at Brindle's suggested I give other men lessons on how to get you to kiss them."

Heat rose in her cheeks. "Oh, yes. The club." The dark, penetrating look in his eyes held her captive, unable to look away.

Panic rolled over her like a backcountry avalanche—totally unexpected and overwhelming.

A whinny from Old Joe provided an escape. "I—I'd better go. My horse is getting up there in years and he's been standing in the snow a little too long. I need to get him back to the stable, and you'll want to go treat Peg-leg's wounds."

She scrambled to her feet and turned toward her horse, but Curran stood up as fast as she did, his fingers closing around her right arm. She swallowed hard, her knees shaking. She'd set a standard for herself with that kiss she couldn't possibly live up to. What would he do now? Nate hadn't been quite so physically powerful, and he'd still been more than she could handle.

She reached deep into herself, pulled out her inner cast-iron-bitch and slid into it. Squaring her shoulders, she met his hard eyes with her best attempt at an equally steely gaze. "Let go."

He took a step closer. She clenched her fingers into fists to keep from shivering when he focused on her mouth. "If I release you, will you promise not to disappear?" His voice was deceptively gentle.

Her palms felt damp inside her gloves. He was bigger than she was, broader, a few inches taller. How fast could she untie Old Joe's reins and mount up if she had to make a break for it? She willed her voice to be steady, strong. "It's time for me to leave."

His green eyes shifted to capture hers again, his gaze revealing nothing. "You started something I'd rather like to finish, Victoria, now that this little bit of serendipity has brought you back to my world." His voice caressed her, sending a spark, bright and hot, trickling through her.

She'd expected something vulgar, blatantly suggestive. She fumbled for her next move, then took a step back, wrenching free of his grip. "You want to finish what I started? Look, I know I left you with a particular impression of me, but I'm not the casual hookup type."

Curran's eyes narrowed and for a moment she felt like he was looking straight into her soul. He stepped toward her again, but made no move to touch her. "Relax, Victoria. My memory of you has fed a number of fantasies over the last couple of months, to be sure, but I don't have sex with strangers." His voice dropped to a quiet, sultry level. "I appreciate your help untangling Peg, but that didn't count as time spent getting to know you."

She sucked in a breath, surprised at the hopeful part of herself shouting *Yes!* Hadn't she learned anything? She couldn't handle someone like him. "I really don't think that's a good idea, Mister—"

"Shaw. Curran Shaw." He raised a hand, and she held her ground as the soft leather of his glove stroked along her cheek. "So, regardless of obvious positive chemistry, you're resistant to getting acquainted. I'm guessing there's bad past relationship baggage?"

Oh, he was good. The touch, the gentleness in his voice, slowly reeling her in. She tensed again. "You could say that."

"You're not the only one." His intense eyes held her gaze.

She tingled inside, her heart pounded. She wanted to turn away, to run, but at the same time, staying right where she was felt so good. No. Bad, very bad. "I'm not looking for anything that would complicate my life."

He laughed, a rumble that warmed her in the chill air. "Neither am I. In fact, I'm absolutely certain this is foolish, but I'm lonely, and you intrigue me." He smiled, crinkling slight lines beside his eyes. He focused on her lips for a moment, his attention sending alternating currents of fear and yearning through her. "Come on, let's make sure Peg-leg got to the barn. I called the vet when I went back for wire cutters, so he should be there to treat him."

Her thoughts snagged on his words. "Hold on a sec, when you went back for wire cutters? What happened to riding with a pair? Because, and I quote, 'with fences like these around, you should.'"

He shrugged and gave her a charming grin. "We both learned something today. Come with me. I'll put on tea and we can talk."

"What about my horse?" Her voice sounded strange in her ears, small and wavering. She sensed the proverbial ice thinning under her with every passing moment.

"Bring him. There are extra stalls in the stable. After talking for a little while, we may decide this isn't worth pursuing and you simply ride away. If we enjoy each other's company, and it gets too late to ride, I'll load him in the trailer and take you both home." Curran took her hand, raising her gloved fingers to his lips, the gold flecks in his eyes glowing in the sunlight reflecting off the snow. "I want to get to know you, Victoria."

She knew his reputation, and he occasionally unleashed a nasty temper. He'd had a volatile breakup with his last starlet girlfriend, but no one ever said he was physically violent.

Oh, yeah, right. Like she'd really have to think about how he'd treat her in a relationship. Men like Curran Shaw didn't have anything beyond maybe a one night fling with women so far beneath their social strata. Besides, if he did by some strange miracle find her interesting enough to date, a few hours with her screwed up psyche and he'd beat a hasty retreat.

Still, he was offering to talk to her. Maybe she could discover the answers to her questions about him. If she could somehow swing this meeting into a formal interview and article, wow, what a serious career boost. She stepped off the edge of the precipice in her head. "All right."

* * * *

They found Peg-leg hobbled in a corral beside the barn, his eyes half closed under the gentle ministrations of the veterinarian. Victoria led Old Joe into a stall and made him comfortable, then waited beside the corral while Curran conferred with the vet.

A wind kicked up, chilling her through the torn parka. She shivered and wrapped her arms tight across her stomach, distracting herself by looking around his property. The corral and barn stood a hundred feet or so from a white brick single-story ranch house. A big red pickup truck sat in the drive, the ever popular snow blade attached to the front. The plowed driveway curved away from the house, beyond the barn, past a similar looking house a couple of acres away. His property looked to be the last one in the exclusive canyon, the mountains finally connecting a quarter-mile beyond his home.

Curran joined her and motioned toward the house. "Time for something hot to drink."

"Is Peg-leg okay?"

"Got himself fairly skinned. There are some awful cuts, but he didn't tear into anything too deeply. Barring an infection, he'll be fine."

When they reached the house and he ushered her through the door, the interior surprised her. She'd expected something horribly Western male, with decorating done in leather and antlers and Indian blankets, or worse, the artsy-cool, look-how-much-money-I-spent method of decorating she'd seen in too many TV specials on homes of the rich and famous. Instead, she found beautiful cherry furniture, an elegant Chinese carpet over polished hardwood floors, landscape paintings adorning the walls and a slight scent of pine hanging in the air. The décor made her cautiously revise some of her assumptions about Curran.

Since he wanted to talk, she decided to soothe her writer's curiosity first. "So, what do you ranch? You have a nice chunk of real estate out there."

He shrugged. "It's not that big. Three hundred acres. I don't really ranch per se. I just play around with the land. I've a few horses. A flock of ducks are rather fond of the pond west of the house, and I must have mice in the barn because a red-tailed hawk likes to hang around. I've had deer all over, and moose in the upper pasture lately. And you're acquainted with Peg-leg." He waved a hand at the cream damask sofa. "Have a seat. I'll get us something to drink."

Victoria shed her torn parka and grimaced at the huge tear across the back and down the arm. Yeah, she'd definitely need to buy a new one.

Too nervous to sit, she dropped the parka on the sofa and nosed around the room. Between paintings, shelves lined the walls, crammed with history books, biographies, atlases, and novels from Tolstoy to Tolkien, from Homer to Crichton. With this many books, he had to be a voracious reader. Major points for him.

She skimmed over the titles, until one she loved caught her eye. "You like *A Christmas Carol*?" she called to him, caressing the frayed edges of the cloth cover and the well-worn pages.

Curran's voice reached her from the next room, the slight rumble in his voice carrying his words to her without an increase in volume. "We all need redemption, right? That story renews hope for mine."

He leaned through the doorway and raised a hand, beckoning her. "Come in here. I'm making Death by Hot Chocolate, heavy on the vanilla and cream."

Chocolate was such a girl thing—she'd yet to meet a man who could create a prime cup. Where had he learned? "Sounds positively sinful."

He grinned. "Calorie-laden, and proud of it." His eyes darkened, and he flicked his gaze over her. Awareness of his perusal made her skin tingle inside the snug black ski pants and white turtleneck sweater she'd hastily pulled on this morning. "Speaking of calories, you have a great body, but please tell me you're not one of those women who diets every minute of their lives."

Now there was a nice line. "No way. I love food." She just didn't make enough money to spend on restaurants, or stock up on her beloved junk food, but she certainly wasn't going to mention that.

Victoria followed him into the bright, open kitchen. Lovely hickory cabinets, butcher block countertops, a big window over the sink. The kitchen opened into an entertainment area, with a huge flat panel TV on the wall, a stereo system that probably cost more than she spent in rent each year, racks full of movies and music, and a comfy looking blue leather sectional couch and recliner. Formal for the front room, decidedly informal in the back. Not bad. She liked his style.

"I'm glad you believe in food," Curran said, crossing to the stove. "I like a woman who's willing to eat and not throw it back up again."

She pulled out a chair at a sturdy wood table. "Ugh. Had a lot of that in your life?"

"You have no idea." He turned his attention to the pot on the stove.

She'd seen the list of models and actresses he'd dated. She had a pretty good idea. He probably had a better understanding of eating disorders and fad diets than any other man on the planet.

Curran came to the table with two tall mugs, each topped with a dollop of rapidly melting whipped cream and a dusting of cocoa powder, and set one before her. He sat across the table corner from her, turning his chair out slightly to face her. He waited while she tried hers.

Thick, perfectly hot, devastatingly rich chocolate caressed her tongue and melted her from the inside. "Oh, this is absolutely decadent."

He nodded. "Mum's recipe. Cheers." He clinked his mug to hers, then sipped. "Tell me about yourself, Victoria. A surname might be a good place to start."

"Linden."

"Middle name."

"Ashley."

"Age." Curran's smile turned wicked. "I know a gentleman isn't supposed to ask but it's on the table now."

She shrugged. "I'm not sensitive. I turned thirty last July."

"Infant. I'm thirty-six." He leaned back in his chair, drank deeply. "Family."

"Not my favorite subject."

His eyebrows raised. "You don't get along with your family?"

Not since they reacted to her fight for her life by saying *we told you so, you're such a disgrace.* "My parents and I had a falling out a couple of years ago."

He winced. "My sympathies. Do you ever see them?"

She shook her head. "They moved to Texas a while back."

"Any siblings?"

"Only child. Apparently, I was such a delight to raise, they decided against ever doing it again." She gave him a half-hearted smile. "I have a cousin I like, but, yeah, I told you it was a negative subject. Move on."

He tilted his mug back and finished his chocolate. Her stomach flip-flopped when he licked the residue from his upper lip. She could have done that for him. Really.

"Where were you born?"

"In Salt Lake."

He nodded. "All right. Family and some of the vital statistics are out of the way. What's your profession?"

Oh, dear. If she said freelance journalist, she was dead in the water. She didn't want to lie, so maybe she could downplay it. "I've done a lot of things. At the moment, I'm a professional house-sitter. It keeps me from starving while I write."

Curran raised an eyebrow. "Interesting. What are you writing at the moment?"

Time to divert the conversation. "No, you see, at the moment I'm supposed to be writing, but instead I'm killing time sucking down incredible hot chocolate and playing the Getting to Know You version of twenty questions."

She smiled at him, allowing herself to enjoy the sparkle in his eyes. The attention felt good.

The diversion didn't last long. Curran shifted toward her, his eyes narrowed slightly. "Seriously. What sort of writer are you?"

The ice beneath her feet thinned and cracked a bit more. For a man who'd been out of the media spotlight for what, over a year, he was still plenty skittish. She'd have to tread lightly. As casually as she could, she said, "Right now, I have clients hiring me for website copy, ghostwriting, that sort of thing. And I'm trying my hand at a novel, but it's intimidating me beyond belief."

"What's it about?" He sounded genuinely interested, and slightly relieved.

"It's kind of a quirky love story, about a man and woman who keep meeting at various stages of their lives but each time is a near miss for them getting together." She heard the enthusiasm in her voice, a little embarrassed about how gung-ho she sounded.

"Do they ever get to happily ever after?"

"Yes, when they're about seventy."

He grinned. "Better late than never."

She swirled the remains of the cocoa in her mug, acutely aware of his gaze on her. The kitchen suddenly felt very warm. He slid one hand across the table, brushed his fingertips across hers, then gently disengaged one hand from her mug and held it in his own. It was the first time he'd touched her without gloves on and the electricity sparked by his calloused hands screamed up her arm and jump-started her pulse.

Now she was in trouble.

Victoria tried to stay objective. He'd probably used this question-and-answer format with dozens of women before. He was likely affecting her precisely the way he intended to, a well-practiced assault on her guard so she'd end up in his bed. Or was it? Didn't his name or his charisma or both usually get him whatever he wanted from women without much additional effort?

He leaned across the table and her heart jumped in response. His voice dropped to a rumbling whisper. "Victoria, your kiss stayed on my lips for weeks. I know this sounds terrible and I'm going way too fast, and it'll likely insult you, but if I don't kiss you again soon, I'm going to lose my mind." He gave her hand a gentle tug.

A battle rose inside her, one side crying for her to run, to avoid this at all costs, to remember why allowing anything to happen again was such a very bad idea. The other side soaked up every flicker of interest in his eyes like raindrops on parched earth, craving his attention with an intensity that stole her breath. Fantasy. It was just a fantasy, and all she wanted was one more little taste before she walked away. She shoved away the fear clawing at her. Heart racing, she eased forward to meet him.

The front door of the house opened and a woman's voice called, "Hi, honey, I'm home."

Chapter Three

Curran sighed as Victoria bolted back to her side of the table. So much for timing.

The flash of frost in her eyes told him exactly what assumption she'd made when she heard Kelli's voice. She pulled against his grip on her hand, and he tightened his fingers just enough to hold her.

She didn't raise her voice, but the anger came through clearly just the same. "Is that your—"

"Sister. She lives in the other house on the property, just down the drive from here." He rather enjoyed the way her fine dark brows rose and the light in her eyes simmered down from the temper he'd managed to provoke. "Tell me, do you always leap to conclusions, Victoria?"

She relaxed slightly. "You have to admit, it was more of a baby step than a leap."

There was a time when she would have been correct to think it was his lover entering the house. He had matured beyond the need to keep more than one woman at a time. "I'm hurt. Do I look like the sort of man who'd try to kiss you if I was already in a relationship?"

"I think most men fall into that category."

Before he could step in that snake pit, a whirlwind blew into the kitchen. He released Victoria's hand in time to catch forty-five pounds of nephew launching at him.

"Uncle Curry, Uncle Curry, look, Mom finally bought me the first-edition foil Charizard! It's way older than me and it's so cool! Look, look, you're not looking!" He waved a plastic-encased trading card an inch from Curran's nose.

Gently easing the boy's hand back so he could focus, Curran gave the prize his attention. He examined it carefully, wearing the most intrigued expression he could manage. "Yeah, it's a first edition all right. Good onya, Robby. I'm very impressed." He ruffled the boy's hair, setting him on his feet as Kelli entered the kitchen.

Kelli dropped several canvas grocery bags on the countertop, sliding her arms free of the handles. "You should be impressed, Curran. Those cards are expensive and you paid for it."

"Mom, can I play video games?"

"Thirty minutes, Rob, then you have piano lessons." The boy tore out of the kitchen as fast as he'd entered and slammed the front door. Kelli turned toward Curran and gave a visible start when she realized he wasn't alone. "You have company."

"Victoria Linden, this is my baby sister, Kelli Davenport. Kelli, Victoria."

Kelli smiled and extended a hand. "A pleasure, Victoria. Do you live around here or are you two old friends?"

Victoria shook her hand. "I'm house-sitting for the Campbells, just west of here. We met untangling Peg-leg from a fence." A slight blush colored her cheeks when he coughed softly. Nah, Kel didn't need to know how they really met.

Kelli shot him a look of dismay. "Is Peg okay?"

"A few punctures, some nasty scrapes. Nothing deadly."

She cast her gaze heavenward and turned to put the groceries away. "That creature would be better off wrapped as steaks and roasts in my freezer."

"Come on, Kel, you love old Peg."

"I loved him until he stomped on my flower garden last summer and ate everything."

Curran eyed the bags on the counter. When he first retired, she'd done his shopping to help him stay out of sight. Now, she did it just to be motherly. "Thanks for the groceries, but I wish you wouldn't do my errands."

She smiled sweetly over her shoulder. "Just racking up babysitting hours, dear."

It didn't matter that she was his sister. Owing anyone for anything made him uncomfortable. He laughed off Kelli's words and turned his attention back to Victoria. She smiled at him, and he slid his hand across the table, lacing her fingers through his. Though she was nearly his height, her bones were small, her fingers long and delicate. The soft skin of her hand felt good against his fingertips, and he couldn't help wondering just how good the tender skin under her clothing would feel beneath his hands.

As if she read his thought—or had the same one herself—her expression changed, her smile tightened. She pulled her hand free of his and stood. "Thanks for the hot chocolate, Curran, but I really ought to be going."

Kelli glanced over from the refrigerator. "Don't leave on my account. I'm just putting the cold things away and I'll get out of here."

"No, no, I have a lot to do today. I've gotten seriously sidetracked. It was nice to meet you."

"You too," Kelli said. "Don't be a stranger."

Curran noted the way Victoria stiffened when she turned back to him. She wasn't planning to come back. The thought made him uneasy. Her spontaneity and self-confidence on Halloween captured his imagination, and he'd spent more nights than he was comfortable with haunting Brindle's, hoping she'd return. A couple of the other waitresses knew her first name, but no one actually knew her. He'd briefly considered buying the place and assigning people to do nothing but watch for her to reappear.

A twist of fate had given him another shot. God bless Peg for his attempt to get through the fence. He couldn't let Victoria walk away a second time. Not until he examined their potential more closely and decided their fate for himself. "I'll help you with your horse."

"Oh, you don't have to do that, really." She sounded cheery enough, but when he looked in her eyes, the deep freeze had returned. Was she always this mercurial, or did he bring out the worst in her?

"I need to get back out there and fix the fence anyway." Vaguely aware of Kelli trying to disappear inside the huge fridge, he lowered his voice. "Please, Victoria. Let me walk you out."

She closed her eyes, turned her face away from him. She nodded. Good, a point for him in this little negotiation. He placed a hand on her waist and guided her out of the kitchen, snagging both of their coats off the sofa with his free hand as they left the house.

They paused on the covered porch and he examined her torn parka. Leave it to Peg to destroy a perfectly serviceable coat. "You can't possibly wear this. You'll freeze."

"It's not that long a ride. I'll live."

He tucked the parka under his arm and held out the sheepskin. "Take mine, until I can buy a replacement for you."

A shadow passed through her eyes, and she shook her head. "Thanks, but I'm fine. Really. Mine will get me home."

"If you insist, but I'm still going to buy you a new one." He studied her, watching for her reaction. There it was again, flitting through her gaze. Wariness, bordering on suspicion. As if she feared he might demand something from her in return.

"You don't have to do that. I was due for a new parka anyway. I'll replace it."

Now, that made no sense at all. Why wouldn't she want him to fix what his animal had damaged? He shook his head, then held the torn parka for her, slipping it up her arms and settling it on her shoulders.

As he pulled on his own coat, she stood watching him, worrying her lower lip with her teeth. He couldn't help focusing on her mouth.

The memory of her sitting astride him in the club, kissing him, slammed home. She noticed his attention and abruptly released her lip and looked away, her cheeks flushing pink. He shook off the memory, but the tightness in his gut didn't loosen.

When she hazarded a glance back at him, he tried to set her at ease. "My nephew does that when he wonders if he should say something."

Her eyes widened. "Does what?"

He reached up, ran a finger along the edge of her mouth. "Chews on his lip. What were you thinking?"

She edged slightly away from his touch. "I don't want to be nosy."

He sighed, his breath a cloud in the frosty air, and thrust his hand in his coat pocket. "Ask. I'll tell you when you're being nosy."

She turned and started down the steps. "Your nephew is a cute little guy. How long have they lived here?"

Well, that certainly wasn't a question he expected. He followed her off the porch, walking beside her toward the barn. "About three years. They moved into their house before I built mine."

He watched her open her mouth to speak and hastily close it again. "You want to know why."

"It's none of my business."

Curran opened the barn door, waving her through. "But you're curious, and I don't mind telling you. More importantly, Kelli wouldn't mind. Her husband was an alcoholic and when he was drinking, his favorite sport was wife boxing."

Victoria gasped, color draining from her already pale skin. Though she clenched her fists, he didn't miss the trembling of her hands.

"Are you all right?"

She blew out a breath and nodded, slowly unfurling her fingers. "Situations like that just make me feel…I don't know. Helpless, angry. I hate that such things happen. She was lucky to get out of there."

"I like to think her husband was lucky. I let him live." That was conditional, of course, on Jonas keeping his mouth shut. He'd be damned if his baby sister would find herself and her son splashed on tabloid pages. "She divorced him and I made sure she got far enough away from him that her ex can't play the 'please baby, I've changed and I want to come home' game. He'll be very, very sorry if he ever tries to get back into her life. Hers or Rob's."

Victoria nodded, then walked over to her horse's stall and lifted the bridle from the hook beside the stall door. "Good. At least Kelli had someone to turn to. So many women don't."

"I wasn't exactly set up to take her in at the time, but I couldn't leave her there. I had a condo in Los Angeles. Plenty big, but it was no place for an ankle biter." He held the half-door open as she stepped into the stall. Her horse whickered softly and nosed her hand, waiting for the bridle.

"What brought you to Utah?" she asked as she slid the bit into the horse's mouth.

"We looked all over the country for a good place. I'd been to Park City before so I was familiar with the area. It's a safe place. Good schools. Besides, Rob is crazy about skiing, so when he found out he could live and ski in the home of the U.S. Ski Team, that settled it."

"And you moved here later."

"About a year ago, yes." He tamped down on the nagging bit of ego inside him that was preening and screaming *she doesn't know who I am? How can she not recognize me?* She'd showed no signs of recognition at all, beyond remembering him from the club, and his more rational self appreciated that.

Victoria led her horse out of the stall, and Curran picked up the blanket and saddle from the rack and swung them up onto the bay's back. As he pulled on the girth, she asked, "Why not go back to Australia?"

"I haven't been back to Oz since I was eighteen."

"Don't you miss it?"

"Not everyone loves the place they came from. And sometimes, you burn too many bridges to go back." That was the standard line. It was far more comfortable than talking about his phobia.

Her gaze shifted to the horse. She rubbed her hand down the animal's wide blaze. "Yeah, I know that feeling," she said softly.

He watched hints of emotion flit across her expression and continued talking to help pull her back from whatever tugged at her. "Once in a while I miss things. Mostly the mountains and wide open spaces, and I have that here. I thought about sending Kelli back. Australia was really the ideal place to put her, but she loves the States and Rob was born here. America is their home."

She smiled, returning to him. "Nice to have such an option. Did your work make it difficult to leave California?"

A wave of tension hit him. He didn't need another woman in his life interested in his image and his money. "Work doesn't hold me in any particular place."

"What do you do?"

It was the one thing she could have said to relax him. Maybe she was one of those people who ignored the tabloids at grocery store check stands, or she simply didn't recall seeing his face on the pages over the last decade. He chose not to lie when he answered but was intentionally vague. "I'm more or less retired, but I consult on occasion."

"There's a lot of freedom in that." She let it drop, turning to lead the bay out of the barn.

Curran hurried to hold open the door for her, breathing a sigh of relief. He liked the idea of seeing where things might go before she found out all the benefits he had to offer.

Outside, she gathered the reins and grasped the saddle horn, settling the toe of her boot in the stirrup. He put a hand on her hip, boosting her into the saddle. The contact set off a wave of heat inside him. He trailed his hand down her thigh to her knee, remembering how her legs felt around his, her pale flesh wrapped in silky stockings. His groin tightened. "I want to see you."

Her expression darkened, but she made no effort to remove his hand. Her gaze seared him the way it had that night at the club. "I told you, my life is plenty complicated. I don't need to add anything else to it."

"If whatever this is between us gets too complex for you, end it. Let me see you."

She directed a hard look at his hand, and he released her leg. "I have things to do. Goodbye, Curran." She laid the reins against her horse's neck and the bay wheeled, kicking up plumes of snow as she encouraged him into a canter out of the yard and toward the trail.

He willed his libido to unwind. She hadn't said yes, but she hadn't really said no, either. At least he knew where to find her now. He had her name; she was no longer a phantom. She was real, the first non-socialite/model/actress he'd dated in a dozen years, and he could pursue her.

He'd never wanted a woman so much in his life.

Curran sighed and turned back to the barn, his craving for nicotine striking harder than it had in weeks. Screw it. He'd try quitting again tomorrow. Tonight, he'd indulge his addiction. Right now, though, he needed to grab a coil of fence wire. It didn't take the winter sun long to slip behind the mountains, and he still had a fence to mend.

* * * *

It took every ounce of strength Victoria had to ride away from Curran, and once she got going, she didn't dare stop. Curran Shaw was absolutely perfect. And he scared the hell out of her.

She rode Old Joe back to the Campbells' barn. No sooner did she open the barn door than the other horse, a gray mare named Aretha, began a high-pitched whinnying. The racket continued as Victoria unsaddled Joe and walked him into his stall. She finally called out to the mare. "I know, Aretha. I'm sorry I left you here alone this afternoon, but I can't ride both of you at the same time."

Talking to Aretha quieted the mare some, as if she were content that she'd been heard. Victoria went to work brushing the old gelding down. Unfortunately, while the action kept her hands busy, her brain was able to skip back to Curran.

He was open, truthful—okay, he pretty deftly skirted around his career, but she would do the same, in his shoes. The big question was, why had he walked away? From the outside, it was obvious that his breakup with Hollywood 'It' girl Amanda Dannen had something to do with his drop out of the spotlight. The breakup and the retirement happened within a couple of weeks of each other. It had to be more than that, though. Why would a man who had everything banish himself to a small ranch property in a high mountain canyon?

The question nagged at her as she finished brushing Joe and buckled his blanket. When she walked past Aretha's stall, on her way to get grain and hay, the mare stretched her neck over the stall half-door, ears laid flat back, and nipped at Victoria's shoulder. She swatted the mare on the nose and glared at the wide-eyed animal. "If you want to be fed, Miss Snotty, I'd suggest you keep your teeth to yourself."

Aretha snorted and grumbled, but pulled her head back into the stall.

Victoria fed the horses, taking time to rub Aretha's neck, since the mare became a much nicer animal when she ate, and promised to take her out for a ride tomorrow.

She went in through the back door of the stucco and stone two-story house, leaving her wet boots on the tile entry, then made her way through the huge house to her room. She loved this room, with the sea foam green walls and the pale gray carpet. The colors made the room a tranquil place. She'd be content to live here forever if the Campbells didn't mind.

After examining the cage in the corner for her rat, finding Sassy sleeping at the end of one of the tunnels, she stripped out of her clothes and slipped into her blue and white chevron-striped swimsuit. She grabbed a towel from the adjoining bathroom, then went downstairs to the indoor pool and hot tub.

She turned on the stereo, playing the CD already in the machine. Handel's Water Music. The appropriateness of the music for soaking in the hot tub always made her smile. She turned on the jets and sank into the water. It occurred to her that wearing a swimsuit to use the tub when she was completely alone seemed a bit silly, but the idea of skinny dipping always made her uncomfortable. It just didn't seem right, especially in someone else's hot tub.

The liquid heat soothed her cold, knotted muscles, but did nothing to relax her brain. Her thoughts swung back to the puzzle of Curran's retirement. He'd lived in the limelight, his picture appearing in tabloids and on news programs almost as often as A-list movie stars. What drove him into seclusion?

Maybe protecting Kelli and little Rob was a factor—oh, no, wait, he'd moved them here well before he retired and joined them on the ranch.

She shifted so a jet of water pulsed against her spine. Still, the fact that he went to such great lengths to care for his sister meant something to Victoria. The flash of anger and protectiveness in his eyes when he spoke of Kelli, of her ex-husband…these were not the signs of a man who would hurt her.

Her brain recognized her fear of him as irrational. Emotionally, she was terrified.

In the past year, she'd finally dated again. Weak, safe men who didn't ask anything of her. She wanted to flirt and date. Too many women who'd been through hell became victims for the rest of their lives, living in the shadow of their abuse. Or worse, moving on to another man just as bad as the last. She refused to let Nate continue to victimize her, and she absolutely would not allow herself to continue the pattern of choosing the wrong guy.

But none of that meant dating was easy. She didn't dare go out with anyone unless she called all the shots, set the pace, and ended it when she wanted to. Keeping all the control protected her.

Her stomach growled and Victoria climbed out of the hot tub, wrapping the towel around her shoulders. She couldn't control Curran. He was way too strong, and she didn't know if she was up to being with someone who was her equal. Or her superior.

And then there was the way he made her skin tingle. He sparked her desire, and there was no way she would travel that road again, unless there was a ring on her finger. The consequences were simply too devastating.

After dressing and feeding Sassy, she grabbed the mail from the box mounted on the wide, covered porch that wrapped across the front of the house and around one side.

She walked back into the ultra-modern, black granite and stainless steel kitchen, sorting through the stack of mail. A couple of utility statements she was supposed to open, just to be sure the bill had been paid by the automatic bank withdrawal her employers had set up. Junk mail, missing person ad, more junk mail. A credit card bill forwarded from her old address—jeez Louise, how hard was it to get an address changed at that company? Maybe she should switch to online statements.

Finally, an ivory linen envelope, also with the yellow Forwarding Address sticker on it. The return address and postmark said San Diego. What in the world? The only thing she was expecting by mail was one article payment that should come from Chicago, and to the correct address.

She set the rest of the mail on the counter and slid her finger under the envelope flap to tear it open. A folded page of the same ivory paper rested inside. A sense of foreboding tingled along her spine as she slid the letter out and unfolded it. It was a sheet of letterhead from the firm of Waddell, Brown, McCaren and Schimel. Her lungs constricted, leaving her unable to breathe as she read the two short sentences.

I've missed you, baby.

Have you missed me?

Her thoughts swam. He wasn't supposed to be able to contact her, not from prison. But then, even though it was his firm's letterhead, the postmark wasn't from the prison or L.A. Was some friend of his delivering a message?

Why now? Nate belonged in the past. What did he want with her now, after two years? Her pulse rushed like the roar of a river in her ears, she fought to draw breath into lungs that felt full of ice.

The distant ringing of her cell phone threw her a lifeline. She focused on the sound, dragging herself out of the panic clawing at her insides. She finally surfaced, finally breathed, and raced to grab the phone from her parka pocket. It stopped ringing before she reached it. She glanced at the display. Mara. She'd call her back later.

She looked down at the paper still in her hand, started to crumple it, then stopped herself. She set it on the nearby table and stared at it, frightened but no longer beyond rational thought. She wasn't ready to handle him again. Fighting Nate sapped everything out of her. If this was the start of some ploy to get back at her, how would she fight it?

She stepped back mentally and reviewed the facts. He wasn't up for parole for another year. She could contact the D.A.'s office. They might be interested in Nate bothering her.

Victoria drew a deep, shuddering breath and straightened her back. She'd panicked, damn it, and now that she was calming down, she hated Nate for still being able to frighten her. If he could do this to her with words on a piece of paper, how would she handle appearing before the parole board to argue against his release? And what if they did let him out and he came after her again?

She picked up the note, went into her room, and tossed it into the side drawer of the desk. Later. She'd deal with it later. Right now she needed people around her, needed some fun to take her mind off Nate until she felt in control again. She pulled out her cell and checked the voicemail. Mara wanted her to come to dinner at the new sushi bar down in Salt Lake's Gateway mall.

Perfect. She'd call her cousin back on the way. A few hours of Mara's bubbly personality should chase away the ghosts haunting her.

* * * *

Curran sat on the front porch stairs just before midnight, ignoring the bitter cold. He watched the path of his sister's torch beam as she walked the distance from her house to his. "What's dragging you over here at this time of night, Kel?"

She stopped in front of him, shook her head, then climbed two steps and sat beside him. She tugged her scarf away from her face to talk. "Rob thinks he left his school backpack over here."

"He did. It's just inside the door." He took a deep drag from the cigarette in his left hand and closed his eyes, feeding his addiction before blowing the smoke from his lungs. He despised himself for relaxing as the nicotine hit his brain, for finding pleasure in something that shouldn't have any control over him.

"Weren't you going over to see Victoria?"

He glanced at Kelli sideways. "She wasn't there. Must've had plans tonight."

She stared at him as he took another drag. "I thought you were quitting."

"I did."

"And now you've started again."

"Bingo. Give the lady a prize."

She swatted his arm. "Don't be a smartass, Curran."

"Careful, you sound like Mum."

They sat in silence. He watched a smoke plume disperse in the slight breeze, then asked, "Robby's in bed?"

"An hour ago. You like her." It wasn't a question.

"Yeah, Kel, I do." Something about Victoria completely twisted him into knots. Her eyes haunted him. He wanted to see her, wanted to touch her. But she'd vanished. Again. And driven him back into the embrace of his addiction. God, he was so damned weak.

Kelli sighed, then stepped behind him and crossed the porch to the door. He looked back at her when she exited the house, Rob's backpack dangling in her hand. "It's freezing out here. I'm going home." She paused beside him on the stairs, touched his shoulder. "Try quitting again tomorrow, okay? I'd like you to see Rob's graduation someday."

He crushed the cigarette butt on the step with his boot, then ran his hands through his hair. "I know. I'll quit. Just not tonight."

"Right, I'll try not to nag you. Goodnight."

He waved at her, watched her click on the light and make her way back to her home. He slipped another cigarette from the pack. Two cravings tortured him. He couldn't do a thing about needing Victoria. The least he could do for himself was soothe the desire for nicotine.

It was a stupid rationalization. Giving in to his addiction would only make it worse, harder to give up the next day. Just like spending time with Victoria again made the desire for her after Halloween seem practically nonexistent by comparison.

Did he like her? Damn, he had it bad. Now he had to convince Queen Victoria to give him a chance.

By the time he finished the cigarette, the wind had kicked up, numbing his nose and chilling him to the bone. He gave up, reconciled himself to a night alone, and managed to fall into a fitful sleep in his otherwise empty bed.

* * * *

The next day, Curran took Rob skiing after kindergarten, like he'd promised. Spending the afternoon on the slopes with an ever-energetic five-year-old left him starving, for the sight of Victoria as well as for food. He cleaned up, changed into a thick fleece pullover and jeans, picked up a Chinese takeout order from Papa Wok and stood ringing the doorbell of the house down the lane at half past six.

When she opened the door, he soaked in the image of her. Barefoot, in plaid pajama pants and an old University of Utah sweatshirt. A headband held her chocolate curls off her face, she wasn't wearing a touch of makeup, and she was frowning at him.

She was beautiful.

"Tell me you haven't eaten."

"Curran—"

"Don't turn me away." He put one foot on the threshold, but forced himself to stay outside on the porch. "Come on, it's not really a date, if that's what you're worried about. It's simply eating together. My treat."

She rolled her eyes. "Curran—"

He dropped his gaze to his boots, trying to look dejected. "She's going to say no. Then I will have failed in my mission to deliver her fortune. Her life will be ruined if she doesn't get the secret message baked into the cookie contained in this very bag."

When he looked back up at her, she wore the hint of a smile, so he pressed on. "Give me a break. It's cold out here and holding all this food is hard work. And I swear—" He stepped over the threshold into the house. "If I don't get to at least have dinner in the same room with you tonight, I swear I will die of loneliness."

She cocked her head and stared at him for a moment, hands on her gently curved hips. The coldness in her eyes faded, and she smiled, sending an unexpected bolt of light through his heart. She gave the door a push to close it behind him, then pointed over her shoulder.

"Table's in there. Did you get chopsticks or do we have to eat with forks like heathens?"

Chapter Four

Curran sat at the table after dinner and checked the takeout boxes, a bit surprised by the smashing success of his idea. A few grains of fried rice in this one, dregs of sweet and sour sauce in that one. A stray lo mein noodle or two. "I don't believe it."

"What, that we ate everything?" Victoria called over her shoulder as she carried dirty plates into the kitchen.

"Yeah." He stacked the little boxes inside one another then carried them into the kitchen. He tossed the stack into the garbage can she'd pointed out earlier, in the cupboard under the sink, then washed his hands.

"You have to understand, this is a first for me," he said, drying his hands on the towel he pulled from the drawer she opened to his right. "I've never had a takeout dinner for two without having leftovers for the next day, unless I ate it with Kelli and Rob."

Victoria shrugged, thrusting her own hands under the faucet. "In defense of your other dining companions, that was a huge amount of food, Curran."

He leaned his hip against the granite countertop, his hands resting on the coved edge. He liked watching her. He'd bet that she'd taken ballet lessons in her youth, given her graceful motions, even in small things like the way she hung the towel over the edge of the sink to dry, then hopped up to sit on the countertop.

For a sharp moment, Curran deeply envied the granite, warming under her lovely curves. He pushed off the edge, taking a step toward her. Amber eyes watched him, locked into his gaze. He swallowed a groan. She made him burn, but he was learning her, bit by bit.

He'd always had a knack for seeing through the facades other people wore. Some were thicker than others. Most people weren't aware they had them, even when they could see them in others.

Though Victoria was friendly, laughing at his jokes, and in all a thoroughly pleasant dinner companion, he wasn't seeing *her*. He was seeing the Victoria Linden mask she wore when she was in a good mood. In the club, he'd seen a bit of that, and a bit of her annoyed self. The kiss, though, was different. Unless his instincts were completely rusty, when she kissed him, it came from the other side of the image she showed in public. He'd caught a glimpse of it yesterday, when he would have kissed her again, before Kelli shattered the mood.

He was going to at least crack the surface of her facade tonight. It was just a matter of poking around, trying various points until he found a weakness. If that weakness happened to be kissing her again, more the better.

Another step and her heat touched his skin. "Tell me something. Everyone has a secret fear. What is yours, Victoria?"

Something flashed cold in her eyes, then the smile returned. "I'm afraid of paper cuts."

"Paper cuts?"

"Yes. For being so small, they hurt like crazy. I worked with a lot of paper as a writer before everything went digital, so you can imagine how this became something of a phobia."

Curran laughed. Agile brain, this one. Quick answers. But he wasn't reaching the heart and soul of her.

She glanced over his shoulder at the countertop behind him. "Coffee's ready. How do you take yours?"

"No cream, two sugar."

Her fine brows rose. "I pegged you for a straight black kind of guy."

He shrugged. "Looks can be deceiving."

"So I've heard. Have a seat in the great room. I'll bring in the coffee."

* * * *

Victoria sipped her heavily creamed coffee, enjoying the conversation as she and Curran worked around from small talk to politics to books. Finally, she set her empty coffee mug on the table, then tucked her leg under herself on the black leather couch, pulling the other knee up, clasping her fingers around it. She watched Curran stretch back into the opposite overstuffed couch arm.

He wanted to kiss her. She saw it in every glance, in every shift of his body toward hers. He'd wanted to yesterday, and the hunger in his eyes had grown worse since then.

She wanted to kiss him, too, so badly that the very thought had her stomach rolling with electricity. What she needed to decide, and fast, was how far she really wanted this thing to go. If she took the plunge, she'd have to give up the idea of writing about him. To do otherwise was completely unethical.

Her attention snapped back to the moment when Curran said, "Tell me your favorite flower."

"Pale purple irises. Tell me your favorite movie," she fired back.

"*Casablanca.* Yours?"

"*Beauty and the Beast*, Disney version. What's your favorite color?"

"Blue. What world landmark would you most like to see?"

"Hmm, have to think about that one."

He shook his head, his dark hair nearly falling in his eyes. "No, give the first answer that occurs to you."

"Fine. St. Basil's Cathedral in Red Square. Same question for you."

He leaned forward, his elbows resting on his thighs. His eyes were bright, warm. "That mountain carved into Crazy Horse in South Dakota." He reached out, lightly touching her knuckles. She unlaced her fingers, allowing him to clasp her hand in his. "Favorite holiday."

She smiled. "Christmas. Yours?"

Curran's eyes narrowed slightly, and he gave her hand a gentle tug. "Halloween."

The quietly spoken word drew a crystalline memory of sitting astride him, tasting him. A hot tide of desire flooded through her. Whether because she failed to conceal it, or because the same rush swept over him, his green eyes darkened.

He rose over her, his hand sank into her hair, the gentle pressure of his fingers on her nape tilted her head back. The anticipation inside her rocketed, and she gasped as his mouth lowered to hers.

His lips caressed hers once, twice. Soft, warm, inviting. The third time, she slid her hands behind his neck and kissed him back, flicking the tip of her tongue against his mouth. A rumbling groan escaped him, and he pulled her up to her knees, his arms folding around her, molding her against him.

Curran brushed his tongue into her mouth, the warmth, the sugared coffee taste of him demanding her focus. Ripples of heat rolled through her, pooling low in her body, pressing thought aside in favor of simply feeling his arms tighten around her, the silken strands of his hair between her fingers.

His mouth left hers to trail along her jaw, down her throat. With one hand, he eased the top of her sweatshirt away from her neck and gently set his teeth against her skin, stealing her breath. She clutched at his soft shirt, reveling in the hard warmth of his chest beneath the fabric. When his left hand found her backside and pulled her against his hips, the hardness of him sent electric shivers through her. Her knees weakened, her senses reeled as she drowned in his heat, in his dark, mysterious, wholly male scent.

Somewhere, at the edge of the sensual cloud enveloping them, she heard a high-pitched sound, climbing and descending the musical scale. Reluctant, her skin screaming in disagreement with separation, she ran her hands between them, pressing his chest. His mouth captured hers again as she tried to disengage herself. For a moment she let herself be swept away before her senses cleared enough to identify the scales ringing from the direction of the chair where his coat lay. She broke the kiss, pushing against him more firmly. "Phone, Curran. Your phone."

The phone sounded again, and Curran leveled a glare in its direction. He growled. "Kel's ringtone." Turning back to Victoria, he swept a quick kiss across her lips. "Don't move from this spot."

He left the couch, snagging the phone out of his coat pocket as it rang up the scale again. Concern shadowed his expression. That worried her, and made it easier to calm her raging hormones.

"Yeah, Kel?" He listened for a moment, then grimaced, running a hand through his dark hair. "Are you two okay? No, listen Kel, I don't care about the vehicle. It wasn't your fault."

An accident. The last of her desire ebbed as she listened to Curran's end of the conversation. His voice held a gentleness that made Victoria's heart ache. She recognized the slight resignation in the way he spoke to his sister. He'd leave when he finished the call.

"Yeah, about twenty minutes, right? Bye." He switched off the phone, dropped it into his coat pocket. He gave Victoria a half-hearted smile, then sighed. "Kelli and Rob were in an accident."

"I figured. Are they okay?"

"A few scrapes, she said. Kelli's religious about seat belts, thank God. Someone going too fast slid through a red light near the outlet mall and nailed their back end. Spun them into a light pole. They're fine, but the SUV's a mess. I have to go."

"Of course." She pushed off the couch as he picked up his coat and followed him out to the entry. "Tell them hello for me."

"I will." He pulled his coat on, then ran his thumb along her cheek. "Thanks for having dinner with me."

"It was my pleasure."

"Do you have plans tomorrow?"

A thrill wriggled through her middle. "Exercising the horses. Writing. Running to the grocery store at some point."

"What are you willing to eat on a pizza?"

"Anything. Everything. If it's pizza, it's all good."

Curran laughed, she felt the rumble under her skin. "Same time tomorrow, then?"

"Please."

He slipped his fingers behind her neck, tilted his head down and kissed her softly. She forced herself to allow him to break the kiss. He pressed his lips to her cheek, then turned and opened the door. "Sleep well, Victoria."

"Goodnight."

She stood in the doorway, the cold night air chilling her through her sweatshirt until the headlights of his truck backed away from the house and followed the curved drive, then turned away down the lane. She closed the door, threw the lock, then wandered back into the great room. Dropping onto the couch, she stared at the vaulted ceiling.

Wow. She lay still, mentally replaying the zinging feeling, the fire Curran's kisses sent roaring through her core. She'd never heated up like that, let alone so fast.

Nate said it was because she was a naturally cold woman. She hoped it was just more emotional cruelty on his part to say such a thing, but she'd dated enough men before him to think he might be right.

Maybe she should revise that conclusion. Her thoughts returned to Curran, to the darkness in his eyes when he looked at her, the secure warmth of his arms around her. She'd never craved a physical connection before, but Curran made her *feel.* She felt alive when he touched her.

She packed up the idea of writing about him in a mental garbage bag and chucked it. The only thing to focus on now was making sure her hormones didn't get the best of her. She couldn't, she wouldn't let her physical attraction to him go too far. The only safe sex was no sex. She'd paid for relying on protection. The price was far too high ever to pay again.

* * * *

Curran tore the top sheet off his desktop calendar, revealing the February page. He leaned back in his leather office chair and rubbed his eyes. The last time he'd dated a woman nearly every day for a month without having sex with her was *never.*

How the hell was he supposed to get anything done when he stared at the computer screen and only saw her? Thinking about her made his blood simmer, and she crept into his thoughts more frequently with each passing day.

He set his jaw and focused on the rows of numbers on the screen. This was the third analysis he'd done for DCS GlobalTech since he retired, and Jamie wanted it by tomorrow...

The ridiculousness of the whole thing suddenly struck him. He paged through the file on his screen, then pushed the laptop away. He picked up the cell, hitting the contact for his best friend.

Jamie Mickelson's clear tenor answered on the third ring. "Curran, how's it going, buddy?"

"She's right, mate. Couldn't be better."

A chuckle sounded in his ear. "Bullshit. You need a massage, I can hear the tension in your voice. I thought retirement was supposed to bring unending days of sunshine and happiness. What's wrong?"

"Jamie, you have a herd of MBAs and analysts filling the second floor at headquarters."

"Yeah, so?"

"Why do you need my input on acquiring Tandena? It's a good company, perfectly viable for purchase, and I'm certain you knew that when you emailed me these files."

"I got some recommendations from the staff, yes, but Curran, you have a gift for this. Your hunches are better than the staff's well-researched definitive answers."

Curran switched the phone to his right hand, leaned back, kicked his feet up on the desk. "Be straight with me, Jamie. You don't need me, and we both know it."

After a moment, Jamie said, "Okay. I'm trying to keep you in the loop. After all, most of this is your money we're spending, Mr. Controlling-Interest Stockholder, and if you stay abreast of what we're doing over here, when you come back—"

"Ah. So that's it. When I retired, mate, I wasn't fooling around. This isn't like a Brett Favre retirement, where I'll keep coming back in a blaze of glory. I'm done. I have other concerns, and I have every confidence in your ability to lead the company. That's why I kept you from taking that piddling CFO job with Horizon."

Jamie laughed. "Quit pulling my chain, Curran. Everyone knows you won't stay underground forever. Running things is in your blood, my friend. I send you stuff because I know damn well you're going nuts not being on top of the heap. You want to oil the gears and turn the works every day, and don't try telling me otherwise."

"I have family and the ranch to focus on now."

"Uh-huh. For how long? How long until that gorgeous sister of yours starts dating? What are you going to do when she marries again and moves away, Curran? Play rancher for the rest of your life?"

"I love the ranch."

Jamie snorted. "Yeah, and I love drinking *cerveza* on the beach in Mexico, but I'm not going to make a life out of it. You know damn well this isn't a permanent arrangement. The last two times I asked for your consultation, you acted like a kid on Christmas morning. So don't tell me you plan to hang out in the Rockies, alone, for the rest... Oh. Oh, man. I get it. You're not alone, are you? Some woman's got you on her hook."

He pushed the thought of soft curls, softer skin, and long, long legs away. She was a siren, calling relentlessly, leaving him on the edge of spontaneous combustion. Nothing more. "Yeah, okay. Remember who you're talking to, mate."

Jamie ignored him. "That's why you don't want to bother with office stuff. Awesome, I'm happy for you, bud. What's her name?"

"I haven't a clue what you're talking about." Curran looked up from the pen he twirled in his left hand as Kelli walked into his office. "Buy Tandena. Here, talk to Kelli."

He handed the phone to her. She quirked an eyebrow at him until he said, "Jamie."

Her face lit up and she pushed him, urging him out of the office chair so she could sit. "Jamie? Hey, handsome, what happened to taking a vacation last month and coming to see us?"

Curran closed the laptop then walked out of the office. He glanced at his watch. Quarter past five. Victoria would have just finished working for the day. He really ought to take her out. She'd never said anything about it, but most women wanted to be wined and dined with some frequency. At least the women he'd dated before insisted upon it. Of course, most of them wanted the exposure and the press.

Victoria was a rather private person, but he doubted she'd mind going somewhere that gave her an excuse to dress up. Spending time together at his place or hers had to be getting old for her.

He strode down the hall to his room. There was a time when being with a woman at home meant dinner and sex, not necessarily in that order. As much as it frustrated him that he failed to steer Victoria into bed, just being with her, hanging out, felt…comfortable.

He'd realized his complete ease with her yesterday, when they spent two hours playing Scrabble with Kelli after Rob went to bed. Laughing and disagreeing over the validity of his native spelling in an American board game made him happy. Having her beside him gave him a strange sense of contentment. It was odd, but he found the thought of losing that contentment disconcerting.

Curran reached for his phone in his pocket, instantly recalling he'd handed it to Kelli, and reversed course back to his office. He really should take Victoria out. The Sundance Film Festival was over, so all the reporters had left town. Besides, he'd surely been out of the media spotlight plenty long enough to come and go as he pleased without wondering where his photograph would show up next. Thank God there were always other people for the public to find interesting. There was no reason at all why he couldn't take her on a proper date.

They'd have a nice meal at a good restaurant. Perhaps catch that new romantic comedy she wanted to see. Then maybe, for once, he'd convince her to stay with him. It was more than just the sexual desire for her. It was starting to be downright damned miserable falling asleep alone every night.

* * * *

Victoria stood in front of her bedroom closet, dripping from the shower, frantically searching for something to wear. Something nice enough to eat at Fusion Cafe. Little black dress would work for there, but not for the movies afterwards. Something nicer than jeans or the pajama pants she lived in. Add expected snowstorm and wind to the mix.

After pairing and discarding a half-dozen outfits in record time, she settled on russet-brown, wool trousers and a muted gold, cable-knit sweater with a V-neck.

Curran had somehow managed to get them a reservation at six-thirty, just before dinner rush. It was a tight squeeze, time-wise, but if he was willing to come out of seclusion and actually take her out, she could certainly rise to the challenge and be ready on time. Luckily, a little anti-frizz gel and a quick blast with the hair dryer made her impossible hair presentable. A brush with the makeup basics later, she slid gold hoops into her ears.

Sassy scampered back and forth through her tunnels for attention. Victoria went to the cage and looked down at the rat. "You were out for hours today, Sassafras."

The rat washed her face, then stared up expectantly.

She reached into the cage and stroked her pet's furry head. "Sorry, girl, I have plans. I'll let you out for a little while when I come home."

Ignoring the spoiled rat, Victoria walked down the hall to the kitchen. She didn't want to be desperately staring out the sidelight by the front door when Curran arrived.

Dating Curran left her giddy inside. He made her laugh. They shared many of the same interests in reading, animals, music, movies. He even passed the acid test—he liked Sassy. There were still certain subjects he avoided, like work, other than that on the ranch. Not that she had room to complain, when she shied away from talk of her past, too.

It was a here-and-now sort of relationship, growing deeper but still uncomplicated. She liked it that way.

An ivory sheet of paper on the counter caught her eye, in the same place she'd dropped it after opening it a few hours earlier. There seemed to be something of a pattern to them, arriving every other week. This was the third. She picked it up, folded it into the original thirds without reading it again. She didn't have to. The words swam before her eyes, simple and to the point.

You and I have unfinished business, baby.

It is far from over.

Anger spiked inside her, and she tossed the note with the other two in the desk drawer. Nate was dictating those notes to someone on the outside. Some creep was helping him reach her, but there wasn't enough to go on for the police to get involved. The D.A. suggested she try not to worry about it, and think about getting a concealed carry permit to protect herself.

She sighed and wrapped her arms around herself. She'd told Mara about the notes, and her cousin simply clucked her tongue and said, "Don't read them, silly, just toss them in the garbage." Victoria shivered. She did need to see them, needed to keep them for evidence in case it somehow got worse.

Icy fingers of fear clutched at her insides as she wondered how it could get worse, but her anger flared, burning away the chill. How dare he still try to frighten her, intimidate her, hurt her!

She basked in the heat of her anger for a moment as she strode to her room, tossing the letter in the desk drawer. Anger made her sharp, kept her in control. Fear made her useless to herself. Yeah, she'd keep the notes. If it ever escalated into something more, she'd have a paper trail to work with.

The doorbell rang. Curran.

Anticipation flooded through her, leaving her tingling from head to toe, washing away both fear and anger. She hurried into the entry, not even feeling the cold when she opened the door.

Curran, wearing a long black leather coat over an electric blue sweater and black pants, moved into the house when she retreated a step. "Evening, Beautiful." He brushed his lips across her cheek, much to her disappointment. She wanted his mouth on hers.

He looked her over, in that quick, sweeping way of his that made her feel appreciated rather than ogled. "Nice outfit. Coat?"

She opened the coat closet and pointed to the street-length red wool coat hanging inside. He helped her into it, waited while she locked the door, then twined his fingers with hers on the way out to his truck.

Instead of opening the passenger door, he backed her against it, leaning into her, his chest and legs flush against hers. Her heart skipped and pounded, a rhythm she felt between her thighs.

"So," she whispered. "Does this mean I get a proper kiss hello?"

"I can't help it. I know women hate having their lipstick mussed, but I very much want to kiss you." His low voice made her heart trip again.

"I use the good stuff, it's not going anywhere. Go for it." The blood rushed from her head when he pressed his lips to hers. He nipped at her lower lip, and she met his tongue with her own, tasting him. Minty.

He rarely tasted of cigarettes anymore. He'd worked hard to quit over the last few weeks, but she knew he could do it. Curran had the strength to do anything.

Pride welled in her heart and she stroked his face and smiled at him when he ended the kiss. He grinned back, crinkling the slight lines beside his eyes, then settled her in the truck.

"Have you eaten at Fusion Cafe before?" he asked as he drove out of their canyon and headed southwest toward Park City.

"Once for my cousin's birthday. It's great."

He nodded. "I went there several times during the film festival, before I moved here. The owner, Dakota Grant, is a real fireball. She dated my friend, Jamie, for a while."

"Ahhh, that explains being able to secure reservations at the last minute."

Fusion Cafe took up a ground-floor wing addition to the Silver Lode hotel, just off historic Main Street in Park City. The interior was spartan, with tables divided by etched chrome and glass half-walls. Sound deadening panels on the ceiling provided a decent atmosphere for conversation even on a busy night. Being a Thursday didn't diminish the crowds much. Several groups and couples waited in the hotel lobby for their tables.

Curran placed a hand on the small of her back, guiding her to the restaurant door. A pretty, petite, delicate blonde standing at the host desk smiled at them, then did a double-take and left her desk to throw her arms around him.

"My gosh, Curran, I heard you were coming in tonight. I haven't seen you in ages."

He laughed. "No one's seen me in ages, so don't feel bad about it." He stepped out of the hostess' embrace and wrapped his arm around Victoria's shoulders. "Honey, this is Georgia Grant. She manages the Silver Lode and is apparently filling in as maitre'd tonight. Georgia, my girlfriend, Victoria Linden."

Girlfriend. Automatic pilot forced Victoria's hand out to meet Georgia's. Huge, multi-colored fireworks exploded inside her, leaving her unable to control the huge, beauty queen grin plastered on her face as Georgia showed them to their table in a private corner. She forced down the urge to run home, call her old high school friends and scream over the phone in delight. God, she hadn't been this giddy since Dale Whitby asked her to the Junior Prom.

Dakota Grant, her lithe form wrapped in a pristine white chef's coat, arrived at their table shortly. Fusion's owner and head chef was Georgia's identical twin, save the hair, which Dakota wore short, spiky and burgundy.

She hopped up and down on the balls of her feet as Curran rose from his chair. She, too, greeted Curran like long-lost family, flinging her arms around him.

In her happy daze, Victoria noticed the way his eyes lit up, the way his innate charm kicked up a notch. He introduced her, then laughed as Dakota badgered him with questions.

"Where have you been, anyway? I thought for sure I'd see you in here during Sundance."

He shrugged and ran his hand along the chef's back. "Sorry, lady. It wasn't that I didn't miss you or your cooking. Just trying to stay out of the camera's eye, you know?"

Dakota snorted. "Whatever, C. Glad to see you, anyway. Try the veal medallions tonight. The sauce is one of my better creations."

She said goodbye to Victoria, then pulled Curran down and kissed him on the cheek before returning to the kitchen.

Victoria noted the glow in Curran's eyes and wondered. In the last month, she had gotten no closer to knowing why he ended his highly public lifestyle. She didn't know quite how to work the conversation around to it, and he didn't volunteer anything.

No matter his reasons, he had obviously missed it. It showed on his face, in his delight at seeing the Grant sisters. She heard the joy threaded through the rumble in his voice.

Tonight, he'd taken himself back into his element. Curran Shaw had returned home, and claimed her as his own.

Her insecurities ate at her self-confidence. The things she'd been told so many times and thought she'd pushed out of her system rose in her mind. She wasn't pretty enough, smart enough, warm enough... anything enough.

Not for a man like Curran. He was simply toying with her. How long could she possibly expect it to last? Especially when she wasn't sleeping with him.

Then he took her hand and gave her fingers a gentle squeeze. His smile, the warmth and sparkle in his eyes when he looked at her helped her chase away those old, hurtful words.

If she were truly that worthless, she wouldn't be here, now would she?

He leaned close and kissed her, his lips firm yet tender slanting against hers.

Here and now. It was all she could ask for. It was all she could handle.

It was enough.

Chapter Five

"I forgot to tell you, Mrs. Campbell called this morning." Victoria dropped onto the couch in her great room after her first real night out with Curran. She pulled her knees up, giving him room to join her on the couch.

"Confirming their plans to return next month?"

"No, telling me they're joining friends on a trip across Asia. Looks like I'm staying here until the middle of April." *And staying close to you.* The comfort of knowing where she would live for the next two months bubbled into a froth with the anticipation shivering in her belly. They'd barely returned from the movie, and though he'd been a perfect gentleman all evening, a palpable tension filled the space between them.

Curran set down a bottle of lotion he'd retrieved from the bathroom and closed his fingers around her left ankle. She raised an eyebrow at him. "What are you doing?"

"Trust me." He loosened the laces on her boot, slid it off, dropped it on the floor. He tugged her sock off.

She leaned back against the arm of the couch, unable to suppress a moan of delight as his strong hands slathered lotion onto her foot.

She knew what was coming. Every time she looked at him, the predatory darkness in his eyes singed her skin. He'd taken his time getting to it, but his intention was obvious. After a month of dating, he intended to change her status from merely girlfriend to lover.

She sucked in a sharp breath when he worked her arch with his knuckles.

"Does that hurt?"

"Ohhh, but it's a good hurt. Keep going, please." She watched him as his hands traveled over her skin, her insides tingling in lazy circles, matching the path his hands massaged around her foot.

He was clearly trying to seduce her, and damn, it was working. Her thoughts fast-forwarded past the obvious enjoyment of making love with him to the very distinct possibility of ending up alone again afterward. That dash of reality helped her focus outside the sensual stirrings in her belly.

Curran continued the massage beyond her ankles, sliding her trouser leg up to work her calf. "Does that mean you're canceling your apartment-hunting plans for the weekend?"

"Yes. Does it bother you that I don't keep my own place?"

He reached for her other foot, discarding the second boot and sock, then filled his palm with lotion. "No, not at all. Why pay rent if you aren't living there? Though I suggest you don't tell your employers about some of the things that may go on between us in this house in the next few weeks."

He gave her a look that sent flames of desire licking over her skin then returned his attention to the foot rub. She sighed, part contentment, part resignation. She couldn't give him what he wanted. What she wanted.

She had to get her mind on something else. "Question."

"What?"

"Why haven't you ever gone back to Australia?"

"I told you, not everyone wants to go home again." He worked her arch, pulling a gasp from her.

"Don't you ever miss your mother?"

Through half-closed eyes, she caught the way his jaw clenched. It was the only outward indication she'd hit a nerve.

"I was hard on my mum. We talk on the phone occasionally. She's even learned how to send email in the last couple of years."

She frowned. "I'm surprised she hasn't flown over to see you, at least."

He paused, his jaw ticking, then rubbed his knuckles against the ball of her foot. "Mum doesn't fly. She's deathly afraid of aircraft. Doesn't do boats, either, so if she can't walk, drive, or take the train, she doesn't go."

"Oh." Heavens, getting information out of him was like herding cats sometimes.

When he was in the public eye, Curran managed to keep his family private. Even with all her research, all she found at the time she wrote the article was that he had a sister, his mother lived in Australia, and his father died when Curran was twenty-five, leaving him DCS GlobalTech. Her curiosity piqued, she gently nudged for more satisfying answers. "You don't speak of your family much, besides Kelli."

He blew out a breath, then glanced sideways at her. "What do you want to know?"

"Anything you're willing to tell me. If you don't want to talk about it, don't."

Curran lifted her feet, slid closer to her, then lowered her legs over his. "All right. Mum and David Shaw were never married. He met her on holiday in Gold Coast—do you know Australia?"

"Uh, sort of."

He nodded and drew a map in the air. "It's on the east coast in Queensland, just south of Brisbane, right? So, they met, spent three solid months together, then he went back to the States, and she was blessed with me."

Victoria shivered. The single-mom subject hit a little too close to home. "Did he know?"

"She didn't tell him until I was three or four years old. She wanted to see if he'd come back for her without knowing he had an obligation. He never came. She finally told him, hoping he'd help provide for me."

"And did he?" Nate wouldn't have.

"Yeah. He was neck-deep in building his business, so it wasn't like he could pick up and move halfway around the world. He wanted us to come to him, but she refused to leave her family, her country, deal with that fear of flying. So, he sent funds, and she raised me with the help of my grandmother."

Victoria trailed her fingers along his arm, enjoying the feel of corded muscle under his soft sweater. "Where does Kelli come into the picture?"

"Mum married Jack, Kelli's dad, when I was nine. He's a decent type, but he wasn't my father. I wouldn't let him be. By the time I was a teenager, I had raised enough hell to get kicked out of the house."

"Where did you go?"

He leveled a look at her. "You know, this is not what I had in mind tonight, talking about my childhood."

"Sorry, I didn't mean to pry."

Curran feathered his fingers into her hair, stroked his thumb down her cheek. "You didn't, but it's a conversation for another time."

Her heart tripped hard as he shifted her onto his lap and kissed her. The room faded away until nothing existed beyond the feel of him, the faint musky hint of aftershave on his skin, the heat of his mouth. Victoria lost herself in the pounding of his heart beneath her hand, the security of his arms, the fiery trail of kisses he imprinted on her jaw, her throat.

He slipped an arm beneath her knees and lifted her, laying her down on the couch and stretching himself out full length beside her. He kissed her, his tongue flirting with hers, dipping into her mouth until her head spun. She gasped when he turned his attention to the hollow at the base of her throat. Nothing else in the world mattered. Nothing but his tongue tasting her skin, his teeth nipping at her collarbone.

A hot throbbing grew between her thighs, achy and demanding. She became more aware of her own skin when he ran a hand down her side, barely touching the curve of her breast, following the path of her waist, along her hip. Down her leg until he tucked his fingers behind her knee, bringing her leg up and over his side as he shifted, resting his own leg between hers. It was so quick, so fluid, it left her no time to think. The throbbing intensified, pulsing against the weight of his thigh. It had been so long, and she didn't recall the prelude ever being this good. It was all she could do to resist the urge to rock her hips and rub herself against him.

She drew a ragged breath, wove her fingers into his thick hair and pulled his mouth back to hers. She tasted him, kissed him deeply. He eased back, his smoldering gaze locked onto hers as he reached his hand under the edge of her sweater, sliding the fine wool up to her breasts.

A pinprick of cold opened inside her, snapping her out of the heat-induced haze. *Think, Victoria, think!* Her mind returned to the day she signed the adoption papers. That was all it took. The chill grew, washing over the throbbing, leaving only wisps of smoke curling in her stomach.

Confusion flickered through his eyes. She hadn't expected him to detect the change, but it saved her from having to work so hard to say no.

She sighed and pressed a hand to his chest. He shifted, allowing her to sit up, then moved to sit behind her. His hand smoothed her hair, likely a wild mass by now. Oh, she wanted him so much. He was a gentle, wonderful man. He was also accustomed to getting whatever he wanted, so how could she expect him to abide by the boundaries she had to maintain? She knew he wouldn't hurt her, but he wouldn't stick around either.

Even in her wildest dreams, she knew he wouldn't want someone quite this messed up.

"Curran, this is going to sound like a line, but I need you to know that it's not you. It's totally me."

He leaned against her back, ran his hands down her arms, pressed his lips to her nape, breathing against her skin and sending a shiver through her. "I want to make love with you." The rumble in his quiet voice seemed more intense, infused with fire.

He wanted her. The ice crystallizing inside her hurt, but it couldn't be any other way. She stood up, took a step, but his fingers closed around her wrist.

"Don't walk away from me, Victoria."

She froze.

"Don't walk away from me, Victoria." Nate's fist
slammed into her ribs—

She shook her head, forcing the memory back to the depths it came from, but she was unable to lose the sick feeling in the pit of her stomach, the panic chilling her. She couldn't look at Curran. She felt him behind her, his hands grasping her shoulders.

"Victoria." His voice, low and quiet, still held a slight edge from the passion ebbing slowly away. He turned her to face him. "You're dead white."

She wrapped her arms around herself, trying to control the shaking. "I, uh, I don't feel very well, Curran. You should go."

"Actually, I think I should stay." He ran his fingers along her jaw, nudging her chin up, urging her to look at him. "What happened?"

She forced herself to meet his gaze. She found warmth in his eyes, his brow knitted with concern. "Nothing. I'm fine."

He shook his head. "Wrong answer. You're not a very good liar, Victoria. I frightened you, and I want to know why."

"You didn't frighten me."

"Oh, really? One minute we're loving up just fine, the next minute, you ice over in mid-step—" His eyes brightened with recognition, his jaw tensed. "I've seen that happen before. When we talked about Kelli's past that first day, I saw a lesser version of this reaction."

She stepped away from him, unable to hold herself together under his gentle scrutiny. "I should have warned you I'm kind of temperamental."

She didn't get far before she felt him behind her. "No, I don't think you are." His voice was low, soft. Dangerous. "I do think you have the occasional flashback from someone beating the hell out of you."

If she'd ever doubted Curran's reputation for zeroing in on the source of problems, she doubted no longer. He didn't touch her, but her skin tingled with the warmth of him standing close.

"I'm sorry I've ruined the evening." She could barely hear her own voice, and wondered briefly if he heard her. She felt so small inside, so cornered. She hated the fear Nate had instilled in her so long ago. Fear she might never completely rid herself of.

Curran's hands settled on her waist, he nuzzled the spot just below her ear. "I don't want an apology, honey. Just tell me his name."

A shock jolted her heart, and she caught her breath as she turned to look at him. She recognized the expression in his green eyes. Anger. Protection.

"Nathaniel Louis Fielder, Jr."

"Where is he?"

Her heart lurched again at the tightness in his voice. He was ready to tear Nate apart. "Serving time in California, thank God."

His eyes closed for a moment and he blew out a deep breath. When he looked at her again, the anger had cooled slightly. He led her back to the couch, sat with her. "Tell me about it."

"Curran, I haven't talked about it in a very long time."

Flickers of warmth skittered across the ice inside her as his fingers laced through hers. "Sometimes it helps to talk it out of your system."

She'd talked to counselors until her throat dried. It had helped as much as it was ever going to. The remainder, well, that she just had to learn to live with. To get past. "It only helps so much. Besides, I'm sure you don't really want the gory details."

"It doesn't help that I'm still practically a stranger, right?" He said it as a matter of fact, without emotion.

"It isn't that. I know you."

He smiled then, a little. "But it's still new. That will change, given time."

Fluttering filled her insides. "I thought I totally ruined this."

"No, not at all. Promise me something, though." He caressed her hair, bracketed her face in his hands. "Don't push me away when I trigger a memory. Tell me. Work through it with me. Otherwise, he wins."

She nodded. He gently nudged the tip of her nose with his, then tilted his head and kissed her softly, carefully. When he pulled back, he lifted her hand to his mouth and kissed her fingers.

"I think the mood I was cultivating earlier is beyond hope of resurrection tonight."

She drew a fingertip along his jaw. "That's hardly fair to you."

Curran laughed softly. "It is what it is." He glanced at his watch. "And right now, it's late. You all right?"

"Yes. I still feel a little out of balance, but sleep is usually a good cure for that."

"I'll check on you tomorrow, after I take Robby skiing." He kissed her cheek, then retrieved his coat. She walked with him to the door, opened it for him, warmed by the brush of his lips across hers.

She stood in the doorway, shivering as the truck engine roared to life, watching until the headlights disappeared up the lane. She sighed and pushed the door closed, leaning her forehead against it. This was hardly the first time she'd been thrown to the past by something someone said. A phrase on a TV show even did it once. Usually, she just shook the memories off and went back to what she was doing. Having such a sharp memory surface while she was with Curran messed with her mind.

He really was wonderful. He made her laugh, he was intelligent, he could converse about anything. He even opened doors for her in a way that made her feel precious. And there was the physical side of things. She'd found a few men attractive in her life, but Curran ignited a heat she'd only felt flashes of before.

Being afraid of him was stupid. The way he treated his sister and nephew told her that much. He'd probably break her heart, but he would never physically hurt her.

Fortified by that knowledge, Victoria settled into bed in the guest room. The more she thought about Curran, the more she wished he was there beside her, holding her.

Then came the thought that snapped her wide awake and filled her with regret.

If it had been Curran, instead of Nate, she wouldn't have given up the baby.

She pressed her face into her pillow and sobbed.

* * * *

Curran couldn't sleep. After reading the same paragraph in his book four times, he knew he couldn't read, either. By three-twenty, he gave up trying. He yanked on a pair of jeans, a thick sweatshirt, boots, a wool hat, and his sheepskin coat, then left the house.

God must have a wicked sense of humor to make it this damn cold. His ears and cheeks burned with cold and his fingertips were freezing inside his gloves before he reached the barn.

He slipped inside, felt along the wall for the light switch, then stopped himself. No sense in waking all the animals. He grabbed a torch from the tack room, clicked it on, then went to Peg-leg's huge box and shone the beam on the bison. The animal stood with his eyes closed, dozing.

"Peg, how's those legs, mate?" He pitched his voice low, but a couple of the horses heard him and whickered. He walked slowly past the other stalls, rubbing velvet horse noses where the curious leaned out to see why he was there. Finally, he returned to the bison's box and unlatched the door.

Peg snorted and stepped back to give him room by the door. He patted Peg's huge head and knelt, checking the scabbed wounds and new, pink skin for signs of oozing or infection. Nothing. The beast seemed to be healing just fine.

He stood and leaned against Peg-leg's massive side. "She's going to be the death of me, Peggy. She took me from rock hard to desperate to defend her in about two minutes flat. What in the hell am I supposed to do with a woman like that?"

Curran closed his eyes, propped up by the bison. His focus was usually so clear with women. With Victoria, it was everywhere at once. He wanted to kiss her, hold her, laugh with her, take care of her. He wanted to watch her face as he slid inside her and made her come, then wrap her in his arms as they slept.

He wanted to look in those hauntingly familiar golden brown eyes and see only himself, none of the ghosts from her past.

He scratched Peg behind the ear. He needed to know what that son of a bitch had done to her. The wrenching in his gut when he thought of someone hurting Victoria might lessen if he knew what had actually happened, rather than letting his broad imagination fill in the blanks. One day, when the time was right, he'd ask her.

One day, when the time was right, he'd make love to her. But she was more fragile than she wanted to admit, and he was willing to wait.

He rubbed the bison's shoulder and left the box. He stepped through the door into a blast of freezing wind. The truck caught his eye, and he considered it for a moment. Drive over there, wake her, love her while she's still half asleep and unable to think too much about her past, her fears…

It sounded like heaven. Hell would follow when dealing with her anger, or worse, her shaken trust, for taking advantage of her. He sighed and trudged back to the house.

One day. Soon.

* * * *

"Come in, Victoria!"

Victoria barely heard Kelli's shout, muffled by the steel and frosted glass door. She turned the knob and stepped inside the woman's house.

Kelli sat cross-legged on the deep blue carpet of the living room, surrounded by boxes. Some were spilling over with photographs, others were stuffed with papers and die cuts. Scissors, glue, colorful stickers, and a massive binder with a few pages in it covered the walnut coffee table. She brushed a lock of dark-blonde hair off her forehead and grinned up at Victoria.

"That glorious hair of yours caught my eye as you came to the door. If you're in search of Curran, he's not here. He and Rob went to lunch. They're having man time."

Victoria shook her head to clear the wistfulness that pricked her. Curran took his responsibility as male role-model to his nephew seriously. He'd make a wonderful father. "I didn't see his truck. Actually, I came to see you."

Kelli beamed. "Oh! How lovely! Here—" She grabbed a box off the pale blue recliner near her. "Take a seat, stay and chat for a while."

"I'd like that." Victoria never had many female friends, and while she hung out with Mara on occasion, Kelli was really the only woman she was close to these days. She craved female company.

She sat down, looking over the explosion in the room. "I never knew anyone who actually made scrapbooks."

"I love it. I started collecting photos and stories and such ages ago. I'm working on Robby's right now. Christmas pictures. I'm a bit behind."

Kelli handed her a stack of photographs. "Rob and I spent last Christmas with my mum and dad. He wasn't quite sure what to make of being able to go to the beach in December."

"How did he handle the flight?"

"Pretty well. Thank God for in-flight movies and video games."

Victoria looked through the pictures. Rob opening gifts. Rob with a smiling gray-haired woman. "Is this your mother?"

Kelli glanced at the photograph. "Yeah."

Same nose, eyes. "Curran looks like her."

"Quite a bit, yeah. I take after Dad."

"Do you go back to Australia often?"

Kelli glued a fancy yellow die cut frame around one photo on a red sheet of paper. "At least once a year." She looked sideways at Victoria. "You know he doesn't go back, right?"

She nodded. "I never quite got him to discuss why."

"Because he's darned stubborn. He's got it in his head that he was a difficulty Mum was glad to be rid of. I was really too young to understand everything that happened, but I remember he fought with her and Dad over everything from money to curfews."

Kelli rummaged through a box and came up with a tube of clear glitter. "He packed a bag one day and moved in with some friends over in Gold Coast. He got into some trouble, partying, stealing, that sort of thing. Total delinquent. Next thing I knew, Mum told me his father took him to the U.S. For a long time, I thought she lied to me, because he didn't contact us. I thought he was dead."

"He sounds like kind of a jerk in his younger years."

Kelli laughed. "Still is, sometimes. He's a good man though. I don't know what Rob and I would've done without him."

Victoria picked up a scrapbook with a dark green cover from the box near her feet. "May I?"

"Feel free. You'll probably like that one. I keep books for Curran, too. That one is childhood stuff. He doesn't appreciate these things now, but even if he never does, someday he might have children. They'll like reading about their dad."

Victoria carefully turned the pages, a feeling of connection growing inside her as she watched the years of Curran's life pass. Infant, toddler, school years. Pictures he drew when he was eight, playing soccer at twelve. She saw him grow taller, watched his face age. The last photograph showed him at sixteen, washing a car. Young, leanly muscled, hinting at the man he would become.

She replaced the book in the box. "Thank you for letting me look at that. You do a great job."

"Thanks." As Victoria stood, Kelli waved her back down. "Stick around, the boys should be home soon."

"Uh, no, I really should go. Lots to do, but I can only chase work assignments for so long at a stretch." As much as she wanted to see Curran, she wasn't at all certain he would appreciate her rifling through his memories. A pang of guilt struck her heart. She'd done quite enough background research on him.

Before his retirement, he'd had a very public yelling match with Amanda Dannen, when he found out she was cheating on him. Curran didn't take things going on behind his back very well. If he ever found out she knew who he was when this relationship started, he'd probably come unglued. So anything else she wanted to know about him, she'd find out the most open, direct way she knew. She'd ask him.

Victoria said goodbye, then glanced out the front window when movement caught her eye through the sheer curtains. A man tall enough to play in the NBA stepped up to the door. "You have company, Kelli."

Kelli looked up from the photo and glue she held as a knock sounded on the door. "Did you see who it is?"

"Really tall, blond guy."

Victoria's heart skipped a beat when Kelli squealed and bolted for the door. She threw the door open and leapt onto the concrete landing, into the arms of the man standing there.

"Hey, if I'd known the welcome would be this good, I'd have taken my vacation a lot sooner." Humor and affection filled the man's pleasant voice.

"How did you manage to get away so fast, mate?"

He hugged Kelli, then set her back, looking her over. "I'd actually had it planned for a few weeks, so, surprise. You look great, Kelli."

"So do you." Kelli glanced back over her shoulder, waggling her fingers at Victoria, beckoning her onto the landing. "Victoria, meet Jamie Mickelson. He's an old friend."

She turned back to Jamie. "This is Victoria Linden. She's off-limits."

His brow furrowed, then his eyes brightened. He extended a long hand to Victoria. "Hi, so you're the bright spot in Curran's life. I knew there was somebody special when I talked to him last. I could hear it in the way he refused to discuss you."

She shook his hand, the blush rising in her cheeks. Was Curran keeping their relationship private because she wasn't important to him, or because he protected the people dear to him? She could take it either way. "It's nice to meet you, Jamie."

"We'll have to go out, the four of us, while Jamie's here," Kelli said.

Victoria nodded. "I'd like that, Kelli. See you later."

She left the house, hearing the door close behind her, cutting off Jamie and Kelli's already lively discussion. Halfway to the SUV, she heard a distinctive bawl from the direction of the barn. She changed course, following the noise along the path toward Curran's house, until she reached the corral beside the barn. Peg-leg stood several feet away from the thick metal bars. The big beast shook his head as she approached, then snorted and moved his bulk in a diagonal shuffle closer to the corral fence.

Victoria scratched his thick coat, rubbing his side. The harder she rubbed, the more he leaned against the bars, into her touch. She laughed. "I hope that corral was built especially for you, Peg-leg, or Curran will have another fence to fix when he gets home."

Crouching so she could look into the animal's deep brown eyes, Victoria rubbed his forehead. "I owe you, you know. It's your fault we got together. Thank you."

If she didn't know better, she would have sworn Peg-leg winked at her. She gave him one last scratch behind the ears, then headed home to drum up some new assignments. Otherwise, work was going to get a little lean in a few weeks.

Chapter Six

A few days later, Victoria stood loading the dishwasher in Kelli's sunshine-yellow kitchen. Mulled cider steamed on the stovetop, the scent overlaying the remains of Kelli's amazing lasagna.

Kelli put the salad dressing away in the fridge then shook her head. "You shouldn't be doing that, Vic, you're a guest."

Victoria filled the detergent dispenser. "Well, you certainly shouldn't do it. You made dinner."

The other woman crossed her arms. "Actually, we ought to make the men do it."

Victoria looked over her shoulder, into the great room. Jamie sat cross-legged on the carpet, helping Rob put together a building-block race car. Curran relaxed on the recliner built into the end of the burgundy floral sectional couch. She smiled, then closed the dishwasher and started it. "Too late, all done."

"They're saved from women's work for another day."

She laughed with Kelli as she washed her hands, then walked to the end of the breakfast bar which separated the kitchen from the great room. She tucked her hands into the back pockets of her jeans and studied Curran. He looked so comfortable in the recliner, eyes closed, the fireplace crackling near him.

Rob whooped and jumped on the couch beside Curran. "My car's done, my car's done!"

Curran opened his eyes and examined his nephew's creation. "Great car."

"Yeah, I know." Rob settled beside him, driving his car in the air, then down Curran's arm and leg. "It had some hard parts. Jamie helped with those."

Kelli leaned over the bar from the kitchen. "That was nice. Did you remember to thank him?"

Rob gasped. "Oh. Oops. Thanks, Jamie!"

"Any time, little bud," Jamie said, stretching out on the other end of the L-shaped couch.

Victoria headed for the couch as Rob stood up, driving his car into the air. He lost his balance, landing full-force on Curran's chest. She flinched, braced herself against the anger, the yelling that would surely follow.

Curran grunted at the impact, then half groaned, half laughed. "Rob, go easy, right? I have old bones, and you're heavy." Not a single trace of anger sounded in his voice.

As he gently set the boy on the couch, Rob patted Curran's cheek. "Did I break you?"

Curran ruffled his hair. "One of these days, you might. Be careful with me, or I'll be forced to tickle you senseless."

Rob giggled and jumped down, driving his car across the front of the couch and around the floor.

Victoria relaxed, watching them. Nothing made the differences between Nate and Curran more apparent than the way he treated his nephew. Rob responded to Curran with open trust and blatant adoration.

Curran glanced at her, then raised his hand and beckoned. She joined him on the couch, leaning against him.

"I'm glad you're here," he whispered, his lips creating a shiver of want in her belly as they moved against her ear.

"Me too."

Kelli came into the room and passed out mugs of cider to everyone, then sat near Jamie. Victoria sipped the tangy spiced cider, its warmth suffusing throughout her body. Conversation flowed freely, though she listened and watched more than she spoke.

The dynamics of family and friends who were comfortable with one another fascinated her. She never spoke to her parents any more, but when she had, her family talked at rather than with each other.

Jamie asked if Curran had any new plans for the ranch, and Kelli laughed. "Yeah, he wants some cows now."

"A ranch should have a cow or three," Curran said.

Kelli raised a brow. "Don't we have enough trouble with the single bovine in the family?"

"Keep up the attitude about Peg, sister, and I'll buy a herd of bison just to make life interesting."

Victoria laughed. Watching the easy banter between Curran and Kelli, she'd never guess the two were separated by a decade in age and, for much of their lives, an ocean as well.

It felt like she'd been zapped into one of those perfect family gathering commercials for tissues. As foreign as this comfortable coziness was, in a way it seemed right. As if she'd always known on some deep level what a family was supposed to feel like, and once within the circle, she recognized the sensation.

She snuggled into Curran's side, contentment brewing within her as he gently squeezed her shoulders.

After a while, Rob hopped onto the couch next to her. "Victoria, wanna see my car?"

"I'd love to." She dutifully examined every side of the brick construction, marveling at the clear blue windshield and the tires that really rolled as he pointed them out to her.

Rob leaned against her, pulling his feet onto the couch. Shock zipped through her at the easy, guileless way Rob accepted her into his world. He took after his mother. Kelli welcomed her with open arms, too. Did everyone in Curran's life feel this acceptance, or was she lucky?

She tried to hand the car back, but Rob patted her arm. "No, it's okay, you can hold it for a while."

Not wanting to hurt his feelings, she set the car on her thigh, patted his head, then tried to catch up on the adult conversation.

Jamie probably couldn't speak if his hands were tied, given his animated motions as he talked. "So, by the day of the tournament, half of human resources is out with food poisoning from that stupid deli platter, including Paul."

Curran said, "And you need a full foursome to play."

"Exactly. So, I'm thinking, who's going to replace him when we have to be on the green in less than an hour?"

Victoria puzzled over the bits and pieces of the conversation, putting two and two together. She came up with the annual DCS GlobalTech-sponsored golf tournament, a fundraiser for a children's shelter in L.A.

Curran nuzzled her cheek then said, "So who did you end up with?"

Jamie shifted to the edge of his seat. "Mike Criszawski."

"Criszawski? Short, skinny, trips-over-his-own-feet, Criszawski? From accounting?" When Jamie nodded, Curran laughed, the rumble in his voice vibrating against her skin, tickling her ear. "Does he even golf?"

"I wouldn't have thought so, but after he birdied twice and sank a hole-in-one on the fourth, I figure I found myself a new ringer. I'm seriously considering making him a vice president so he won't be tempted to jump ship and make some other company look good in the future."

"Go ahead," Curran said. "You don't exactly need my permission to advance him."

Kelli giggled and Jamie rolled his eyes. "Thanks for handing over the mantle of authority, boss, but you'd kick my ass if I brought someone up that high without your blessing."

Victoria felt Curran stiffen beside her. In the weeks they'd been seeing each other, he'd never brought up his company, and she'd never prodded. She sat up slightly and met his gaze, unsure what to say, if anything. The conversation with Jamie clearly went somewhere he hadn't anticipated, and would have left her with questions, had she not already known about his company.

But he didn't know she knew. The rock-hard tension in his muscles told her he realized she'd want an explanation. Finally, he gave her a half-smile and whispered. "We'll talk later."

She nodded, and turned slightly against his side, realizing as she did that the warmth and weight against her right hip wasn't moving. She looked down at the top of Rob's blond head, resting against her waist. One small fist curled against her thigh, his other arm rested limply across his stomach.

He'd fallen asleep.

For one crystalline moment, Victoria pictured herself sitting this way in Curran's home, his ring on her finger, their child snuggled against her, asleep. It was merely a glimpse of what it would be like to have a family. *Her* family. A husband. A child. A wave of longing washed over her, threatening to overwhelm her completely before she blinked and swallowed hard, forcing the emotion back.

She coughed, covering the hitch in her breath, the tiny cry clawing at her throat. The realization struck hard. This wasn't what she'd given up when she signed away her parental rights. With Nate, it would never have been like this. Everything about him diametrically opposed the comforting warmth, the happiness surrounding her. And that baby—that child, now—was far more a part of Nate than of her.

But what she felt now…this is what it would be like with Curran. If she'd even briefly considered giving in to her physical craving for him, the incredible sense of belonging bolstered her resolve. Too great a risk, to feel this much or more and have it ripped away when whatever this was between them eventually broke apart.

Kelli left her seat and crouched in front of the couch, looking at Rob. "What I wouldn't give to fall asleep as easily as he does. Come on, sweet thing." She eased Rob into her arms, then smiled at Victoria.

She managed to smile back. Apparently her internal shattering had gone unnoticed by the others. Thank God. The flash flood had left her shaken to the core, but if no one saw it, she could pretend it never happened.

Rob stirred as Kelli hoisted him higher on her shoulder then took him down the hall to put him to bed. Her feelings settled somewhat with the boy gone, but the level of comfort Victoria knew before this emotional revelation was beyond her reach.

When Jamie excused himself to use the bathroom, Victoria smiled at Curran, then wandered into the kitchen, on pretense of needing a drink of water. All she really needed was a moment to breathe.

* * * *

Curran rose and stretched, then found Victoria's coat on the rack by the front door, along with his. He pulled on his own then went into the kitchen. Victoria poured the last of the water in her cup into the sink, then set the cup on the counter. He liked watching her. Even in simple motion, her natural grace came through.

He crossed to her, pressed his lips to the top of her shoulder, his touch making her jump slightly. "Come outside with me."

She turned to him. "Why outside? It's freezing."

He held out her coat. "It's starting to snow, but there's no wind. Come walk with me."

She smiled, an expression that hit him in his gut, infusing him with warmth. She took his hand and he led her through the door that exited the kitchen onto the wide redwood deck. Together they descended the stairs to the yard below. The snow fell slowly, in thick clumps rather than individual flakes. It hadn't snowed recently. The storm would certainly revitalize the ski runs.

Curran wrapped his arm around her shoulders, and they walked through the silent snowfall, across the open yard and through the grove of bare scrub oak and aspen trees. Magical quiet cocooned them, separated them from the rest of the world.

He enjoyed holding Victoria, walking with her. Seeing her with his family contented him. She fit in his world, his most personal world, in a way that women with designer bodies and flashy careers never had. He wondered if he lifted her spirits the way she did his, at least more frequently than he jogged her painful memories.

He felt comfortable with her. A bit too comfortable, or he never would have slipped and allowed Jamie to talk about work-related topics. Well, how long did he think he could date the woman and skirt around that subject? She wasn't the pushy type, but she had to wonder precisely how he afforded his relatively lazy life.

They stopped when they reached the three-rail pasture fence. Victoria climbed up and sat on the top rail, then raised her face to the sky and stuck out her tongue, catching a snowflake. Just watching her made him smile.

He needed to tell her. He'd known her long enough to figure women didn't get much more down-to-earth than Victoria. He seriously doubted anything he could offer her would change her into something else. He crossed his arms over the rail beside her. "Inside, when I said we'd talk later?"

"Yes?"

"It's later." He looked up at her, brushed the snowflakes from one of the thick curls beside her eyes. "Victoria, you know the company Jamie heads, DCS GlobalTech?"

She nodded. "It's not exactly a household name, but yeah."

He took a deep breath and said, "I own it. Well, seventy percent of it, anyway."

She ran her fingers down the side of his face, the feather touch sending a shiver through him. "Good for you."

Interesting response. Rather anticlimactic, it left him at a bit of a loss. "I just thought you should know."

"Thank you." She smiled at him, and his heart felt perceptibly lighter.

What an amazing woman. So many things about her appealed to him. He liked the way she moved, with a dancer's grace and elegance. She wasn't moody and bitchy over stupid little things the way so many women in his past were. For once in his life, he'd found an intelligent woman. She had her share of complexity, and peeling back the layers intrigued the hell out of him.

Somehow he couldn't picture growing tired of her company. That surprised him. Usually, within the first few days, he knew how long a thing was going to last.

She gazed down at him, a quizzical expression in her amber eyes. "What is it? What are you thinking?"

He stepped forward, pressed his hands against her knees until she opened her legs and he settled between them, wrapping his arms around her hips. "I'm thinking that I thoroughly enjoy your company, and I'm happy you came tonight, and I need to kiss you."

Victoria tilted her head down to meet his lips. He kissed her long and deep, sliding his hands up inside her coat, across her back. He nuzzled her neck, reached one hand up to release her coat zipper, explored the vee of delicate skin inside the open neck of her shirt. He trailed the edge of the fabric with his finger, finding the first button. He released the button, drawing a sharp gasp from her. She was pulling back inside herself, the way she had the other night when his touch grew too intimate.

He kissed the creamy skin revealed by the opened button, then leaned back to look at her. "Victoria, you've said you're not afraid of me, yet every time I try to touch you, you ice over. Is that part of how he hurt you? Did he force you?"

Her brow furrowed. "No."

"Then what's holding you back, honey?" He ran his fingers through her hair. "I'm not trying to pressure you, but I need to know what the problem is."

She shrugged. "Why does there have to be a problem? I just don't think having sex outside of marriage is a good idea."

He pondered that for a moment. "Are you telling me that you're a virgin?"

"No." Her smoky voice was quiet, her tone unreadable.

"Was Nate your only one?"

She threw a frosty look at him. "What does that have to do with anything?"

Touchy subject, he'd better tread lightly. "Knowing whether or not your abusive lover was your only lover tells me a great deal."

"Look, Curran, I've had a decent experience or two. I assume you have as well, so let's leave it at that, okay?"

"But since Nate you have a moratorium on sex?"

"Yes."

This was not what his body wanted to hear. "Why?"

She sighed deeply. "It creates too many problems."

"Such as getting hurt in a breakup."

Victoria looked away from him, out over the snowy ground. "There are worse things."

Okay, now he was getting somewhere. He lifted her down from the fence and turned to lean back on the rails. She held herself stiffly in his arms, not settling against him as she normally would. He loosened his hold on her, giving her more space before he continued his questions.

"What's worse than hurt feelings? Honey, if it's practiced safely—"

She met his gaze, and the pain in hers startled him. "There is no such thing as safe sex, Curran."

If Nate Fielder had given her some disease, God forbid it be AIDS, prison walls wouldn't protect him. "I'm starting to think the worst here, Victoria, so please, tell me what happened. Are you ill?"

"No." She blinked hard and looked away. A tear trickled down her cheek, tearing a hole inside him as he watched her fight for composure. Finally, she crossed her arms against her stomach and returned her newly hardened gaze to his.

"Curran, I'm not having sex again until I'm in a secure relationship, which in my book means married. If you can't handle that boundary, then, hey, it's been nice knowing you."

He'd never heard the final word on a subject laid down with quite that much steel behind it, from a man or a woman. He may not be getting all the answers he wanted, but he had to admire her strength.

Curran raised his hands in surrender. "Fine, enough said. I'll stop trying to seduce you."

She managed a half-smile. "Thank you." She leaned up, brushing her lips across his. "Listen, this sounds awful coming on the tail end of such a conversation, and I hate to say it, but I'd better say goodnight. I promised my cousin I'd drive her to the airport in the morning so she doesn't have to leave her car there."

"All right, I'll see you out." He wrapped his arm around her waist as they walked back to the house in silence.

He waited as she got her purse and said goodbye to Kelli and Jamie, then he followed her out front. She kissed him goodbye, a sweet kiss that seared him nonetheless, scattering his thoughts. In a tiny little corner of his mind, his promise to stop trying to seduce her flickered. He'd have to be careful how much kissing they did, or that promise would gutter and die.

Curran watched her leave, then kicked at the snow on the walk and went into Kelli's house to say goodnight. He entered to the sound of laughter. In the great room, Kelli and Jamie sat together on the couch, big silly grins on their faces as they both turned to look at him.

"Having a good time, are we?" Too good a time. He'd better stay for a bit. He tossed his coat on the back of a chair at the breakfast bar, then took a seat on the unoccupied end of the sectional.

"Yeah, actually," Kelli said. "You, um, came in to say goodnight, I suppose?"

The movement was small, but he caught it. Jamie, his arm resting across the back of the couch, stroked Kelli's shoulder with his thumb. He turned a hard look on his best friend. "Watch that, mate."

Kelli groaned. "Oy, wary brother alert."

Jamie, his grin full of his usual cocky exuberance, raised his palms. "Relax, Curran. I'm calling it a night." He leaned over and kissed Kelli on the cheek. "I'll see you tomorrow."

He walked around the couch, pausing to clap Curran on the shoulder. "Go skiing with us in the morning, bud. Late, maybe eleven. You need your beauty sleep."

Curran shook his head. "I don't know. Maybe." He lowered his voice then. "Be careful with her, you bastard."

Jamie looked heavenward. "We've had this discussion before. Chill. G'nite."

When the front door closed behind his friend, Curran leveled his gaze at his sister. "He's a terrible flirt, Kel."

She smiled. "Yeah, I know."

"He doesn't have a serious bone in his body outside of business."

"Know that, too."

"He'll hurt you."

Kelli leaned forward, her elbows on her knees, hands clasped before her. "Curran, nothing short of steel-toed boots counts as hurting any more. I like him. I'm thrilled he's here on vacation. I'm going to spend time with him. If it doesn't work out, fine, no worries. I know Jamie. He may not have a serious bone, but he doesn't have a mean one, either. And you know it, so leave him alone."

He studied the floor, struggling with the protectiveness welling in his chest. He'd never forget the swollen, purple flesh around her eyes, the cast on her arm. The terror etched on Robby's little face. When he'd arrived to collect them, they were huddled behind the locked door of the bathroom, wondering if he'd get there before Jonas did.

Kelli was right. Jamie would never, ever raise a hand to her. "Robby seems to like him."

"Why wouldn't he? Jamie is Uncle Curry's best friend, so he's a safe person."

He sighed. "I'll try to fight the urge to kill him while he's here."

"I'd appreciate that." She stood and stretched. "I'm going to bed. Hey, Victoria likes to ski, doesn't she?"

"Yeah, we've been a few times."

"Good. Bring her tomorrow. She can keep your mind off me and Jamie."

Or perhaps Kelli and Jamie would keep his mind off Victoria. She was carting around complicated baggage, including abuse of one form or another, and she wouldn't talk about it. She barely let him touch her. Curran left, trudging back through the snow to his own home. The way his thoughts were nagging at him, sleep would be long in coming tonight.

* * * *

Victoria stood by the window in her room, watching the snow fall in the middle of the night. She absently petted Sassy, perched on her shoulder.

She drew a deep breath, blew it slowly out again, trying to relax. Her thoughts refused to let her.

Once, maybe twice. That's all the time she had left with him before he decided to move on. Curran Shaw never stayed with one woman very long, and now that she'd forced herself to tell him her hard limit, it should be over soon. Sex wasn't everything in a relationship, but for most men it was a pretty big part of the whole. Add to the mix that she refused to explain why she felt the way she did, and it would be *hasta la vista* any time now.

She couldn't tell him, though. Not about the baby. If the lack of sex didn't drive him away, knowing she was the sort of woman who could walk away from a child would send him running.

If all else failed, the old article would destroy everything. He was going to find out eventually. Somehow, somewhere, he would find out, or remember, that she had interviewed him, written about him.

She should tell him. He'd probably be irritated, to say the least, given as much as he disliked the press. But surely it would be better to tell him herself than to have him find out on his own.

Her insides twisted into a knot. How could she tell him? She couldn't read him well enough yet to know how for certain how he'd react. It wasn't like she made him look bad in the piece, though it did include a paragraph about the rowdy fun he had that weekend, when he grew sick of interviews. Other journalists had made a much bigger deal of his nasty attitude and wild, noisy parties in their coverage of the junket.

Sassy tugged at her hair and squeaked. Victoria helped the rat into her exercise ball and let her loose on the bedroom floor. She slumped onto the edge of the bed and watched her pet without really seeing her.

She should have told him tonight. His confession about his company made a great lead-in, but she chickened out. If not telling him gave her one more day with him, she'd take it. Since it was going to end anyway, she wanted to enjoy every minute, not ruin it faster by bringing up the article.

The night passed in a haze of staring at the ceiling, playing with Sassy and half-formed dreams during those moments when her eyes finally closed. She started awake at the ringing of the phone beside the bed. She rubbed her eyes, clearing the gunk out of them enough to read the red numbers on the clock. Who on earth would call at five-thirty?

She picked up the phone, barely registering her cousin's voice. "Mara, why are you calling so early?" The words barely crossed her lips when she bolted upright. Mara's flight. She needed to leave in about five minutes in order to get her cousin to the airport on time.

"Hey, cuz, just called to tell you I canceled my flight. So you don't have to wake up early and take me. Oh, sorry, guess you're up early already, huh?"

Victoria took a couple of deep breaths to calm her racing heart. "When did you cancel?"

"In the middle of the night practically, but I got my cards read last night, and I am so not supposed to go to Florida this week."

She fought a yawn and lost. "Mara, I thought tarot readers weren't supposed to predict the future. Doesn't that break some sort of psychic code of ethics or something?"

"Well, yeah, but this was a total emergency, so she bent the rules a little. She didn't want me to get hurt down there, isn't that thoughtful?"

Victoria dropped onto her back. "Lovely, Mara. I hope you tipped her well. Can I go try to get some sleep now?"

Mara clucked her tongue. "You've been up all night, haven't you? Your voice gets really rough when you haven't slept."

"I've had a lot on my mind."

"Ohhh, cuz, you've got it bad. You've been replaying the evening."

Victoria rolled her tired eyes. "What are you talking about?"

"It's a chick thing. We are genetically wired to revisit every word, every expression and search for the deeper meanings. We just don't realize that there isn't a lot to read between the lines with men. What you see, what you hear, is generally all there is to it."

Victoria cringed at the hoarseness of her laugh. She really, really needed to sleep. "Thanks for the advice, Mara. You're right. Curran is a great guy. He's straightforward, and so far, he's pretty understanding of my limitations and my baggage. But I don't expect that to last. Besides, I'm going to blow the whole thing sky high when I tell him about my original connection to him."

"Back up, what did I miss? What original connection?" Her cousin sounded miffed.

Victoria shivered, pulled the covers back over herself. "Several years ago, when DCS GlobalTech bought Pieron Pictures, Curran threw a huge press junket. I covered it as part of an article I wrote about him for a magazine."

"So?"

Victoria sighed. Sometimes Mara had to have things completely spelled out for her. "So, he doesn't remember meeting me before.

Curran doesn't know that I already knew who he was. He thinks I'm just some regular, normal woman he met. The right time to discuss it has just never come up, and frankly, he doesn't strike me as the kind of man who takes deception very well."

Mara blew a tongue-raspberry in her ear. "It's not deception, Vic. So you knew about him already, big deal. It's not like the person he's been dating doesn't exist. Who knows, maybe you've seemed familiar to him all this time, and finding out the truth will just tell him why. But if you're worried about it, I'd discuss it with him sooner rather than later."

Sooner rather than later. Yikes. "So, did Madame Psychic tell you when it's okay to go play in Florida?"

"In a week or so. Go get some sleep. I'll talk to you later."

Victoria let the phone slip from her fingers, not caring where it landed. How Mara could possibly sound so perky this early in the morning was a mystery. Did she have that much energy when she was twenty-one? Nope, too far back, she didn't remember. One thing for sure, her flighty cousin would never get her feet on the ground until Uncle Martin stopped financing her life of leisure. The only thing that made Mara's parental spoiling tolerable was her relative lack of brattiness.

Victoria rubbed her thumbs over her eyes and ran a hand through her hair, wincing when her finger caught on a tangle.

Sooner rather than later.

If by some miracle, the truth didn't bother him, and he could live without sex, as if, then maybe there would be hope for this relationship after all. She glanced at her watch. Way too early, and she was way too tired. Besides, this wasn't the kind of discussion one should have over the phone. She'd go see him later today. She'd tell him.

Really.

* * * *

Victoria dragged herself out of bed after ten in the morning, when Sassy scraped her food dish across the bottom of her cage for the fifth time. Showering and slipping into a cozy fleece pullover and pants made the morning a little more bearable.

She lit the gas fireplace before braving the cold to get the morning paper. She found a letter wedged in the jamb when she opened the door. A yellow sticky note clung to the front of it, from the neighbor a quarter-mile to the west. The letter was delivered to her house yesterday by mistake.

She carried the letter and the newspaper into the kitchen and dropped the paper on the table. She leaned her hip against the counter, turning the ivory envelope over in her hands. The letters came regularly now, at least once a week. What surprised her was how little they bothered her lately. They never said anything new, and she was kind of accustomed to them.

Besides, what could Nate really do to her from where he sat?

A knock sounded on the door as she slid her finger under the envelope flap. She pulled the paper from the envelope. Not the usual ivory, but white copy paper. She unfolded it, and the kitchen around her vanished as she realized what she held.

A copy of her medical file from the obstetrician in Los Angeles, showing the dates of her prenatal visits. A red-ink note scrawled in the margin drew her attention.

Where is my child?

She couldn't breathe. He'd given up his rights to the child, before the trial was over. He didn't want the baby.

But he wanted him now.

The adoption records were sealed. He'd never find the boy.

Someone was talking to her. She forced her whirling thoughts to calm and focused on the sound.

"Victoria?"

She jumped, recognizing the low rumble of Curran's voice. She wrenched herself fully into the moment and pasted a smile on her face as she jammed the paper back into the envelope. "Curran, where did you come from?"

"I knocked a few times. The door was unlocked, so I let myself in. I hope you don't mind." Through narrowed eyes he looked down at the envelope in her hands, then back up at her face. "You were in another world for a few moments there. What's going on?"

"Nothing, just…lost in my thoughts, I guess."

"What's the letter?"

No. Oh, no. This was definitely not for his eyes. "It's nothing." She cringed inside at the waver in her voice.

Curran's eyes darkened. "Nothing. Except your hands are trembling and you won't look at me." He crossed the room slowly, like a predator on a hunt. He grasped her shoulders, his hard gaze snaring hers. "Victoria, you're keeping a lot of things from me, and I'm quite aware I've just stumbled onto one of them. I want to know what is going on, and I'm not leaving until you explain it."

Chapter Seven

Victoria steeled herself under Curran's gaze. Standing here in the kitchen, Nate's latest twist to the note game in her hands, Curran awaiting an explanation…she felt exposed, vulnerable, with no visible means of escape.

Curran's thumbs brushed the sides of her neck. "What is going on, Victoria?"

She was tired of keeping secrets from him. How could she even dream of growing closer to him if she constantly hid things from him? As long as he didn't insist on seeing the letter in her hands, she'd break one of her secrets open right now.

"I've been getting letters from Nate." The tension unwound slightly inside her, providing an amazing sense of relief as she let the secret go.

His brow creased. "What sort of letters?"

"Annoying ones. One line, sometimes two. Reminders that he isn't finished with me until it is on his terms."

"The hell he's not. Isn't there something the police can do?"

"Not really." She turned away from him, out from under his touch. She wanted to save all the letters for evidence, just in case, but this one should never, ever see the light of day again.

She strode into the great room to where the fireplace blazed, opened the glass front and tossed the envelope into the fire. It blackened and curled before bursting into flames.

There. The worst part of her life was still a secret, and safe for now.

Victoria shut the door, only then becoming aware of Curran's gaze locked on her. She turned and found him leaning against the wall, arms crossed over his chest. A muscle in his jaw ticked.

"You did a lovely job of acting unconcerned about his letters. I almost believed it, until you destroyed that one in such a panic." He pushed away from the wall, striding toward her with an air of almost lethal grace. Was he angry with her?

She stood her ground, waiting. When he reached her, Curran grasped her fingers in his, gently but insistently unfolding her grip on her own arms.

"Just because someone sends you something doesn't mean you are obligated to read it. He wants to continue hurting you, and if you read these things, it's not that far removed from standing there while he bloodies your nose."

How the hell would he know? "Wrong. It's not nearly in the same category."

He gently touched her cheek. "Ignore them, Victoria. Toss them all in the fire unread."

Oh, if only it were that easy. If she did ignore the letters, she'd have no warning at all if he upped the ante again, like he had today. At least through the notes she might have some clue what to anticipate. "It isn't that easy."

"Hmm. Perhaps not. Where is he incarcerated anyway?"

"I told you, California."

"Be more specific."

A quiet threat hung in his tone, and the way he shifted closer to her combined with the hardness in his eyes sent a chill shuddering through her. This was a side of Curran she'd heard about but never witnessed. When he set his mind on something, he could be ruthless. "Why does it matter?"

"It's time for someone to have a word with Mr. Fielder about the way he chooses to spend his spare time."

"Someone like you?"

"Of course. I'm not fond of men stepping into my territory."

"And I'm your territory." It had such a caveman sound to it, part of her bristled. A greater part nearly melted into a puddle at his feet. He wanted to protect her.

"Yeah, honey, you are." Curran drew her into his arms, pulled her tight against him, and tilted his head, capturing her mouth with his. The bottom dropped out of her stomach the way it did shooting down the first hill of a roller coaster.

Then the kiss ended and he brushed his fingers along her cheek. "I won't allow him to hurt you, Victoria. If I have to have a personal sit down with him to stop this, I will."

She swallowed hard against the lump that swelled in her throat. She didn't deserve his protection. "What if that isn't enough?"

"There are always legal means."

"He comes from fairly old money, Curran. I don't think his family would appreciate any more legal problems."

"Good. The threat of further public humiliation hangs over their heads. They might pressure Nate to stop this behavior."

She shook her head. "They fought for him before, against me. They have deep pockets."

Curran laughed, but there was little humor in it. "Honey, I really doubt their pockets are deeper than mine. If they decide to back him against me, they will be very, very sorry."

She took a deep breath and buried her face in his shoulder, unwilling to let him see her get all choked up. It was such a silly, girly thing to get teary eyed.

Still, how could she not? It wasn't every day a man offered to be her champion, to go to war for her. Even her thick armor was little defense against a hero.

He held her for a while, then gently set her back and smiled. "We're going skiing. Come."

She smiled back, blinking hard, hoping he didn't notice the sheen of tears in her eyes. "We?"

"Jamie, Kelli, Rob. Me."

"I'll be ready in ten minutes."

* * * *

Nate's latest letter vanished from Victoria's thoughts once her skis hit fresh powder at Park City Mountain. The scent of pine and aspen infused the thin, brisk air, and she didn't feel the cold as she spent a few hours speeding down the runs and laughing with her friends.

Curran lit up on the slopes, racing with Robby and teasing her. He was a far better skier than she was, but she'd never cared for moguls or black diamond runs anyway. Fear wasn't fun. She loved the freedom of a wide, fast run like Temptation and Carbide Cut, where she tucked low over her skis and all but took flight.

They broke for a late lunch at Mid-Mountain Lodge, a meal full of laughter and undisguised flirting between Kelli and Jamie. Curran seemed to ignore it, but she noted his tension in the stiff way he held himself and his subdued laughter. Clearly, the combination of his sister and his friend didn't sit well with him, though she couldn't fathom why. They seemed so happy together, and Jamie appeared to be equally enamored of Rob, who climbed all over him and talked him to death.

Finally, when the meal was over and Rob was yawning, Curran said, "Time for hitting the bowls. Anyone want to join me?" He looked pointedly at Jamie.

Kelli said, "You boys go on ahead and do your crazy rough skiing. I think Rob needs a break. How about it, Victoria? Want to hang out and have coffee while the boys go tempt fate and broken bones?"

Victoria took the hint. Curran clearly wanted to talk to Jamie alone. "I'd like that, Kelli. If we move fast, there's a spot over by the fireplace we can claim."

"Good. Robby can settle on the coats and take a nap."

"Mom, I'm not a baby. I don't need a nap, but I can sit and play my game."

The fatigue on the boy's face belied his claim, but Kelli nodded. "Fine, no nap then. But you will plant yourself beside me and take it easy. Clear?"

"Yes, Mother."

Victoria stifled a laugh at the resignation hanging in the boy's tone.

Curran kissed her on the cheek then lifted his parka from the back of his chair. "Right then, ready to give it a go, mate?"

Jamie sighed. "Why do you do this, Curran? We're going to get up there, you'll want to put money on it, and then I'll kick your ass."

"I'm a gambling man, Mickelson. I'll take that chance."

The men left, and Kelli and Victoria moved to a more comfortable spot by the fire, Kelli half dragging Rob as he concentrated on his game.

Victoria's muscles turned to jelly, sitting in a soft, cushiony chair before the fire. She'd skied harder than normal today to keep up with Curran, and between the workout and her lack of decent sleep last night, she now realized just how tired her body was.

Kelli sipped her coffee. She was a pretty woman, and when Jamie was around, she positively shone.

"How long have you known Jamie?" Victoria asked.

Kelli broke into a grin and set her coffee cup on the hearth. "I met him a few years back, but I didn't get to know him really well until this last year. Curran's known him forever, though. They attended UCLA together."

"He seems like a nice guy."

"I could go on about his qualities forever, but I don't want to bore you."

After chatting for a while, Victoria glanced over at Rob. "Oh, Kelli, look. He conked out."

Rob's game hung in his limp fingers as he lay on their coats near the fireplace. Kelli reached over and smoothed his pale hair.

The motion hit Victoria hard. Was her child's mother as gentle? "He's a sweetheart. Is he always as well-behaved as he's been today?"

Kelli laughed softly. "I wish. He has days when I dearly wish Jonas could be trusted with him, because I'd send him on his merry way for a week. He's a very typical little boy."

Outside of counselors, Victoria hadn't talked to another abused woman. She'd never wanted to. "Kelli, can I ask you a personal question?"

The woman's smile put her more at ease. "Ask away."

Part of her desperately wanted to know what it was like to raise a child fathered by an abusive man. Did seeing his father in him ever bother Kelli? Her voice caught on the edge of her question. How could she ask such a thing? She switched to a slightly less delicate topic. "What happened with your husband? Did he always hurt you?"

Kelli raised an eyebrow, but her expression was unreadable. "Interesting question."

"I'm sorry, I shouldn't have asked, it's just...I've never really talked to another woman who—" She broke off as Kelli's eyes widened and her mouth sagged open.

"Victoria, were you in a violent relationship?"

"Didn't Curran tell you?"

Kelli shook her head. "No, Curran is intensely private when it comes to relationships. He didn't tell me anything. Wow." She hugged her arms around her knees and sighed. "We were married for three years before anything ever happened. They were great years. In fact, when I look at Robby, I see the better parts of Jonas."

Were there any better parts of Nate she could have seen in their child? She couldn't seem to remember any, aside from his great looks. "What changed?"

Kelli gave a smile touched with sadness. "He lost his job. The bank was going to foreclose on the house before he found another, and Curran bailed us out. He hated taking money from my brother, thought it made him less of a man. He started drinking heavily. One day, he slapped me and shoved me against a wall. He felt terrible later, but once the door was opened, it never quite closed again. It was easier for him to do it the next time he was drunk and angry. And after a while, he was drunk and angry all the time."

Victoria nodded. So she had good times she could remember when she looked at her child. A well of sadness tried to open inside her, but she locked the lid on it. She knew better than to revisit her own choice. Adoption was the very best thing she could have done at the time. Hindsight sometimes clouded the clarity, the surety with which she'd made her decision.

Kelli's voice jolted her from her thoughts. "Do you mind my asking what happened?"

She shared a kinship with Kelli, a bond of sisterhood born in pain. She'd never shared her experience with a friend, only with counselors.

Even her parents, not that they cared, heard the skeleton version. Now, the words poured out of her.

"I started dating Nate five years ago. He was a successful attorney, I was a struggling writer. He pampered me and I fell hook, line and sinker. My roommates drove me nuts, and when he invited me to move in with him, I jumped at the chance."

"When did it start?"

"He was subtle at first. He'd tell me to change my outfit because I didn't look good in what I'd chosen. He convinced me to bleach my hair because he preferred blondes."

"What a bastard."

"Yeah, and if anyone tried that now, I'd give them explicit directions to Hell. But he worked on me so gradually, I just sort of believed him. He'd pick my meals at restaurants so I wouldn't gain weight. He started leaving me home from social events because I wasn't intelligent enough to follow his law friends' conversations."

"I don't know if anyone has told you this, Victoria, but emotional and mental abuse is every bit as bad as the physical kind."

She smiled weakly. "I know. Thanks for that."

"How did you finally get away from him?"

"I decided either I was better than he said I was, or I might as well just die and get it over with. I chose to believe I was better, and I told him I was leaving. He went ballistic, beat me badly enough to put me in the hospital. I testified against him in criminal proceedings, and he's still a year away from his first parole hearing."

"Good onya, Victoria," Kelli said, her eyes bright with support and understanding. "He's right where he belongs."

"Yeah. For now."

After a moment, Kelli said, "Tell me, does your experience make it harder to let yourself go with Curran? Are you more defensive?"

"Sometimes."

Kelli sighed, laid her head back on the chair. "Starting a new relationship is so hard. I adore Jamie, and he is the polar opposite of Jonas. Still, I find it difficult to let down my defenses, even when I know he would never hurt me."

"You feel scars you'd forgotten you had." And the ones she hadn't forgotten grew raw again.

"Exactly. Jamie's so great with me, though. I'm not expecting it to go anywhere, really, but it is wonderful for now."

Victoria didn't dare question what future she might have with Curran. The fact that he showed up this morning to take her skiing was a minor miracle in her book. Trying to envision a happy ending was foolish at best. She'd take every day as it came, and soak in all the wonderful moments to sustain her when it all ended.

* * * *

Jamie turned his skis and stopped on the open snowfield near the lodge. He winced as he rubbed his thigh. "Curran, if I do any more moguls today, my legs are going to give out on me."

Curran cut to a stop nearby, sending a tail of snow into the air. He slipped his goggles off, leaving them hanging around his neck. "Wuss."

"Hey, now, is it my fault you get to play ski bum every day and I have to sit in an office and rule your empire?"

Curran snorted. "Yeah, I know just how much you hate being in charge, mate."

"I could get used to it. You'd better hurry back before I redecorate your office."

"Very funny." Curran used the end of his pole to release his boot bindings, then stepped off his skis. He thrust the poles into the snow and leaned down to lift his skis and slide them together for carrying. "Well, Jamie, now that you've had plenty of time to ponder, stop avoiding the question. What are your intentions toward my sister?"

Jamie released his own bindings. "What am I supposed to say, Curran? Anything I say outside of 'I'm going to marry her' will probably be wrong. Hell, saying I'll marry her is probably not what you want to hear, either."

He stared at his best friend. "What exactly is that supposed to mean?"

Jamie slid his skis together before turning narrowed eyes on him. "It means I'm well aware you don't think I'm good enough for Kelli."

Where had he gotten that idea? "Mate, I think you'd be great for my sister. If you're serious. If you're toying with her, then I want you on the next plane to Los Angeles."

Jamie hefted his skis onto his right shoulder and took a few steps towards the lodge before glancing back. "How can I tell you what my intentions are when I don't even know?"

Curran picked up his own skis and joined his friend on the walk to the lodge stairs. "Do you love her?"

The question jolted him the way Curran hoped it would. Jamie went stock still, his frown and furrowed brow a reflection of his internal war. "Don't ask me that, bud, okay? I can't answer it yet."

He widened the crack in Jamie's armor. "Can't, or won't? I know you loved Alexa, Jamie, but she's been gone for eight years. Do you honestly think she'd want you to live the rest of your life alone?"

He knew he'd hit the nerve too hard when his friend tensed, then rounded on him. "Tell me something, why do you presume to lecture me about love and relationships when you have the worst track record I've seen and you've never been in love?"

"What makes you think I've never been in love?" Now why did he say that? The conversation had somehow turned around on him. He had to get it righted, refocused on Jamie.

Jamie stalked across the snow and leaned his skis against the rack by the stairs. "Because the loss of a woman has never turned you inside out and left you to dry, that's why. You take it all in stride. Even with Amanda. All she did was seriously bruise your pride. She didn't break your heart."

Curran set his skis against the rack and wrapped a cable lock around them. Thinking about Amanda still pissed him off. "That was a damned public bruising. Let's not forget the picture of her half dressed and wrapped around her other boyfriend at Aqua. Half a dozen entertainment shows and every tabloid in the market splashed that one around. And let's not talk about what showed up on the internet."

"She was bad news from the start, Curran. You should have never hooked up with her."

"Hindsight's perfect."

"And you should've never let her chase you out of your life."

Curran blew out a deep breath, pulled off his glove and rubbed his hand across his eyes. "I didn't choose this life because of Amanda. But she showed me I'd never find a long-term relationship. Not there. Not with the women in my circle."

"Is Victoria long-term?"

He weighed that for a moment. She was pretty, smart, kind. She also had enormous strength and kept him on his toes. Falling in love with her took no effort at all...and it was a direction he wasn't prepared to go. He swore and pushed her image away from his mind's eye. This discussion wasn't supposed to be about him. "I don't know."

"Well, figure it out, and if she is, marry her, have a nice honeymoon, and get your ass back to work."

Marry Victoria? He hadn't even come close to crossing that line of thought yet, nor did he want to. "Jamie, how many times are we going to have this conversation? Retired. Need me to spell it for you?"

Jamie shook his head. "Answer me this. Have you sold your condo in L.A.?"

"The market's in a slump right now."

"Uh-huh. And you don't check the stock quotes five times a day and watch competing companies like a hawk either, do you?"

"Force of habit."

Jamie snorted. "Admit it, Curran. You miss the big bad business world. You're a shark trying to act like a goldfish."

The conversation had seriously gone off the proper track. He started out warning his flighty friend off his sister and somehow now had to justify his own path in life. He tossed a curse at Jamie, and strode into the lodge, ending the discussion before it grew any more complex.

* * * *

Later that evening, after dinner with everyone, Curran stood with Victoria on her porch, waiting to see her safely inside. Safer in the house than in the truck, where he'd been unable to keep his hands off her.

She unlocked the door and turned to him. Her eyes glittered with passion and her kiss-swollen lips curved up in a smile. "Do you want to come in?"

Curran groaned and wrapped his arm around her waist, pulling her body into his. "Only if you'll change your mind about letting me make love to you."

She drew a deep breath. "Don't tempt me. I want to, but I'll hate myself in the morning."

The resignation in her voice dampened his raging desire. He covered her lips with his own in a gentle kiss, then released her. "In that case, I'd better be a gentleman and refuse your offer. If I walk in that house, I may not leave."

She trailed her fingertips along his jaw, over his lips. "And I may not let you. Goodnight, Curran."

He waited until she'd closed and locked the door behind her before leaving the porch. He opened his parka, grateful for the cold and the way it helped knock his libido down a few notches.

Victoria continually hovered at the edge of his thoughts now. In a way, he regretted promising not to seduce her. It might prove the most difficult promise he'd ever had to keep. Her scent drew him to her. Her pale, tender skin tantalized him, and every time she looked at him, he felt the light in her eyes deep in his gut.

If it was purely a physical reaction, it would be easier to manage. But it was more than that. She warmed his soul in a way he craved. His life seemed a little darker when she wasn't nearby, and the more time he spent with her, the less he liked leaving and missing her.

When he neared Kelli's house, the lights were on, but Jamie's rental car was already gone. He needed something to take his mind off Victoria. Finding out if anything had happened between his sister and his friend should do the trick.

Kelli let him in, then settled back into her workspace on the living room floor. He wove his way around the scrapbooking boxes to the lone empty spot on the sofa. He pushed at a heavy box with his feet, trying to move it out of his way so he could stretch out his legs. Frustrated, he gave the box a swift kick.

"Hey, be careful with that, Curran! I work hard on these scrapbooks."

"Sorry. Where's Jamie?"

She crossed her legs, then picked up a photo and decorative scissors from the pile on the coffee table. "He went back to the hotel. He was tired. You really put him through his paces."

"Does it bother you that Jamie is staying at the Silver Lode?"

Kelli shrugged and leaned across the table for a glue stick. "Why should it?"

"Because Dakota Grant's restaurant is there, and he dated her for over a year." He winced as he finished speaking. His words sounded petty. He chalked it up to crankiness brought on by lack of sex.

Kelli cocked her head at him. "If he wanted her, he would have stayed with her. He was rather quiet before he left, though. I certainly hope you didn't say anything to mess up what we have going."

He'd meant well, but he didn't think Kelli would appreciate his discussion with Jamie. "Of course not. I have nothing but good wishes for you two."

He reached into the box he'd kicked and pulled out a blue leather book. One of his, he noticed as he opened the cover. "Why do you do this, Kel?" He never understood why she felt the need to chronicle his life, his rise to the top of the business food chain. He turned page after page of years-old articles. He remembered all these events. What did he need a scrapbook for?

"Even your memory isn't perfect, dear. Someday, you may want to look back on your accomplishments. Or your kids will, if you ever settle down."

"It still seems ridiculous to me, but whatever makes you happy." He flipped another page and froze, his brain clarifying what he'd just seen. Slowly, he turned the page back. A profile of himself from a business magazine, done around the time the company moved into the filmmaking arena.

The world tilted slightly as a sick burning grew in his gut. He read the author's byline again. The words stared back at him.

Victoria Linden.

Chapter Eight

Curran's hands trembled as his fingers grasped the scrapbook. Victoria Linden. Her name stood out in small, bold type under the yellow block headline, "Shaw Sets Out To Conquer Hollywood."

The scrapbook seemed to fade as his focus turned inward and he concentrated. He sifted through memories, back to that weekend when Victoria must have interviewed him. It seemed so far away, such an utter blur.

He'd announced his acquisition of Pieron Pictures. He'd held a press conference on Friday morning at company headquarters, then holed up in the Four Seasons hotel for the weekend, along with executives from Pieron, and a few actor and director friends involved with the film company. It was a Hollywood-style press junket and he gave interviews until he lost his voice, then partied with his mates every night. It was enormously fun, if dreadfully long, and he must have met a hundred journalists there.

"You're lost in thought." Kelli crouched beside him, tugging him back to the present.

He sat back in the chair and refocused, weaving through the images in his mind. She had to be there somewhere.

"Earth to Curran."

He absently tapped the scrapbook page. "Give me a minute. I'm trying to remember."

Kelli lifted the scrapbook from his knees and examined the article. A sharp gasp of breath told him she'd read the author's name. "Maybe it isn't her. It's been a few years since this article, but I'd think you'd remember meeting Victoria before."

"There's always been something familiar about her eyes, I just couldn't place her." Suddenly, he sorted her image loose from the jumble of others in his memory. "I remember. If I'd only sat and really thought about those eyes of hers, I might've figured this out sooner."

He glanced at Kelli, who wore her concern like a mask. "Her hair was different. Long, blonde. She wore glasses then, I think."

His heart shuddered. It had been wonderful while it lasted, to have her in his life. To have who he thought she was, at any rate. "Kel, do you have any idea how much a current article about me would be worth to her?"

She grasped his arm. "No, no way. You can't possibly think—"

"Why not? It makes sense. She spends a while getting to know me, then writes a lovely in-depth report for her pick of major magazines. She gets a huge scoop, a big fat check, and probably pushes her career up several notches in the process."

His fingers tightened on the chair arms. His chest ached with the tension twisting through him. His lungs wouldn't work properly. It wasn't the first time he'd been betrayed, but strangely, this was the only time he could recall it causing him pain. "When did I become such a poor judge of people?"

"Curran, you're hurt, I can hear it in your voice."

He pushed up out of the chair. "I'm not hurt. I'm furious, dammit! None of this was real."

"I've seen the way she looks at you. She cares for you, enormously."

"And you're such a skilled judge of character."

Kelli's eyes clouded. "That was harsh, Curran."

Curran forced himself to control the whirlwind building inside him. She was right; he didn't have any cause to take out his misery on her. "I'm sorry."

Something inside him trembled and cracked, threatening to break. He'd be damned if he'd let it happen in front of his sister. He sidestepped between her and a stack of boxes. When he reached the door, she called out to him.

"Curran. Please. Talk to her, calmly, before you do something you're going to regret."

He looked over his shoulder at his sister. She looked small, fragile, standing with her arms wrapped around herself as if for support. For a blinding moment, he saw Victoria standing that way, pale and trembling, the night of her flashback. The sudden ache nearly split his heart. He shook off the image. It was all some sort of grand act. "Oh, I'll talk to her all right. After everything I gave up for a modicum of privacy, she owes me some answers."

"Maybe she truly doesn't care that you used to be a bit of a celebrity. Give her the benefit of the doubt, at least. Think about the Victoria you know."

"I have. She doesn't exist." He left, bracing himself against the bitter wind as he crossed the snow-crusted ground between the houses. The women he dated all wanted something more than companionship, in the long run. Usually, they wanted to share his spotlight for a career lift, to siphon off what they could use from the image he'd crafted over the years.

As a journalist, Victoria would strip him of his carefully built privacy for her own gain. Stupid. He knew she was a writer, but he let himself believe that what she wrote had nothing to do with him.

He kept his anger and his pain leashed until he entered his home. He stalked down the hall to the fitness room and sent the door crashing shut behind him. Here, completely alone, he could let loose.

He stripped off his shirt and boots, pulled on a pair of running shoes and stepped onto the treadmill. He sped it up to a full run, uphill. His quads screamed in protest, still tired from hours on the slopes.

It didn't matter. He touched the remote control attached to the treadmill console. The blare of music answered him. He cranked up the volume, letting the thunder of drums, heavy bass and a wailing guitar wash over him as he spit out every curse in his repertoire.

How in the hell had this happened? People with ulterior motives never slipped in below his radar. If they did, he'd have been screwed a hundred times over in the expansion of his company. He read people too well to be surprised. Even when Amanda cheated on him, he'd expected it. The only curve she threw him was making a public spectacle of it and embarrassing both of them.

Victoria kept secrets well. Not well enough to conceal the fact she had them, but her skill kept him from figuring everything out on his own. Even after she told him about those threats in the mail, he'd known that wasn't all she hid. She was the first person he didn't have pinned down before the secret surfaced.

Which probably meant he'd really lost his touch, and needed to get his ass back to work so he could sharpen up again.

Or, it meant she was somehow innocent. Maybe she really was the woman he perceived—sweet, fun, with a fascinating steel-edged fragility that made him desire her and need to protect her all at once.

No. She could have told him that first day, untangling Peg. She could have told him when they talked about her writing over hot chocolate. She could have told him every time he asked about what she'd worked on that day.

She could have. She should have. She chose not to.

Therefore, the only possible conclusion was his first. She meant to write some sort of an exposé that would destroy everything he'd gained by disappearing from public view and moving here.

Yeah, he'd talk to her. Right now, he needed to shut down his mind, and run himself to exhaustion.

* * * *

Victoria hadn't heard from Curran in two days. She thought about calling him, but her own insecurities made her put down the phone every time she picked it up. She expected it to end, didn't she? True to Mara's prediction, she spent much of her quiet time, when she should be writing, stewing over everything he'd said on Sunday, on the way he'd kissed her before he left, trying to recall the exact expression in his eyes.

Finally, on Wednesday afternoon, the doorbell rang. A glance out her bedroom window confirmed Curran's truck sat in the driveway. A thrill shot through her, and she ran for the door.

Victoria glanced in the hall mirror. At least she'd worn mascara today. Her stomach lurched with delicious tension at the thought of seeing him again and she drew a deep breath before she opened the door.

He stood on the porch, sheepskin coat closed against the breeze, gloved hands clasped before him, dark hair tumbling over his forehead and collar. His expression was so composed, so hard, she couldn't read anything in him. The tension in her belly took a sickening dive. Something was wrong.

"Hi. Come in."

"I'd rather not. Get your coat and talk to me out here." A distant coldness hung in his voice, making her shiver.

She slipped her coat from the closet and pulled it on, then stepped onto the porch and closed the door behind her. "Okay. We're outside. I missed you the last couple of days."

"I'm sure you did."

Where did that attitude come from? "Curran, what's going on?"

He took a step closer to her. "I know who you are now, Victoria. I remember you."

Sooner rather than later. Oh, God. Later had come.

"You were different then," Curran said. "Bleached blonde. Glasses. Professional, very quiet. I might not've remembered you at all, but Kelli, being the good little sister, kept scrapbooks. Every article, every mention of my name ever written."

The scrapbooks. She'd talked with Kelli over those books, she'd flipped through one. And another held her article. "I thought about telling you, so many times—"

His voice sharpened. "But you didn't, did you? Now I'm left wondering if you'd ever have told me at all. I have to believe you wouldn't have until the new article comes out."

She had thought of writing a piece about him, hadn't she? Until he kissed her that first night, after he brought Chinese takeout over.

Curran stepped toward her again, close enough to touch her. He reached a hand up to her face and fear flashed cold through her stomach. She cursed herself for trembling, but old responses died hard.

He paused for a moment, something she couldn't read flickering in his hard green eyes. Then he brushed the backs of his gloved fingers gently down her cheek. His jaw ticked and she got the distinct impression he was fighting with himself.

"It's the kiss that doesn't fit into the equation," he said, rough emotion in his voice. "Obviously you recognized me when we met over Peg-leg's fence adventure. But I'd like to think the kiss at the club was pure."

Yeah, the kiss was pure all right. Pure fantasy. Heat rose in her cheeks and when she dropped her gaze from his, he swore.

He paced away from her then turned back. "None of it was real. You knew me on Halloween, didn't you?"

He'd apparently seen the truth in her reaction, so she'd better fess up. "Yes. Your voice gave you away."

"I should have known. It was rather convenient how you ended up house-sitting down the lane from my home. Took a while for you to track me down, but you managed. I owe you a round of applause for your resourcefulness."

Victoria clenched her fists. *Don't cry, don't cry.* She concentrated on his words.

"The only other thing I can't make fit is why you haven't slept with me. You never explained, you just said no. The nearest I can figure is you had too much pride to stoop quite that low for a story."

Anger fused into the hurt pressing on her heart as she connected exactly where he was going with all of this. "You think I was just playing you? That going out with you, kissing you, is all about a story?"

"An exclusive story worth a healthy amount of money, I'm sure. Tell me, just how much am I worth in print these days?"

Her anger boiled over, sweeping her pain away. "How can you stand there and accuse me of being some sort of media prostitute?"

"You're right; prostitute is too harsh considering you refused sex. I'll settle for unethical tease."

She shifted her stance, mentally measuring the time it would take to get through the door and lock it behind her if she needed to escape. She should let it go, but he'd scratched her fragile pride and the strength to stand up for herself surged in her veins.

"How dare you! I've spent years earning a solid reputation as a writer. You think I'd risk it to write a piece without your consent and cooperation? I can't believe you think I'd toss my ethics aside that easily. You want the truth, fine. I'll give you the truth. Yeah, when we ran into each other over Peg, I thought about asking you for an interview. I thought about it for twenty-four hours, until you kissed me again. An article was no longer an option at that point."

His brow creased and confusion lit his eyes. "Then what were you hiding? Why not just tell me about the Pieron interview?"

She spread her arms wide. "This is why! You never hid your dislike for the press, Curran. If I'd told you that first day when we talked at your house, you'd have kicked me off your property."

The heat of her anger kept her tears at bay, but the tingle in her face told her they wouldn't stay away much longer. "I should have told you, but I was afraid of this very reaction. Dating you was something I didn't want to lose. So I struggled to tell you and couldn't do it."

He released a mirthless laugh. "Uh-huh. And Brindle's. Explain the club to me."

She tapped her index finger against his chest. "Hey, you approached me on Halloween, remember? Yeah, I recognized you. And you know what? I wanted to kiss you. I was dying to find out what you were really like. I never in a million years expected to run into you again."

He scrubbed a hand through his hair. "What am I supposed to make of all this?"

Victoria's anger peaked. "You've already drawn your conclusions. You stormed over here armed with what you thought you knew, wanting to play judge, jury and firing squad. So I suggest you take your damned self-centered ego off my porch, Curran. If you can't recognize something sincere and real, if you can't see it when it's right in front of you, then I want you gone. Get out of my life and don't ever darken my doorstep again."

Victoria marched into the house and slammed the door behind her. She threw the deadbolt, then held her breath, listening. He cursed and slammed his fist against the door once. Finally, she heard an engine turn over. A moment later, the truck rumbled away down the road.

In the silence that followed, she sank to the floor and wept.

After a while, her brain overrode her emotions. *I'm acting like such a girl.*

Grateful not even Sassy was there to witness her meltdown, Victoria pulled herself to her feet and trudged to the bathroom. She splashed her face with water. It didn't accomplish all that much in the way of soothing her red, puffy eyes, but she felt a little better.

Funny that she reacted so strongly to all of this. She'd known it would end, she'd expected it soon. Heavens, she'd even thought it would end because of that old article. It shouldn't have surprised her.

She'd apparently given Curran Shaw more of her heart than she thought. Now she'd relearned one of more important lessons of her life. Letting a man into her world led to pain. Well, she wouldn't be doing that again any time soon, would she?

* * * *

Curran slammed the door of his truck and stormed across the yard to the pasture fence. Peg-leg gave a snort as he approached and lumbered over to meet him, but he wasn't in any mood to pet the beast.

He pulled the cigarettes he'd picked up at the convenience store out of his pocket and ripped off the plastic wrap.

The barn door slammed open and Rob approached at a dead run. "Uncle Curran, can you saddle Sparkler for me? I wanna ride."

Curran pulled the cigarette from his lips and tucked it into his pocket, but not in time. Rob skidded to a stop, his eyes widening into saucers. "Oh, man, are you gonna be in trouble!"

"Rob, you don't need to tell your mother—"

His plea came too late. His nephew was already running across the snow to his house.

Curran swore and returned the cigarette to his lips. Peg snorted at him when he flicked his new lighter. He growled back at the bison. "Shut the hell up, Peg. I'm already going to hear it from Kel, I don't need it from you, too."

Peg's eyes rolled and he let out a long bawl. Curran leaned against the fence, slowly releasing the smoke from his lungs.

How the hell did Victoria do that? How did he go over to confront her and end up being the one who got dumped? She'd jerked control of the situation right through his fingers and turned it around on him.

Peg butted the fence rail and rolled his eyes again. Curran pointed at the bison with his cigarette. "Don't look at me like that, mate. You weren't there, you're not entitled to have an opinion."

He pushed away from the fence and started pacing along the line. When he'd smoked halfway down his second cigarette, Kelli cleared her throat behind him.

He waited, but she kept her silence. He glared at her over his shoulder. "What?"

"Did you give her a chance to explain?"

"Pardon me? Nothing about falling back into the clutches of my addiction?"

Kelli crossed her arms and nailed him with one of her stern mom stares. "You know how I feel about it, but I can't exactly punish you. If you want to kill yourself with those things, that's your business. Just don't you do it around your nephew."

She stepped closer to him, her expression softening. "Now then, did you really talk to her, or did you just shove the article in her face and walk away?"

Curran dropped the cigarette butt into the snow. "She admitted she'd considered writing about me again."

Kelli's mouth hung open. "She said that?"

"She also claimed she decided against it after I started seeing her."

"I told you so!"

He glared at her. "Don't."

"What else happened?"

He kicked at the snow, sending a flurry in Peg's direction. The bison snorted and shied away from the fence. "She said I can't see something real when it's right in front of my face."

"Well, can you?"

"Thanks, Kel. Whose side are you on?"

She stepped closer to him and patted his shoulder. "I'm on yours, Curran. But I want to see you happy, and I think you're going to regret letting her go."

He turned away and crossed his arms over the top fence rail. "I won't regret it. It wasn't honest. It wasn't real."

Kelli heaved a sigh. "Okay, if you say so. I won't bring it up again."

He listened to her footsteps crunch across the snow, until the sound grew too faint. He stretched out his hand toward Peg-leg and waggled his fingers, offering a scratch. "Come on, Peg. Come over here."

Peg snorted and walked away.

"Fine, you bastard, be that way."

She'd kept secrets from him. She'd lied to him. Just like Amanda.

Only getting rid of Amanda didn't fill a corner of his heart with an intense ache.

Curran tapped another cigarette out of the pack and slid deeper into the only thing he ever allowed to get the best of him.

* * * *

On Friday afternoon, Victoria yanked herself out of a deep, writing-induced haze when she finally processed that the doorbell had rung.

It was probably Mara. Who else would be visiting? That's all she needed right now, when the only things going right in her life were extra writing jobs lining up: Mara's preternatural perkiness.

She opened the door to a woman stepping off the porch. "Kelli?"

Curran's sister looked back over her shoulder, a smile tugging at her lips. "I—I'm sorry, did I disturb you?"

Aware that she looked like she just crawled out of bed, in her T-shirt, flannel pants, and bare feet, Victoria shook her head and leaned against the doorjamb. "I was writing. It took me a while to register the sound of the doorbell."

"Oh, good." Kelli grasped the hem of her long purple parka with her fingers, looking every bit as awkward as Victoria felt.

She pushed the door open a bit wider. "Come in. Would you like a cup of tea or something?"

Kelli managed a smile. "I'd love a cuppa, thanks."

She stepped into the house and Victoria closed the door behind her, then took her coat to hang in the closet. Kelli followed her through the entry and into the kitchen.

Victoria waved Kelli into the great room while she filled a teapot and placed it on a burner. She joined the other woman on the couch.

Kelli said, "I suppose you're wondering why I'm here."

Victoria set her elbows on her knees, balanced her chin on her fists. "Does it have anything to do with Curran?"

"Only a little, but let's get it out of the way." Kelli drew a deep breath. "Curran has convinced himself that everything about your relationship was a sham."

Victoria grimaced, the constant ache behind her heart intensifying. "Figures."

Kelli reached out, patted her hand. "I think he's wrong. I spent enough time with you two to see your feelings for him."

Victoria looked away, unable to halt the shudder passing through her as the hurt sharpened. "Can we not talk about this?"

"Right, sorry."

The tension twining between them grew uncomfortable. Finally, Kelli cleared her throat and said, "Look, Victoria, I really came to say I've enjoyed getting to know you and…goodness, I feel like a little girl back in primary school. It was so much easier to make friends back then because you could just waltz up to another girl and say, wanna be friends, mate?"

Victoria's brows rose and her eyes widened at the surprise. Did she interpret that correctly? "You want to be friends, Kelli? Even after this disaster between your brother and me?"

Kelli waved off the question. "Vic, if Curran wants to cause himself strife, so be it, okay? We can agree not to discuss him, if you wish." She leaned forward and grasped one of Victoria's hands. "You're heaps of fun to be around, and I think we discovered at the lodge that we can really talk to each other. I don't know about you, but I haven't had a true girlfriend in so long, I'd forgotten what it was like."

Victoria's heart leapt, lighter than it had been in days. "Me, too! I haven't had a close girlfriend since before Nate cut off all my outside acquaintances. And I like you, Kelli, I really do. I hadn't realized how much I need another woman I can confide in until we started talking."

Kelli laughed. "Oh, thank God. I was so terrified to talk to you. I was certain you'd turn me away."

Victoria sobered somewhat. "You're a braver soul than I for making the attempt. I wouldn't have dared come out to your house."

The teapot whistled, and Victoria went into the kitchen to make up a tray. She set the tray on the side table, started the teabags steeping, then folded her legs under her on the couch. "I'm a little surprised, though, Kelli. You're such a nice, fun person, I expected you to have dozens of friends."

The other woman shook her head. "The canyon is pretty sparsely populated. Only a few of these homes up here are year-round residences, and most are older couples or people with teenagers."

"Aren't you close to the mothers of Rob's friends?"

"No, not really. Most of them have the perfect lives, perfect families—"

"Perfect hair."

Kelli giggled. "Oh, you've met some of them? I don't fit into that world. Frankly, I'm not sure I want to try."

Victoria waved a hand at her friend. "My mother is the same way. I'm uncomfortable with anyone that perfect, because I am so very not. On that note, since you know how my imperfect life as altered in the past week, fill me in on yours. How is Jamie?"

Kelli sighed, wistfulness darkening her eyes. "He flew back to L.A. on Monday."

"He flew back and…what, end of story?"

"I don't know. He was very quiet Sunday after skiing. He dropped by on Monday before he left for the airport, gave me a kiss and said he'd call. That was it."

"Is this typical Jamie behavior?"

Kelli lifted a shoulder, let it drop. "He has a reputation for being flighty with relationships. I knew that, I just sort of hoped I'd be different. The only woman he ever totally committed to was his wife, Alexa, and she died of leukemia just before their second anniversary."

"Poor guy." Victoria reached for the teacups, passing one to Kelli.

Kelli stirred a bit of sugar into her tea then leaned back. "I know I said I wasn't expecting this thing with Jamie to go anywhere, but now that it clearly isn't progressing, I'm—"

She coughed and blinked hard, but Victoria noticed the tears glimmering in her eyes. She gave Kelli's arm a gentle squeeze.

Kelli's laugh sounded somewhat forced. "This is what I don't understand. I knew full well this was just a fun little fling, right? So why does it bother me that it might be over?"

Victoria nodded and sipped her tea. "Just because you expect the outcome doesn't make it sting any less."

"True. What's strange, though, is the fear. On one hand, I'm afraid to care about Jamie, but on the other hand, I'm afraid to not care. I don't know if I can take the misery of another relationship failure, but at the same time I'm afraid the perfect man is there for me, and I'll pass him up out of fear he'll be like Jonas."

Now that she understood. "I know exactly how you feel."

"Do you think men experience this much mental anguish over relationships?"

Victoria snorted. "Hell, no!"

She finished her tea then changed the subject. "Where is Rob today?"

"My brother, whom we shall not mention, took him to Salt Lake after school to check out the Children's Museum. Hey, do you want to get some lunch? I was so nervous about coming here, I couldn't eat this morning, and now I'm starved."

In response to the suggestion, Victoria's stomach growled. "Come to think of it, I haven't eaten yet today. Let me throw on some shoes, and we'll go."

They laughed and ate and ended up talking most of the afternoon. When Victoria finally waved goodbye to Kelli and walked back into the house, she realized how much the anguish inside her had lifted, at least for a while. Hopefully, she helped ease Kelli's misery in return.

Another thought occurred to her as she went to play with Sassy. As glad as she was for Kelli's friendship, spending time at her house wasn't an option. The last thing she wanted to do was run into Curran again. Ever.

Chapter Nine

Curran came into the house through the back door, pausing in the mud room to shed his coat and gloves. He kicked out of his boots and stripped off his wet, freezing jeans. He tossed the soaked denim into the utility sink, then grabbed a pair of black fleece pants from the shelf and pulled them on. Damn, he hated being so cold.

Peg-leg was possessed. That was the only explanation for the three fences the beast ripped down in as many days. How he managed to break off fence posts and go on walkabout without hurting himself again, Curran couldn't figure.

He passed through the kitchen into the entertainment room, backtracking to the front door when the bell rang. A delivery for his sister—the Express guy said she wasn't home. He signed for it, then set the box by the door and made his way to his recliner.

Three times since his blowup with Victoria, he'd ended up wading through hip-deep snow, wet and freezing his ass off. The worst part of mending those fences was the memories of her that surfaced and ate at him, killing him one bite at a time.

He thought about the way her eyes lit up when she laughed, and the way they glowed like gold after he kissed her. He missed the slips of paper with smiley faces drawn on them, spritzed with her perfume. She used to tuck them into his coat pocket, or into the cushion on the recliner, or in one of the cupboards, for him to discover long after she'd gone.

It took hours to shove the memories back down in the depths of his mind where they belonged, every time he had to repair a fence. If he didn't know better, he'd swear the damned bison was doing it to him on purpose.

Curran settled onto the recliner where he'd left the murder mystery he was reading. The warmth of the house soothed him, melting both cold and tension from his body. He re-read a page in his book to get back into the story. Shortly, he was fully engrossed in the characters.

"Uncle Curry!"

He sighed and closed the book. His nephew had a talent for interrupting.

Rob barreled into the room at full speed, fresh from his half-day of kindergarten. He flung his backpack on the floor beside the recliner and dropped down next to it. "I got cool stuff at school today, Uncle Curry."

"Really? What sort of cool stuff?" The joy radiating from the boy made him smile. Rob's zest for life always rubbed off on him. He put the foot rest on the recliner down so he could sit forward and examine the treasure trove his nephew dumped from the backpack.

Envelopes, mostly small white ones with a few reds and pinks mixed in, cascaded from the backpack as Rob turned it upside down. Curran snagged one from the pile and examined it. "What's all of this?"

Rob rolled his eyes as if Curran had suddenly dropped a few IQ points. "It's Valentine's Day, of course. And, see, these are all my valentine cards from my class."

Something inside him twisted and compressed like a tourniquet around his heart. Valentine's Day. His mind filled with the plans he'd made—and subsequently canceled. A fabulous dinner in Deer Valley, dancing, a sleigh ride. He still hadn't gotten around to returning the pearls he'd intended to give her.

How long was he going to hurt over her?

Rob waved a pink heart backed by a frilly white doily. "This one is my favorite."

In a painstakingly perfect child's writing, the card said *To Robby, Love Melissa.* "Why is this your favorite?"

Rob ducked his head and a bright blush stained his cherub cheeks. "Because it's pretty. It's from my favorite girl."

He missed her smoky voice, and the tiny lines beginning to form at the corners of her eyes. The tourniquet cranked harder. "Do you like Melissa?" He missed the way her fingertips circled lightly on his wrist when he put his arm around her.

"Yeah, she's my friend, and she's funny. She burps louder than I do." The clear respect in Rob's voice kept Curran from laughing.

"She sounds like quite a girl."

Kelli walked in from the kitchen. "Rob Taran Davenport, haul your backside back home. It's almost time to go to the dentist."

Robby made a face. "Okay, Mommy. I have to give Uncle Curry his valentine first."

"Make it quick."

Curran waved at her. "Kel, an express mail came for you. It had to be signed for, so they brought it here. It's by the front door."

Kelli left the room and Rob opened another compartment in his backpack. He pulled out a folded piece of red construction paper. "I made this for you. I hope you like it."

Curran accepted the paper and unfolded it. Inside, he found crayon drawings of stick people skiing down a hill, decorated with silver glitter. His throat constricted as he read the crooked words.

> *You are my best friend cause you take me fun places*
> *like to ski. I love you, Uncle Curry.*
>
> *Love, Rob Davenport*

A rush of tears filled his eyes, and he swallowed them back. With all the good things he enjoyed associated with being an uncle, he imagined how much better it would be someday when he was a father.

"Is it okay? Do you like it?" Rob looked up, hope shining in his face. Curran swept images of curly-haired children from his mind and opened his arms. The boy leapt up from the floor and threw his arms around his neck. Curran hugged him hard. "Of course, I like it. I love it, Rob. It's the best valentine I've ever received."

Rob pulled back, his eyes alight, his mouth shaped in a wide grin. "Really?"

"Yeah, really. Thanks, mate."

"Welcome." Rob scrambled off his lap and went to work stuffing his cards into his backpack.

"Did you make a card for your mother, too?"

"Yes. I gave it to her after school. It was pretty nice. Wasn't as cool as yours, though." Rob zipped his backpack closed.

"Did she like it?"

Rob laughed. "She cried."

Curran laughed too. "Then you did well, Robby. Making a mother cry happy tears is quite the accomplishment."

Kelli returned to the entertainment room, holding the large brown box. "Rob, go home and brush your teeth."

"I can use my toothbrush that's here." Rob trudged across the room, his head low, trailing his backpack along the floor. "I hate going to the dentist."

"It's a necessary evil." Kelli sat on the couch and examined the box.

Curran didn't know what it was, but the return address was Jamie's. She frowned and picked at the edge of the packing tape until she could pull it up. She ripped off the tape and opened the box, spilling packing peanuts around her feet, then gasped and withdrew a figure covered in bubble wrap.

He smiled to himself. Jamie obviously knew the way to Kel's heart was through the door of a porcelain doll shop.

Kneeling on the floor, Kelli carefully unwrapped the doll, then set it into its rosewood stand and placed it on the floor. She straightened the doll's frothy lavender organza and lace gown and arranged the long blonde ringlets around the doll's shoulders.

Rob ran in, a bit of toothpaste foam clinging to the corner of his mouth, and plopped onto the floor beside her. He gingerly touched his finger to one of the doll's ringlets. "She's pretty, Mom. Is she a Valentine's present?"

Kelli nodded. "Jamie sent her to me."

Curran grinned. Major score for his friend.

Rob turned his attention to the packing box and rummaged through the peanuts. "Did he send me something, too?" He tossed an envelope at his mother, then whooped and pulled out a small package wrapped in blue paper. "Look, this has my name on it!"

In three seconds, Rob destroyed the paper and jumped to his feet. "It's a new game, *Mechazoid 3-D*! This is the best game, and even Chad in my class doesn't have it! Look, Uncle Curry."

Kelli glanced up. "Hold everything, Robby. What's it rated?"

Curran examined the game box. "E for Everyone, Kel, it's fine."

Rob snatched the box from his hands and bit into the plastic wrap at the corner until he could rip it off.

Curran propped his elbow on the chair arm and rested his head against his palm, watching his sister slip a sheet of Jamie's pale blue letterhead from the envelope. She sniffled, wiped her eyes with the back of her hand. Another point for Jamie. "Must be a decent letter if it's made you cry."

Kelli started, as if she'd forgotten he was in the room. She brushed her fingers across her wet cheek. "Yeah, it's a good letter. He misses me."

"I'm not surprised."

She cocked her head at him. "You miss Victoria, don't you?"

Curran tensed. Here he was bursting with pride over his best friend rising to the occasion. Why did she have to spoil it? "Don't ask me that."

Kelli sent Rob to get his coat from the bathroom, then stood, cradling her new doll in her arms.

"Curran, you're being stubborn."

He glared at her. "You're treading on unwelcome territory, Kel. I know you're friends with her, but don't think you can intervene on her behalf."

She sighed and walked toward the hall. She paused at the doorway and looked back at him. "Maybe I'm trying to intervene on *your* behalf. Life's too short to spend it miserable and alone. You pushed away the best thing you ever had."

"I didn't push her away." *In the end, she broke up with me.* "I couldn't trust her anymore."

"I'm sure that old article startled you, but admit it, deep down, you never believed Victoria was using you. It just provided an easy way to end the relationship."

Her words stunned him. "An easy way? You think I was looking for a way out?"

"Yeah, I do, because it was getting too deep." Her voice softened. "Curran, you're my brother, and I love you, but sometimes you are every bit as superficial as your Hollywood mates you complain about."

He bristled at the offense. He'd changed, dammit. "I am not."

"Look, you say you want something real. I reckon real is the one thing that truly scares you, or you would have found it a long time ago."

He barely noticed when she left the room. For a long while, he sat staring into the mirror Kelli made with her words.

He didn't like the man who stared back.

* * * *

The front door of the house slammed open just after seven in the evening on Friday, sending Victoria's pulse into orbit. She dropped her book on the couch in the great room and scrambled to her feet, her instant fear morphing into relief and irritation when Mara walked in through the kitchen.

"Hiya, cuz. How's tricks?" The woman had the audacity to grin at her.

Victoria sank back onto the couch, breathing deeply to calm her pounding heart. "Mara, could you maybe not burst into the house like that? You scared me to death."

Mara cocked her head, her grin widening. "Sorry. If you didn't want me letting myself in, you should've locked the door." The redhead sauntered over and plopped onto the couch, looking at the magazine in Victoria's hand. "Whatcha reading? Oh, *Uglies*, I love that one."

"Yeah, well, don't give me spoilers. I'm enjoying it. When did you get back from Florida?"

"Yesterday. I had serious jet-lag to sleep off or I'd have called sooner. And I got sunburned, but it was so great." Mara shrugged off her white parka, revealing a tight, black, low-cut wraparound blouse, matched by clingy black pants and spike-heeled boots.

The woman might as well have 'I'll show you a good time' tattooed on her forehead. "You obviously have plans tonight."

"Yeah, but I was in the area, and thought, hey, I'll drop by and say howdy." Mara craned her neck, looking around the room, down the hall. "Imagine my surprise at finding you here alone at primetime on Friday night. Where's Curran?"

Oh, that's right. She didn't know. "We broke up."

Mara's jaw dropped. "What? Why?"

Victoria picked up her book to give her something besides her own crashing wave of hurt to concentrate on. "Because he's a jerk."

"That's real specific."

"I don't want to talk about it."

Mara shrugged. "Fine. Whatevs. Have you heard from your prison penpal lately?"

Victoria knew she meant Nate. "Nothing in the last couple of weeks."

"Good. Maybe he got some sense knocked into his head and gave up." Mara turned on the TV and started flipping through the satellite stations.

As much as she liked Scott Westerfeld's writing, Victoria just couldn't get back into the book, not with the TV on and her own thoughts churning. She didn't believe Nate was through. She wanted to relax and not worry about him any longer, but a knot of apprehension took up space behind her heart. Instinct told her whatever game Nate was playing still had a few hands to go.

She settled a bookmark between the pages and returned the book to the end table, then watched the picture on the TV switch every five seconds while Mara channel-surfed.

A couple of minutes of that were all she could take. Her patience frayed. She grabbed the remote from her cousin and switched the TV off.

Mara mumbled an apology then turned her attention to the silver rings on her fingers, twisting them around and around. In that moment, Victoria realized her cousin's innate happy-go-lucky spark had gone out. "Mar, are you okay?"

A feeble smile crossed her red-painted mouth and she waved a hand in the air. "Oh, yeah, of course."

Victoria took her hand. "Be serious with me, cuz. Just once. What's up?"

Her lower lip quivered. "Dad called me last night and yelled at me."

The very idea shocked Victoria. Uncle Martin never raised his voice that she could recall. "What for?"

Mara rolled her eyes and made a face. "Because I'm wasting my life. I mean he understands that I'm traveling a lot to get some culture and some experience, but he thinks I'm spending way too much money doing it."

"But you've always spent too much money. What changed?"

Her cousin ducked her head, avoiding her gaze. "He ran into a friend of mine when she was in town last week. I guess he asked her how I was handling school. Like a total dunce, she told him, oh, yeah, didn't you know she dropped out last quarter?"

"You dropped out?" Victoria knew her cousin was socially flaky, but she also worked hard to keep good grades. She never expected her to do something like quit school. "Why?"

Mara heaved a huge sigh and looked at her with the most serious expression she'd ever seen on the woman's face. "I realized I don't want to go the direction I'm headed. I thought all my life that I wanted to be a nurse, because, you know, helping people was cool."

"And you could work in your dad's practice."

"Yeah, that, too. Then last summer, remember when I went to Europe? I spent all this time in the great museums and stuff, and it totally fascinated me." Mara grasped her hand. "And you know what? I loved it. I want to learn about that stuff, Vic. I want to be a curator."

"That's a pretty big switch."

"Oh, I know. Totally different classes, for sure. And a different school. Since I have an associate's degree already, I'm using that in my application to other universities. I'd love to get into a program in New

York. There are so many great places there to get an internship. So, hopefully I'll hear something in time to start classes this fall."

Wow. Mara actually put thought and effort into this. Would wonders never cease? "How did your dad take it?"

"He blew a gasket, but that was mostly after I admitted that I withdrew from school. Once he chilled and I explained what I want to do and why, he was okay with it. I had to promise to stop running up my credit cards though, if he's going to support me in New York. I could get a job, but I have enough distractions from school without working, too."

"Well, good for you, then. I hope everything goes the way you want it to." Victoria stamped on the envy rising deep within her heart. She couldn't hold such support against Mara, just because her own parents withdrew all financial support the day she declared a journalism major instead of the pre-law track her mother expected her to take.

Maybe that's part of what drew her to Nate in the first place. If her mother couldn't have an attorney daughter, she could have had an attorney son-in-law. Yeah. Like it ever had a chance at going that far.

Mara studied her for a moment then said, "You haven't been out to do anything fun since your spat with Curran, have you?"

"No."

A grin spread across her wide mouth. "Well, cuz, my personal cure for a lousy, boyfriendless Friday night is a bunch of rowdy friends and a beer. In fact, I'm meeting a group of just such friends at Brindle's. Want to come?"

Rowdy friends in Mara-speak meant guys. Usually gorgeous twenty-somethings. How long had it been since she had simply hung out, surrounded by a bunch of friends and loud music? Nope, she couldn't remember back that far. "I need to change. Give me five minutes. I'll even play designated driver."

She bolted to her room to change clothes, since going out in her ratty old flannel pants wasn't appealing. She grinned, thinking of Mara's choice of friends. Most of the guys her cousin knew were a little insane. They were a parent's worst nightmare, living for dangerous sports, getting plastered and chasing girls. But they were a lot of fun to spend a few hours with.

Victoria pulled on navy leggings and a clingy baby-blue, V-neck tunic sweater. Yeah, this was exactly what she needed to chase away her lingering Curran blues. Mara's guy friends flirted relentlessly. She could use a little ego-stroking. Feeling desirable should boost her spirits.

In half an hour, she and Mara had joined her friend Brian in commandeering two tables at Brindle's. Over the next twenty minutes, their group grew to eight, including Brian's girlfriend and three guys who worked on ski patrol at The Canyons resort.

The last to show up was Danny Holt, one of Mara's many ex-boyfriends whom she still claimed as a buddy. Danny slid into a chair beside Victoria. He pushed his black forelock out of his dark blue eyes and gave her a wicked smile. "Hey, gorgeous, haven't seen you in a while. How've you been?"

When he took her hand in his and kissed her on the cheek, Victoria sidled closer to him. "Been better, been worse. Are you getting into trouble these days, Dan?"

He laughed and kissed her fingers. "When am I not in trouble, babe?" So true. Danny partied way too hard, and had been in rehab once already that she knew about.

He wasn't her type, not by a long shot. On top of his partying habits, he was five years her junior. Besides, she most definitely wasn't looking for anything, not even a fling.

But with his killer good looks and easy, seductive manner, Danny's flirting soothed the empty, aching space inside her. It was harmless, friendly fun that would go absolutely nowhere, and he knew it as well as she did. She willingly gave herself over to it.

* * * *

Curran thirsted for a crowd tonight. He craved the energy, the electricity, needed to feel it coursing through him. Thoughts of Victoria tormented him, but a couple of drinks and the flow of the crowd should dampen his need for her.

He drove into town, intent on going to one of the microbreweries that should be hopping on a Friday night. Maybe he'd drop by Fusion later and say hello to the Grant girls.

Reflexively, he glanced at the Brindle's parking lot as he passed. A white SUV caught his eye.

His heart kicked into double-time and his breath vanished from his lungs.

Surely it wasn't hers. There had to be a score or more identical vehicles in town. He signaled and pulled into the lot. He drove slowly behind the SUV. Fuzzy purple dice and a miniature disco ball hung from the rearview mirror, singling this vehicle out from all others like it.

Victoria. Raw need punched him square in the gut.

A horn honking behind him cleared his head and he took his foot off the brake and circled into the next parking row. He found a space for the truck and parked.

Her silent call drew him through the club doors like a sailor to a siren. He looked around, his eyes slowly adjusting to the low light, the pulses of color. The steady stream of people through the club doors gradually filled the dance floor and the bar. Many of the tables still stood empty, but they wouldn't stay that way long. He scanned the club for her.

The smoky sound of her laughter caught his attention. She sat at a table with her cousin and several others, primarily men. He quickly found a table that afforded him a view of her and ordered a beer.

He leaned back in his chair, watching her. Every move she made, every peal of laughter added tinder to the smoldering pit inside him. When the guy to her left leaned into her and whispered in her ear, the embers erupted into flames and lit the fuse on his temper.

It was nothing like the protective anger that flooded him when Victoria told him about Nate's letters. The rancor building inside him was far more primitive.

The guy was coming on to her. The fire grew hotter as he watched his rival wrap his arm around Victoria and draw her close to him. Hearing her low laugh in response to the guy's whispers twisted and pulled the fire inside him. It drew itself up into a beast, straining to be set free.

His temper flared with every flirtatious movement between them. Then she stood up and the guy stood with her. He slid his hand across her waist and down her hip, then pulled her to him, kissing her on the temple.

The leash on the beast snapped.

She was his, dammit.

He rose and strode across the club, never letting the guy out of his sight. Somewhere beyond the sound of his own blood rushing through his veins, he heard Victoria call his name as he approached.

Her voice checked him enough that he didn't throw a punch. He grabbed the guy's shirt, lifted him, planted him hard against the wall.

The guy spat out a vulgar curse. "What the hell?"

"Keep your hands off Victoria, mate, or I'll break every bone in your body."

Chapter Ten

Electricity crackled through the air in the club. Chairs scraped the floor and Curran heard movement around him and a collective holding of breath as he leaned his forearms against his rival's chest, holding him to the wall. He sensed Victoria standing behind him.

The guy glared at him, then looked over Curran's shoulder and said, "Does this jerk belong to you, Vic, or can I kill him now?"

Oh, yeah, give me a reason to hurt you. Curran adjusted his hold on the guy's shirt, edging him higher against the wall. "Just try it."

Then Victoria stood beside him, her hands pressing against his shoulder. Her touch sent sparks shooting through his veins. Her scent twined around him, weakening his knees.

"Curran, what are you doing? Let Danny go!"

The beast of his temper faltered at the anger in her voice. Beneath the haze of jealousy, Curran realized how much trouble he'd make for himself if he did pummel this Danny guy and leave him broken and bleeding. He took a deep breath and backed up without releasing him.

The movement allowed Danny to slide down. Once his feet hit the floor, he shoved his hands against Curran's chest. He grunted at the impact and loosened his hold on Danny's shirt.

"Victoria—" Curran turned to drink in the sight of her at his side. In that moment, he caught movement in the corner of his eye and ducked as Danny threw a left hook.

He heard her call his name as he came back up, catching Danny in the ribs with his fist. He stopped his other fist when Victoria forced her way between them.

"Curran, stop!" Cold light flashed in her eyes. She thrust a hand against his chest, her heat branding the mark of her slender fingers into him through his shirt. She braced her other hand against Danny and glared at each of them in turn.

"Knock it off, boys." Anger gave her voice a knife edge. "I'm drowning in the testosterone you two are putting out."

"He started it."

She glanced over her shoulder at Danny. "Do me a favor. Be a grownup and walk away. Please."

I win. Curran grinned as Danny flipped him off and walked back to the table. His superiority lasted until Victoria rounded on him, eyes blazing, shaking her index finger at him.

"As for you, Curran, wipe that smug look off your face. I don't know what you think you're doing, coming in here and destroying my fun with my friends—"

"Your friend wants to get into your pants, Victoria, in case you hadn't noticed." He chafed under her angry glare.

She set her fists against her hips. "So what? I'm enjoying myself and if I want to flirt with Danny, I will."

He stood close to her, her heat drawing him. Visions of pinning her against the same wall and devouring her with kisses danced in his head. He ached to touch her.

Victoria slapped at his hand when his fingers reached her jaw, then pushed against his chest. "Back off, Curran."

"No. I can't sit back and watch you with someone else."

A harsh laugh burst from her. She waggled her left hand at him. "Do you see a ring on my finger? As long as you don't, I can and will do whatever I please. Besides, you made it pretty clear that you don't want me, so take a hike."

"I want—"

"I don't care what you want. Leave me alone." She turned and walked back to her table.

Curran gritted his teeth, forcing himself not to grab her as she left him. He glanced at the crowd. Some seemed to be minding their own business, but plenty were staring. A big man, clearly a bouncer, stood beside Victoria's table, his thick arms crossed over an even bulkier chest.

Curran swore and stormed out of the club, pausing only to collect his coat. He welcomed the icy air hitting him when he burst through the doors.

That certainly went well. He hadn't lost his temper in years, but his father was right. When he let his temper run loose, everything he did concentrated on the moment, with no thought to later.

He'd managed to refresh his memory of her scent, sharpen his need for her, and make a complete fool of himself in public all at the same time. *Good onya, Curran. Way to go.*

* * * *

"What was that all about, Vic?"

"He looked just like Curran Shaw."

"I'm pretty sure he thinks you're still together."

Victoria nursed her hot chocolate, waving off the questions and comments about the confrontation from her friends. Danny sulked beside her, stewing in his injured pride. From other tables, she noticed people throwing her furtive glances and chattering amongst themselves. Great. So much for a fun evening.

Mara gave her a worried look. "Are you okay?"

No, she wasn't. Curran's jealousy and the elemental need blazing in his eyes left her heart aching, but his behavior made her ill.

Forget it. The carefree mood was beyond her grasp now. She gathered her coat and purse. "Mara, I'm going home."

She sighed. "Okay, cuz. Steve isn't drinking, I'll get a ride home from him. I'll call you tomorrow, figure out how to get my car back from your place."

Victoria nodded then turned to Danny. She pressed her lips to his cheek. "Sorry about all of that."

Danny shrugged and gave her a half-smile. "I'll live."

He squeezed her hand, which made her feel a little better. Then she slipped on her coat and walked away. She needed to get out into the cold before her nausea got any worse.

She hadn't felt that kind of violence crackling through the air since Nate's brother lunged at her in the hall after the trial. Her stomach churned again at the memory of the black rage contorting Greg Fielder's face, the way he screamed at her for ruining his brother's life.

She passed through the club doors into the foyer. She had to take comfort in discovering some strength in herself. That she hadn't cowered, but instead put herself right in the middle of Danny and Curran, was a minor miracle.

That she stood up to Curran and he took it was another. Not many men would take such a public dressing-down in stride.

She stepped out into the icy night air and sucked in a breath. She headed for her SUV, watching the ground so she didn't lose her footing as she went. She rounded the rear corner of her vehicle, looked up and froze.

Curran stood with his back against the driver's door, his arms folded across his chest. He tilted his head sideways and looked at her, his eyes glittering in the glow of the nearby streetlight.

She swallowed hard against the panic cascading through her. She'd shamed him. Nate was furious, and she'd only argued with him in private, and oh, God, it hurt…

Stop it, she hissed silently to the chill fear lumped in her stomach. Curran wasn't Nate.

She stiffened her spine, narrowed her eyes and fixed him with what she hoped was a hard look. "You know, there are laws against stalking in this state, Curran."

"Very funny." His voice was quiet, the natural rumble more pronounced than usual. "I want to talk to you."

He pushed away from the car and stepped toward her. Instinct took her a step back.

Curran halted, and his brow knitted. Hurt flashed in his eyes, hammering a fissure into the armor she'd worked so hard to reconstruct after their breakup.

He wasn't Nate. She drew a shaky breath and blew it out, steadying herself, then closed some of the distance between them. She tucked her hands into her pockets and leaned against the SUV. "What do you want, Curran?"

"I miss you." He moved closer, until the toes of his boots touched hers.

Her traitorous pulse tripped. "Do you?"

His gaze traveled over her hair, her face, halting at her lips. "Yeah, honey, I do." He raised his hands, drew his fingertips lightly across her cheeks and jaw.

Her heart crashed against her ribs in response to his touch. No, no way. He was running on jealousy and hormones, and when he came to his senses, it would be over again.

Curran shifted closer still, moving his feet to bracket hers. He threaded his fingers into her hair, leaving her skin tingling wherever he touched.

"I'm going mad without you, Victoria," he said softly, tilting his head until his nose nearly touched hers, sliding his hands down her arms, finding her waist inside her open coat. "I feel like I've been turned inside out and left to dry. Nothing is quite right anymore."

Her breath faltered, caught. Every nerve ending stood at attention, straining in anticipation. Her pulse hammered at the emotion churning in his eyes.

"I need you."

His head dipped, and then his mouth was on hers, and her soul caught fire.

A groan rumbled from deep in his throat, the sound setting off fiery tingles that shot straight to her core, leaving her pulse points throbbing. He pressed for access and she opened her mouth to him, a delicious shudder coursing down her spine as his tongue brushed hers. He deepened the kiss and she twined her arms around his neck, giving herself over to the firestorm whipping between them.

His hands found her backside and lifted her against the side of the vehicle. She ached for him, and without thought, she wrapped her legs around him. His hips rocked against her in response, his erection barred from her only by his jeans and her thin leggings and damp panties. She kissed him hard, then his mouth left hers and he captured her earlobe between his teeth as she tightened her thighs around his hips.

"Victoria, please." His voice rumbled against her ear. "I want you. Please. Come home with me."

Part of her soul strained toward the warmth he offered, but at the same time, her brain snapped back into place. In a split second, she processed everything he'd said, separating it from the incredible rush flowing through her body.

She lowered her legs and slid a hand down to his chest, pressing against him. He shifted back, confusion and need lighting his eyes.

"Hold on a second." Silently she berated her libido, hating her emotional and physical craving for him.

"Why? What's wrong?"

She pushed against him, completely disengaging herself so she could gel her thoughts together. "Two things. Number one, I didn't hear an apology of any kind from you, and frankly, you owe me one."

His eyes widened, but he held silent as she continued. "Number two, why is it everything revolves around you?"

"What are you talking about?"

She clamped down on her need for him, using her anger as the vise. "You only wanted me in the first place because you didn't think I knew who you were. You came unglued thinking I might disrupt your life with my writing. Now you miss me, you need me, you want me…are you detecting the trend here, Curran?"

His bewildered expression hardened. "This is not all about me."

A bitter laugh escaped her. "Oh, really? Tell me, did you ever, in all your misery, consider how I might feel? You broke my heart, you jerk, and I am *so* over you!"

His gaze darkened. "Yeah, I don't think so. That kiss didn't feel like you were over me."

"You kicked my hormones into gear, nothing more. In fact, I should have never given in to them in the first place with you. If I could take back kissing you on Halloween, God knows I would."

She turned and opened the vehicle door, climbing inside. She pulled on the door, but he grabbed the edge, preventing its closure.

"Don't tell me you regret that kiss and everything that came after it." Heat tinged with desperation flooded his low voice, flickered in his eyes.

Anguish pricked her soul, sharp and fresh. "Curran, I regret every day I spent with you."

This time, when she yanked on the door, he let it go. She glanced at him one last time. His hands dropped to his sides and he stared at the ground. She thrust away the rise of sorrow for him as she reversed out of the parking spot and drove away.

He didn't love her. Wanted her, yes. Needed her. Even ached for her, if she could believe the expression in his eyes. And that was what really pulled her back, enabled her to leave him standing there, looking dejected.

Better to be alone than with a man who didn't love her. She had to believe she was worth being loved. She'd cobbled a life together again because she clung to that belief. If she settled for a man who didn't love her, what was the point?

One thing was clear to her as she returned home. She couldn't take another round with Curran. No matter how much she craved him, body and soul. She'd trap herself in a relationship without love because of her own weak need for him.

She was worth more than that. If not, she might as well have stayed with Nate.

* * * *

A snowstorm snarled into the mountains before dawn the next day. Curran leaned against the window in the living room, watching the snow fly.

You. You. You. Are you detecting a trend here, Curran?

She was right.

He set his forehead against the cold glass and closed his eyes.

Did you ever consider how I might feel?

He hadn't. Until now, after he'd sorted through his memories of her and catalogued her expressions when he confronted her with the article.

He'd hurt her, cut her deeply. He'd seen it in her eyes then, in the tears she'd choked back before she turned the tables and unloaded on him. He hadn't cared at the time, in his quest for self-preservation. Thinking about it now, what he'd done weighed him down with her pain.

I reckon real *is the one thing that scares you.*

He'd stripped a lot of insulation from his soul in the last several hours, looked deeper into himself than he ever really wanted to. It all came down to this—part of him was missing, and Victoria held it. He needed her in his life, and the idea of committing to her, of letting her permanently into his heart scared the hell out of him.

Scared him enough to send him to his baby sister for advice. He pulled out his cell phone and dialed. After a couple of rings, Kelli's sleep-rusted voice said, "Hello?"

"I need to ask you something."

"Curran, you're up early." She yawned. "Or did you never go to bed?"

He went back into the entertainment room, dropped onto the couch. "Couldn't sleep."

"So you deprive me of mine. Thanks, dear."

He needed a woman's perspective. "Kel, am I selfish?"

"You woke me up this early and you have to ask?" She yawned again and grumbled, "Of course you're selfish. You're a guy."

"That doesn't help."

She drew a deep breath, blew it out slowly. "All right, seriously then. Sometimes you are. You aren't with Rob, though. I've never seen you behave in a self-centered way with him. Why?"

He considered her words. Maybe there was hope after all. "I'm trying to figure some things out."

After a moment of silence, Kelli said, "Curran, what do you want? Deep down inside, what do you really want, most of all?"

The words passed his lips before he could stop them. "I want Victoria in my life."

"Is that it?"

His throat swelled and stung. His voice came out rough. "I want her to love me."

"Then you have to love her."

Curran released a dry laugh. "Easy for you to say. After last night, I doubt she'll have anything to do with me."

She cleared her throat. "What did you do?"

Some things didn't need discussing with his sister. Besides, she'd probably hear every detail from Victoria later. "I saw her at Brindle's and let's just say that I made a real ass out of myself and hurt her feelings again. She regrets every day we were together."

Kelli laughed softly. "I know Victoria, and I know you broke her heart. That doesn't mean she won't give you another chance."

"Of course it does."

She sighed. "No, you clearly don't understand her. Or, women in general, for that matter. If you go about it wrong, then yeah, she won't give you the time of day."

The complexities of business never bothered him. In fact, he thrived on the challenge, puzzling out how to bring companies together and manage to please the stockholders, how to restructure debt in a way that raised the company's worth rather than undermined it.

Complexities in relationships meant it was time to break up, like selling off a stock just as it started to dive. But ending things hadn't helped with Victoria. His feelings were plenty complicated and getting worse every day. "How do I do this, Kel? How do I get her back?"

"I told you. Love her. If you don't, it won't work, and frankly, I won't help you."

Love her. How? His heart was too hard; he'd kept it that way rather than lose his ability to concentrate on work every time a relationship ended. He didn't have time for injured feelings, so he never let any feelings build.

Wasn't this constant ache for her proof that he'd slipped, that she'd gotten under his skin? "I'm serious about this, Kel. What do I do?"

"Let her in. You're good at keeping people out of your heart, while you demand they let you into theirs. You try to dissect them, to find out everything—"

"No, I don't."

She laughed. "Curran, you did it to me. That's how you operate."

When he didn't reply, she said, "You have to let her in. Open yourself up to be hurt. You can't feel deeply if you continue shielding yourself. And you can't ask for something from her that you're not willing to give."

He rubbed his eyes. Kelli made a lot of sense. He didn't like what she said, but he couldn't argue with it, either. Only one question remained to ask himself. Did he want her enough to lay himself open?

"I'm going to bed." Curran switched the phone to his other ear and rose from the couch. "I need to get some sleep so I can think clearly."

"Maybe you shouldn't make this decision with your head, Curran. Maybe this should be the one decision you make with your heart. Just a suggestion."

"Duly noted."

Curran found sleep quickly once he climbed into bed. When he awoke late that afternoon, the wisps of dreams floating in his head combined with the ache in his heart to tell him what he needed to do. Now, how did he talk Victoria into giving them a chance to start over?

* * * *

Three days after a storm had dumped an extra twenty inches of snow in the mountains, Victoria stopped by the post office to pick up a package. She'd missed delivery while picking up groceries a day earlier. The clerk returned with a box that was too big to fit in the mailbox. Victoria left the counter and waited until she had the SUV turned on and the heater blasting before she examined the box.

It was postmarked in San Diego.

Nate was at it again.

She hesitated, her heart pounding. She wanted nothing more than to toss the box in the garbage unopened. Her need to know what he was up to made her pull open the pocketknife on her keychain. She slid the blade through the packing tape, then took a deep breath and opened the box.

She withdrew a note, a toy truck and a rag doll from the shredded paper filling the package. The note was far longer than the others.

I want to see the child. Does he look like me? Or does
she look like you?

Bring him, her, whatever. Come see me, we can get
married in the chapel here.
   We can be a family.

The air vanished from her lungs. He didn't know. He thought she'd kept the baby.

She didn't have the resources to raise a child on her own. She knew she wouldn't be able to look at her son without seeing Nate. A child deserved more than that, deserved a solid home, with both parents who loved it and wanted it, and a fenced yard and a dog. She'd given her child those things.

And she'd saved her son from his father. She was glad she'd let him go. He would never have to face the devil behind Nate's handsomely chiseled features.

She drove behind the corner gas station to the dumpster. She ripped the note into a dozen pieces, then threw the toys, the box and the paper into the garbage. She drove home on autopilot, trying to forget about the package, until she pulled into the driveway and found the left side filled by Curran's truck.

Nate's latest ploy left her drained. Pulling up the energy for sparring with Curran was impossible with her reserves emptied.

He opened his truck door and climbed out when she did. He let her walk past, then he followed her onto the porch.

She unlocked the door and drew a deep breath before turning to Curran. He didn't appear his normal, confident self. He stood with his hands buried in his pockets, his shoulders slightly rounded. He clearly hadn't shaved today, and the shadows under his eyes told her he hadn't slept much recently.

The sight of him looking so out of sorts made her heart twinge. She'd sworn to herself she wouldn't miss him any longer. Did she really think she could turn off her feelings that easily?

He gave her a half-smile, but didn't quite meet her gaze. "I know you're not thrilled to see me."

No, she wasn't, but that didn't stop her soul from yearning, tugging her emotions out of their hiding place like a crocus surfacing to early spring sunshine. "I can think of people I'd rather see. I suppose you want to come in?"

"For a moment. I have some things I need to say to you."

Victoria shrugged. She doubted he could hurt her any more than he already had. Being polite wouldn't kill her. "All right." She opened the door and hung her coat and purse in the closet, then led Curran into the living room. She faced him, crossing her arms before her. Her heart thumped in anticipation, though part of her feared what he might say.

Curran nodded toward the love seat, the largest piece of furniture in the elegant burgundy room. "Will you sit with me?"

"Go ahead. I'll stand." If he touched her again, in this drained state, she'd shatter.

His gaze dropped to his boots, then he nodded. He drew a deep breath and looked up, his eyes capturing hers. The swirl of blatant emotion in his normally composed gaze shocked her.

"I, uh...damn. I'm not good at this. But I wanted to apologize. I've not been careful of your feelings. You're right, I was a jerk. Actually I was a lot worse than that. I truly am sorry."

She doused the internal spark of hope. "You're forgiven, Curran. I owe you an apology too. I should have been upfront about the article."

He nodded. "Apology accepted."

Okay, that cleared the air, right? "Good. Now we can go our separate ways without these things hanging over our heads."

His head jerked back. "Go our separate ways? I don't want...I mean, um, is that what you want?"

She couldn't answer. Her throat constricted so hard she could barely breathe, let alone say anything. He stepped toward her. "I'll do whatever you ask, Victoria. I'll leave you alone, if it's what you really want."

She gripped her arms tighter, wanting to say no, wanting to beg him to stay. "Do you want to start over?"

"What I want doesn't matter. What do you want?"

She shivered, fighting the intense need for him, trying to use her brain for once. "I don't know."

His crestfallen expression broke her heart. He nodded, looked at the floor. "I suppose that's my cue to leave, then." He walked to the door, pulled it open. "You know where to find me, Victoria. If you ever need anything, I'll be there."

He stepped out, closed the door behind him. The click of the latch ripped through the protective bands around her heart and set her feet free. She ran to the door, yanked it open.

"Curran." Oh, she had to be completely insane to subject herself to this again.

He turned at the foot of the stairs. "Yeah?"

"Do you have a plan for starting over?"

Relief flooded his eyes as he climbed the stairs to reach her. "Nothing specific. Dating. Taking it slow." He leaned against the post supporting the porch roof, ran a hand through his hair. "Victoria, I am truly sorry. I didn't mean to hurt you."

She raised an eyebrow. "You came over here that day to chastise me and break up with me, and it never occurred to you I might be hurt?"

He leveled his gaze at her. "You have to understand something. Whenever I've dated a woman, it's been with the understanding that it was all fun and games, and when it ended, that was it. No hard feelings, we both just walk away. Remember, that first day at my place, before you rode off. I told you if things got too complex for you, end the relationship. That's the way it always worked."

"Sorry I wasn't sophisticated enough to pick up on the don't-get-emotionally-involved angle of dating you." She heard the bitterness in her voice, but didn't bother to soften it.

"Dammit, that's not what I mean. I never expected this thing between us to become so different from what I was accustomed to."

"Different how?"

"No one ever cared enough to be hurt by me, just pissed off." He stepped toward her. "I never cared enough to be hurt before."

She desperately wanted to believe she was different, unique from the other women in his life. "Do you hurt now?"

His eyes darkened, as if her very words pained him. "God, yes." He drew a shaky breath. "Victoria, I'm walking on totally unfamiliar ground with you."

Now there was something she could relate to. But if Curran could bare this small part of his soul to her, the least she could do in return was take another chance. "Maybe it's best to walk unfamiliar ground together. I'm willing to start over if you are."

Curran smiled, some of the shadows lifting from his eyes. "I can't promise I won't screw up a few dozen times."

"Neither can I."

He reached out and grasped her hand. She squeezed his fingers in return but retreated a step when he slid a hand behind her neck as if he meant to kiss her. She shook her head in response to his confused expression. "Take it slow, Curran. I'm too raw to pick up right where we left off."

He released her and raised his hands in surrender. "Fine, no worries. Since we're going slow, may I call you tomorrow?"

Had a guy ever asked if he could call her? "Sure, I'd like that."

Curran gave her a wave, then strode off to his truck. She watched him back out of the drive before she retreated into the house.

They were starting over. She didn't know which feeling was stronger, the elation, or the dread.

Chapter Eleven

Curran promised he'd take their relationship slow, and he followed through. He called Victoria every couple of days over the next week. As much as he disliked phoning women, fishing for something to say after the first five minutes, he found himself eager to call her. Somehow, they found things to talk about for more than an hour at a stretch, covering everything from the activities of the day to their earliest childhood memories. With Victoria, each call was an adventure, an exploration.

Finally, when the gnawing need to see her grew too great to subdue, he picked up Chinese takeout and rang Victoria's doorbell at half past six.

When she opened the door, his heart leapt. She stood in bare feet, wearing blue flannel pajama pants, an oversized white sweatshirt with sleeves long enough that her fingers just peeked from the ends. She pushed her riotous curls out of her eyes and grinned at him.

Her smile lightened his heart. "Tell me you haven't eaten."

She laughed. "Come in."

He stepped into the house. "You mean I don't have to convince you to have dinner with me?"

She shrugged and waved him into the dining room. "I thought about teasing you, but I'm too hungry to follow through."

Curran set the bags of food and the thermos on the table, then took off his leather jacket. "Long day at the office, honey?"

She met him at the table with plates, serving spoons, and cups. "Yeah, productive though. What's in the thermos?"

"Jasmine tea."

Delight brightened her eyes. "You remembered! Great night for it, too. I can't seem to get warm today."

I can think of ways to warm you. Curran swallowed that thought, shaking his head to clear the image of exactly how he'd warm her in his bed. He pulled the food boxes from the bags and opened everything on the table. He broke out the chopsticks and they filled their plates. "How's the feature on the quilting lady?"

She swallowed a bite of Kung Pao chicken. "Great, almost finished, well ahead of deadline."

"I'm impressed. Any inspiration on chapter eighteen?"

"Nope, still stuck. I'm thinking of jumping over the scene at the train station and writing a later scene, just to keep the juices flowing. I'll figure it out eventually."

"I'm certain you will." He smiled, then took a drink and dug into his lo mein.

The way her brain cooked up fiction fascinated him. His own creativity extended no further than occasional pranks and schemes he pulled off as a kid. Some called his approach to business imaginative, but knowing how to work people until they came around to his way of thinking wasn't on the same plane as Victoria's inventiveness.

They ate and chatted until, during a moment of silence, they heard Sassy scrabbling loudly in her cage. Victoria excused herself to see to her pet, and Curran watched her walk down the hall, the gentle sway of her hips leaving his mouth bone dry.

A few moments later, the rat came rolling into the room in her exercise ball. Sassy bumped against Curran's foot and paused to look up at him. He waved. "G'day, Sassafras." She blinked, then rolled on her merry way.

Victoria rejoined him and swallowed the last of her tea. After a moment, she sighed. "I talked to Kelli today. I guess she's taking a trip home in May."

"For Mum and Jack's anniversary, yeah." He finished off his egg roll, watching Victoria push the few remaining noodles around her plate with her chopsticks. When her teeth caught her bottom lip, he pushed his plate forward and crossed his arms, leaning on the edge of the table. "What?"

She looked up at him, her eyes wide. "Hmm?"

"You're chewing on your lip. What are you trying not to say?"

"It's nothing." She stood and picked up her plate.

He followed her into the kitchen with his own plate, placing it in the sink. He knew what was going on in her head. The few times they had spoken of Australia, he'd been vague. Her detail-oriented mind didn't handle vague very well, and knowing Kel was going back probably had Victoria's brain in a stew.

She refilled her teacup and headed for the great room. He grabbed his own cup and followed her, nearly tripping over Sassy as she rolled ahead of him.

He sat opposite Victoria on the comfortable leather couch and studied her as she mulled her thoughts. "Just ask and get it over with."

She gave him a sheepish smile. "You don't have to answer."

"I'm aware of that."

"Why don't you go home for a visit? I'm sure your mother wants to see you, even if there were problems in the past."

He rolled his eyes. "You've been talking to my sister about more than her vacation plans."

"I didn't ask, Curran, she just told me one day how strained the relationship with your mother is, and that you haven't been back because you're stubborn."

Terrific. He blew out a breath and ran his hand over his face, then through his hair. "Kel made up her own explanation about why I don't go home because I've never given her a straight answer on not going back."

Victoria's brow creased, her eyes reflecting concern and confusion, but she waited for him to continue.

He didn't particularly want to talk about this. Yet, what had Kelli told him? If he wanted her to love him, he had to let her in. Well, hell, if he couldn't tell her something this simple, stupid though it made him feel, he had no business trying to get closer to her.

"I can't go home, Victoria."

"Why not?"

"I literally, physically can't."

She cocked her head at him. "I don't follow you."

Why did it make his heart pound just to think about it? He rubbed his suddenly clammy palms on his jeans. "I can't get on the plane."

"Are you saying you're afraid to fly?"

He swallowed hard, the very image of sitting on a plane to Australia making him sweat. "Yeah."

She shook her head. "Curran, you used to fly all over the place when you were at DCS GlobalTech."

"All over the country, yes. To Canada. Even points south, if the flight was well planned."

The understanding light in her eyes told him she'd connected the dots. "You're afraid of flying over the ocean."

"I've tried over the years. Time comes to board the plane and my feet freeze. If I manage to move, I suddenly can't breathe."

"Panic attacks."

He nodded, watching her face for signs of rejection. Finding only warmth there, relief flooded through him.

Victoria tapped her index finger against her chin. "I know the company held annual conferences in London and Tokyo."

"Yes, and I was always conveniently busy, available only via satellite. I sent Jamie."

"But, if you're afraid to fly over the ocean, how did you get to the U.S. in the first place?"

He hated the memory of that flight. "That's where it started. I was nervous about the flight anyway, when my father made me leave Australia with him. In the air, I calmed down a bit, actually didn't mind the flight too much until we flew into some turbulence. It got severe all of a sudden and dropped us a good five thousand feet in a few seconds."

The terror of that drop surfaced sharply inside him. "When we flew out of the clouds, I looked out the window. Nothing but ocean in any direction. I realized that if we went down, we'd be a thousand miles from anywhere. If I didn't die in the impact or drown, I'd be left trying to swim for my life, avoiding sharks and God knows what else, for however long it would take for a rescue."

She set her teacup on the end table and reached out to him, clasping his hand in hers.

He squeezed her fingers, grateful for the gesture. "I didn't think anything of it, once we landed, though I've never been so grateful to stand on solid ground. When I tried to go back home for a visit a few months later, I couldn't do it."

She frowned. "So you're marooned here."

"I never thought of it that way, but I suppose so."

"How sad." She leaned forward, brushed her lips across his cheek. "Thank you for telling me."

To lighten his own mood, he said, "Keep it to yourself, right? It'd be bad for my image if word got out."

She laughed. "Your secret is safe with me."

He believed her, and realizing that surprised him. He'd let her in, and in the bargain, tied himself to her, but the security he felt knowing she held one of his secrets shocked him.

Perhaps Kelli was right. Perhaps intimacy did have more to do with sharing souls than with sharing bodies. Because right now, he felt closer to Victoria than he'd ever been to another woman.

It was great. He wanted more.

* * * *

For the beginning of March in the mountains, forty-eight degrees was a veritable heat wave. Victoria basked in the sunshine that made wearing a coat over her cream fisherman's sweater and jeans unnecessary. She and Kelli found the stores at the Factory Outlet clogged with shoppers brought out by the warmth. Kelli picked out jeans and a few shirts she wanted for her son, then they drove to Main Street for shopping of the more eclectic variety.

Victoria loved shopping the historic district, even if she rarely purchased anything. The western-Victorian architecture delighted her. The boutiques always sold the funkiest stuff. The art galleries refreshed her senses, though she couldn't possibly afford the paintings, sculpture and photographs she fell in love with.

For a woman with a frugal income, she had extravagant taste. Nearly every time some piece of art or eclectic item of clothing resonated with her, it was the most expensive thing in the place.

Finally, their stomachs rumbling, she and Kelli ducked into The Eating Establishment for a late lunch. The restaurant was still busy, and they were lucky to get a window table.

She worried about Kelli. She hadn't been her fun, bantering self today, and the skin under her eyes was shadowed. By the time Victoria was half finished with her Silver Queen salad, her friend had pushed more of her salad around than she ate.

"So what did you say to the principal?"

Kelli lifted one shoulder, let it drop. "I told him if he didn't want me to make his life difficult, he'd best punish the girls for hurting the boys and not just the other way round. I know girls usually pick on boys because they have a crush on them, but the double standard is outrageous."

"You're right. By that logic, when boys fight it should be excused because 'boys will be boys.'"

"Exactly." Kelli stabbed at her salad, with more force than necessary.

Victoria deliberately set her fork next to her plate and clasped her hands, leaning against the edge of the table. "Kelli, what's bothering you? It's more than just Robby's school problems. You look like you haven't slept well in days."

Kelli left her fork in her salad and placed her elbows on the table, dropping her head into her hands. "Jamie's driving me mad."

"I thought everything was going fine. What happened?"

"He can't seem to make up his mind what he wants. One minute, he's telling me how much he misses me, and that he can't think about anything else, and then he takes off on some conference in New York, and he doesn't call, doesn't email. I know he's unsure of himself, but this is insane."

Kelli ran a hand through her hair and sighed. "When we're together, the emotion between us is deep enough to drown in. It's like we're two halves of the same soul or something. But then...I don't know if he's thinking too much, or what the problem is."

"Does he still have issues with his wife?"

"Apparently, she was an intensely possessive person. Near the end of her life, she told him if he ever replaced her, she'd come back to haunt him."

Victoria speared a black olive with a chunk of feta cheese. "Poor Jamie! Even if he didn't believe her, that must give him pause."

"It does. He's a little hesitant with Rob, too. He's wonderful with him, but sometimes I catch Jamie watching him with worry in his eyes. He may be a bit afraid of becoming a parent if this thing between us goes that far." Kelli finished off her lemonade, then rubbed her chin. "Some days, I could kick myself for becoming emotionally involved with a man who isn't sure he's ready for it."

Victoria reached across the table and patted her friend's hand. "How are you holding up, letting emotions go?"

Kelli gave her a half-smile. "Not bad. I really shut everything down while I was with Jonas. Now that I've remembered how to feel and how to care...I suppose I'd forgotten that as wonderful as the up days can be, the down days are pretty damned miserable."

She knew those extremes well, from her time with Curran. Hopefully, the rock-bottom after their breakup would be something she'd never hit again.

After they finally finished lunch, Kelli dropped her off at home. Victoria snagged the mail from the box and glanced at the stack of ads and envelopes on her way into the house. None of the ivory linen that always made her gut clench. She hadn't received anything from Nate in weeks. Maybe he'd finally given up his sick little game.

She went into the house and checked on her sleeping pet before sorting through the mail. Halfway through the extra heavy dose of junk mail, she found a letter for her from the Los Angeles County District Attorney's office. A flicker of fear lit in her belly as she set the other mail on the counter.

Why would the D.A. be contacting her, unless something had happened with Nate. Had he been released? Her hands shook as she tore open the flap and slipped the paper from the envelope. She unfolded the letter and two newspaper clippings fluttered to the floor. She looked at the letter as she knelt to retrieve the clippings. It was from Deanne, one of the assistant attorneys who helped shore her up during the trial.

I thought you'd appreciate these, and you might never
see them if I didn't send them to you.

She dropped the letter and focused on the clippings. One was a short article. As she read it, the breath vanished from her lungs.

He was dead. Another inmate had killed him.

She fought for air, then read the other clipping. His obituary. She deliberately ignored the photograph.

Nathaniel Louis Fielder, Jr. Gone to the arms of God
at age 34.

"Gone to the arms of God? Who are they kidding?" She scanned the rest of the column. Mentions of his family, his schooling, his achievements...

There it was. "We will dearly miss his sweet soul, taken from us too early by mistakes, lies, and a crime committed in a place he should never have been."

Mistakes. That must be the night he put her in the hospital. Lies. Every word she spoke on the witness stand, in the mind of his mother.

"You lying bitch!" Brenda Fielder's shrieks echoed
through the halls of the court. "How can you do this to
him, after everything he has been to you? He's given you
everything, and this is how you repay him?"

She folded the clippings, tucked them into her back pocket, mentally beating back the ghosts inside her. She grabbed her purse and keys and left the house.

She drove over to Curran's place, trying to sort out the conflicting emotions weaving through her. She turned off the engine at the top of the drive, got out of the vehicle and closed the door as the front door of the house swung open.

He stood in the doorway, looking somewhat rumpled in faded jeans and a blue plaid flannel shirt loosely buttoned over a T-shirt, a hand braced against the doorjamb. She drank him in, as if she hadn't seen him in weeks.

"Come in." His low voice rumbled to her across the crusted snow.

She approached him, her skin tingling at the way his gaze traveled over her. "If you're on your way out, I can come back later."

He touched her arm as she reached him. He cocked his head to the side and smiled. "I've a lot on the plate today, but none of it is more important than seeing you."

Her breath caught when he dipped his head, but an acute disappointment followed when his lips brushed her cheek rather than her mouth. Two weeks and counting since he kissed her last, that night at the club, pinning her to the side of the SUV. What was he waiting for?

Victoria walked into the house and dropped onto the sofa. When he sat beside her and took her hand, she said, "Some interesting news came in the mail today."

"What sort of interesting?"

"Nate is dead." The words left her with a strange taste in her mouth. It occurred to her that of all the things she wished on Nate, death wasn't one of them.

Curran's brows raised. "How?"

She slipped the newspaper clippings from her jeans pocket and gave them to him.

He studied the short articles. "Where did you get these?"

"One of the attorneys in the D.A.'s office thought I'd sleep better if I knew."

His gaze locked with hers. "And will you?"

A sheen of tears clouded her vision. Frustrated at her own emotions, she blinked and swallowed hard, forcing them back. "Isn't it wrong to be so happy that someone lost his life?"

"Not when that someone hurt you the way he did."

A bitter laugh escaped her. "How the hell would you know? We've never discussed it."

His eyes darkened, but he said nothing as she pulled her hand free of his and paced across the room. She turned back to him and compelled herself to give voice to the thoughts churning at fever pitch. "Curran, he did hurt me. He cracked three of my ribs, knocked my front teeth loose, gave me a serious concussion, and broke my right arm in two places with his golf club. The club was considered a deadly weapon and it's the only reason he served longer than six months."

"So why are you feeling guilty?" The low, even question cut to her heart. How did he do that? How did he see through to her inner thoughts?

She pressed her fingers against her eyes, willing the tears back again. "In the two and a half years I was with him, that was the only time he ever physically hurt me. I mean, yeah, he said cruel, horrible things to me, and by the end my self-esteem was practically non-existent, but to lose his life because he wouldn't let me leave?"

She wrapped her arms around herself, her soul shrinking inside her. He was dead, and she still felt cornered. "Look at Kelli. Her husband hurt her all the time. He deserved to serve his two years and lose his wife and his son. Nate flew off the handle one time. One time! He didn't deserve to be stabbed to death with some makeshift knife in a prison shower."

Somewhere along the way, Curran had crossed the room to stand by her side. The security of his arms beckoned her, but she turned away. She didn't belong in that comfort, not after what she had done. She wasn't worth a man's life.

Warm hands settled on her waist. Heat radiated against her back as his body shifted closer to hers. His breath stirred the hair beside her ear.

"You didn't make his choices for him, Victoria." The quiet rumble of his voice vibrated deep in her chest. "He chose his path, and the consequences that came with it."

He turned her, sliding his hands up the sides of her neck, gently bracketing her face. She met his gaze, and her knees weakened at the stern protectiveness in his eyes. "This is not your fault. I swear to you, honey. You didn't do anything wrong."

Oh, God, she wanted to believe him. Her bruised soul needed to believe him, the desperation clawing for relief the way the drowning want air.

"Victoria. How can I help you see the woman I see?"

She wanted to laugh. He saw a woman who didn't exist. She knew who she really was inside. A woman capable of sending away her own flesh and blood forever, a woman able to send a man to his death.

He stared at her, his eyes narrowed. "I know what you're thinking, but you're wrong. You haven't fooled me. As Jamie is so fond of telling me, I'm a shark. I got where I am in this life by seeing through other people. What surprised me with you is that, under the surface, you're the same woman you present to the world, just a hell of a lot more complex."

He slid his hands back to her shoulders, a smile tugging at his lips. "There is nothing about you that is bad or evil. There is nothing about you that is worthless."

She didn't try to sweep away the tears before they trickled down her cheeks. "But I shouldn't be happy he's gone."

"Are you happy about it? Or, are you simply feeling tremendous relief that he can't ever frighten you or hurt you again?"

Relief. Now that the foreign spot of weightlessness inside her had a name, it went supernova, expanding at light speed. She threw her arms around his neck, security enfolding her as his arms molded her to him. "I feel so free."

He gave her a squeeze. "Don't give him another thought, Victoria. It's over."

He gently disengaged her arms, pressing a kiss to her forehead before setting her back from him. Her heart skipped into an ominous pounding. Wrapped up in her own blind need, she hadn't realized something was bothering him. A fresh edge of guilt knifed through her.

"Are you okay?" She touched his face, and he pressed her palm to his mouth, then released her.

"Fine. I need to go, though. One of the horses is ready to be picked up at the vet."

I'll go with you. She stopped the words before they formed on her tongue. Sometimes Curran needed solitude, and since they were back to seeing each other every day, he likely wasn't getting as much as he needed.

He'd kept her from shattering just now, helped her regain her footing. The least she could do in return was let him have the time to himself she'd interrupted.

Curran walked her to the SUV and dropped a quick kiss on her cheek before helping her into the vehicle. Before he closed the door, she reached out, drew her finger along his jaw. "Thank you."

He took her hand in his, kissed her knuckles. "Do you feel better?" "Yes."

His smile lent lightness to her heart. "Good. I'll call you tomorrow, right?"

She nodded and let him close the door, then watched him walk toward his truck, in the smooth, purposeful gait that spoke of a man who knew what he wanted and knew how to get it.

He'd call her tomorrow. Yeah, he definitely needed to be alone. Oh, well. She needed to exercise the horses anyway.

* * * *

Three days later, Victoria let Curran into the house and promptly handed Sassy to him. "I'm almost finished cleaning her cage, but she wants to cuddle and I can't do both at the same time."

Curran set the rat on his shoulder. "Okay, I'll trade you. Here. This might make a good cage liner." He waved a newspaper at her.

One of the weekly tabloids. She examined the cover, showing various stars surrounded by garish headlines. "What's this?"

He gave her a half-smile, then scratched the rat under her chin. "That is karmic justice for you, honey. I hate it, but after the way I accused you, I deserved it."

She raised her eyebrows at him, then flipped to the page marked by a slip of white paper. A series of photographs with a short article. Now this was surreal. A murky photo of Curran holding Danny against the wall at Brindle's. Another of her telling him off. She shook her head at the weirdness of seeing her face in a national tabloid. "Oh, my."

"The one at the bottom is my favorite."

Another of Curran storming out of the club. The final one, at the bottom, of her wrapped in his arms, against her vehicle. Wow. The kiss looked like something out of the movies, and her stomach flip-flopped, recalling the fire in that kiss.

She thought back to the club. "I didn't see anyone taking pictures that night."

Curran picked Sassy off his shoulder and held her against his chest, petting her. "I'm usually aware of paparazzi cameras, but everyone has a cell phone camera. It could have been anyone."

Victoria scanned the article. The infamous 'sources' said Curran was in Park City to ski, but may have purchased recreational property in the area. Something about his lover—oh, that would be her. Heat rose in her cheeks, but she had to laugh when she read the last of the article. "Oh, I've been identified as a European model, have I?"

"You're tall, you're striking. Natural assumption for them to make."

"Oh. Thank you." She'd never thought of herself as anything close to model material. It made her feel good, until the implications of seeing photos of Curran in a tabloid hit her. "This is the first time you've shown up in one of these things since you retired, isn't it?"

The frustration in his eyes overshadowed his fleeting smile. "I did it to myself. I lost my temper and made a scene, and I earned this."

She followed him as he carried Sassy into the great room and sat on the couch. The rat scooted up his chest, curled into a ball under his chin and closed her eyes.

Victoria sighed. "I'm sorry, Curran. It's been so long since you dropped out of sight, I wouldn't have thought you'd be a camera magnet anymore."

"Sitting there having a beer wasn't story-worthy. The fight made me tabloid fodder. Though they seemed to like my attempt at making up with you." He growled in his throat, stabbing his fingers through his thick hair. "You'd think after I spent so long trying to stay under the media radar, I'd have known better than to go off like that."

There really wasn't anything to say other than agreeing with him, which he wouldn't appreciate. When he picked up the TV remote and started channel surfing, Victoria returned to the kitchen to finish washing out Sassy's food and water dishes.

She listened to the TV as she worked. The picture channel changed through a dozen satellite channels, then stopped on a Los Angeles station's evening news broadcast. Curran didn't care for television much, but she knew he watched the L.A. news regularly, and had kept his subscription to the L.A. Times. He clearly missed living in

California, missed his old life more than he would ever admit if she asked him about it.

So why had he retired and left in the first place? She'd never dared to flat-out ask him. He was starting to open up to her, but she wanted to ask that question when she could be reasonably sure he'd answer it.

She put the cage back together, dumped in fresh aspen shavings, then retrieved Sassy from her cuddle spot under Curran's chin and put the rat back into her home.

Curran was channel-surfing again when she entered the great room and sat beside him on the couch. He shifted, draped his arm around her and hugged her, kissing her on the temple.

She snuggled into his side, watching the channels flick by. Something was clearly eating at him, and she had a feeling it was more than the tabloid photos.

Victoria tilted her head up and kissed his throat. His body tensed, his heart shuddered under her palm. Hmm, maybe she could distract him a little from whatever was on his mind, and get the kiss she'd been craving for what felt like forever.

He stilled, his breath shortening as she tasted the slight saltiness of his skin. She straightened her back, pushing herself higher against him. Her own pulse speeding, she flicked her tongue along his earlobe, then down into the hollow below.

A growl sounded in his throat and he grasped her shoulders, setting her apart from him. With a quiet curse, he stood.

She frantically tried to align her thoughts in confusion. What had she done to upset him? She rose beside him. "Curran?"

He turned to her, the unmistakable glow of desire in his eyes. "I'm going home, Victoria."

Her hands trembled, and she tucked them into her pockets. "Why?"

"Because the only thing I want to do tonight is make love to you and fall asleep with you."

Her heart ached, and for a moment, she lost sight of why that would be such a bad thing. It would be so easy to fall into his arms. And hate herself in the morning, and be sick wondering if the past had repeated itself. "I'm sorry."

His eyes squeezed shut and he drew a deep ragged breath. "Believe me, so am I." Finally, he looked at her again. "I can abide by your rules, but my strength only holds out so long. I'll kiss you when I feel like I can handle it. Otherwise, don't tempt me."

Curran feathered his fingers into her hair, kissed her on the forehead and said goodnight.

Victoria sat on the couch for a long time afterward, searching her soul. She could tell herself it would be different this time. Perhaps protection would never fail her again, and making love with him might bring nothing but joy.

And if it did fail? The idea of maybe having a child with him wasn't entirely terrifying. God knew he could and would support his offspring. But where would that leave her? He wanted her, yes, and he enjoyed her company, but he wasn't in love with her, let alone formally committed to her.

The most frightening thing of all was realizing that she loved him. She loved him heart and soul, in a way she'd never dared feel for anyone.

If they broke up again, loving him meant she'd find herself on an entirely new level of Hell. Losing him, after discovering what it was like to become one with him, would surely kill her.

Chapter Twelve

"Ah, the sweet smell of rural life."

Curran leaned against the manure fork and wiped his forehead on his sweatshirt sleeve, then glared at Jamie, who stood in the doorway of Sparkler's stall. "When did you get here, mate?"

"A few minutes ago. Kelli wasn't home."

"I didn't know you were coming up this weekend."

Jamie scratched his head. "Neither did I. But I ended up with a pretty slow schedule today, and I got a great last minute fare, so here I am."

"Good. Grab the other fork out there and get to work. I've three more stalls to do. Make yourself useful."

Jamie snorted and suggested another physically uncomfortable place to put the fork.

"Care to try that, mate?" Curran lifted another soiled clump of straw and swung it into the wheelbarrow.

"Hey, I got my fill of ranch stuff every summer at my uncle's place. I've shoveled a lifetime quota of manure, not to mention the kind I put up with on your behalf."

"Wuss."

Jamie called him a vile name, but Curran laughed when his friend stomped over to the tack room. "You got my boots out here? Oh, never mind, I found 'em."

Jamie went to work on the next stall. Curran called over the wall to him. "Thanks. It's nice out now, but those horses aren't going to be happy if they have to stay out in the corral when the sun goes down."

"Yeah, yeah. You owe me a beer."

"I'll buy you a case. Put your back into it."

They turned the last horse into its clean, food-stocked stall as the sky grew orange and pink. Curran opened the second corral, calling to Peg-leg. The beast snorted and made his goofy, diagonal way to him, following him into the barn and through the door of the huge box stall. Curran scratched the bison's shoulder, then closed the stall door. He and Jamie changed out of their rubber boots and washed their hands in the barn before heading to the house.

As they walked, Jamie pulled an envelope from his coat pocket and handed it to Curran.

"What's this?" He opened it as Jamie talked.

"An invitation that came to the office yesterday. I usually decline them like you asked me to, but I thought this one might interest you."

Hmm. A fundraiser for the children's hospital in Salt Lake, hosted by Sophia Holt. He recognized the name. Her husband was a well-known developer in the state, but Sophia spent her time on charity work, organizing the kind of galas that appealed to people with the ability to dump big money into donations. He checked the date. The event wasn't until July, but for these sorts of things, he supposed issuing invitations well in advance got it marked on far more calendars.

A short note accompanied the invitation. He read it, then grimaced. "Oh, she's heard rumors I might be in the area, and if said rumors are true, she'd love to have the honor of my company."

Jamie laughed. "Everybody reads the tabloids, Curran, you know that, especially those who would never admit to it. Speaking of which, my own, ahem, sources, say those club photos were snapped by some schmuck at a party and sold to the paper. So you weren't tracked by the paparazzi, if that makes you feel any better."

"It doesn't."

They entered the house through the mud room, then went into the kitchen. Curran leaned his hip against the sink, considering the invitation for a moment longer before tossing it on the counter. He rubbed his eyes with the heels of his palms, listening to Jamie open the refrigerator.

"You want a beer?"

"No." The children's hospital did incredible work. He would definitely donate to the cause. But should he actually attend the event?

Perhaps he should go. A distinct craving surfaced inside him. It had been so long since he'd attended a big event. Immersing himself in a crowd was one thing, but prancing around at a gala, dressed to the nines, to see and be seen was another matter entirely. The rush never wore off.

Unfortunately, he didn't do a terrific job of controlling the need for it, either. It had consumed him before, drained him to a shell of a man. Attending this thing might be lifting the lid on the proverbial Pandora's box. Still, he'd like to think he was more grounded now. Maybe he could handle it.

Something cold nudged his hand. He mentally shook himself and looked at the bottle of beer Jamie held out to him.

"Whatever it is, bud, you're thinking about it too hard. Pop this open and hang with me until Kelli gets home."

He humored his friend, but this was a subject he'd have to revisit. Could he resume the parts of his old life he craved without sacrificing everything he'd gained since then? Because if he could, hell yes, he would.

* * * *

The next evening, Curran made a pathetic four-inch putt to finally sink the ball into the third hole at the indoor miniature golf course.

He retrieved the red ball from the cup and eyed his companions, standing just off the fake turf green. Robby's mouth hung open in shock, Kel was turning red from trying so hard not to laugh. Jamie didn't bother to hide his mirth, chuckling as he wrote on the group score card. At least Victoria had the decency to walk over, wrap her arm around his waist and kiss him on the cheek in sympathy.

Robby touched his hand as he stepped off the green. "Are you okay, Uncle Curry?"

"I'm fine." Before he could say more, Jamie dropped to one knee beside his nephew.

"It's okay, Rob." Jamie glanced up at Curran, that damned competitive grin on his face. "We finally found an activity that your uncle isn't naturally good at."

Curran swallowed the nasty name Jamie had coming, if only so it wouldn't enter Rob's vocabulary. "Do I dare ask what my score is so far?"

Kelli giggled. "Fifteen."

"I thought I counted more than that."

Victoria gave his waist a gentle squeeze. "You're allowed a maximum of five strokes per hole."

He pulled her against him. "Are you telling me you let me flail around for three holes, trying to get the damned ball into the cup, when struggling to finish was futile after that fifth stroke?"

She broke into a laugh. "You wouldn't have walked away until you'd sunk the ball anyway."

"She has a valid point, Curran." Jamie gave his green ball a toss straight up, catching it again without much effort.

He glared at his friend. "Just lead on to the next hole."

Rob skipped the few steps to the fourth hole, where it appeared the object was to hit the ball into the haunted house as the door swung open and closed, in order to get onto the main green and have a chance at making par. Rob set his orange ball down and planted his feet apart. "Watch me, Uncle Curry. I'm good at this game, I'll teach you."

Curran laughed. "Right, mate. I'm all eyes."

If only it were that easy to stay focused on his nephew. With Victoria tucked under his arm, the curve of her hip against his, the swell of her breast pressing his side, her warm floral scent teasing his nostrils...paying attention to anything but her proved more difficult as the evening drew on. Wanting her was absolute torture, but sweeter than any desire he'd ever known. She belonged right where she stood beside him. She fit, as if she'd been fashioned just for him.

Robby hit his golf ball, but not nearly hard enough. It went halfway to the haunted house and rolled down to him. He bent and put it back on the white dot on the floor, then looked imploringly at the half-circle of adults. "Would you help me, Jamie?"

Curran couldn't help the broad grin that spread across his face in response to Jamie's own surprised but happy expression. Jamie hunkered down behind Rob, his big hands over the boy's on the club grip.

He glanced at his sister and wasn't at all surprised to see the love shining in her eyes as she watched her son with the man she wanted in her life.

Damn you, Jamie, don't you dare hurt her. Or my nephew.

They took their turns through the hole, everyone cheering for Victoria when her ball made it into the haunted house, and rolled down directly into the cup. Her grin infected him, filled him with happiness. God, she was beautiful.

When his own turn at the hole came, he timed the speed of the little door opening and closing. When he had it right, he whacked the ball. Too hard. The door swung down and smacked the ball, sending it flying off into the miniature blue river trickling beside the path.

Curran rubbed his forehead. "Exactly how many holes do I have left to suffer through?"

They answered him in chorus. "Fourteen."

He'd gone nearly thirty-seven years without playing miniature golf. He could easily go another thirty-seven and never miss it.

An hour later, and more points on his scorecard than he wanted to count, they reached the eighteenth hole. Anxious to be done with the whole mess, he set the ball down and gave it a half-hearted whack. He no sooner stepped away than a red siren above the skee-ball styled hole lit and shrieked.

Rob jumped up and down. "You did it, Uncle Curry, you did it! You won!"

He looked at Victoria, baffled. "What did I do?"

She was laughing so hard she could barely answer. "You hit a hole-in-one on the last hole."

"I did?"

An attendant in a maroon vest approached, turned off the siren, and handed him a card. "Congratulations, dude."

Curran had never won anything like this before, but as he looked at the card, the delight melted. "Just what I need. A free mini-golf pass."

He handed the card to Rob, who whooped and tucked it in his pocket. Curran snagged Victoria's hand in his and pulled her to him. He drew a deep breath filled with her scent then kissed her lightly. "Enough of this game. Let's get something to eat."

"My sentiments exactly," Jamie said, holding Robby's hand on one side, his arm draped around Kelli on the other.

* * * *

A few burgers and fries later, Curran drove them all back to Kelli's house. Victoria enjoying the way Curran wrapped his fingers around hers and held her hand against his thigh, driving with his left hand on the wheel.

What a great time she'd had. Good friends, lots of fun. She enjoyed miniature golf anyway, but seeing Curran tackle something new to him enlightened her. With his natural competitiveness, his reaction to the game came as a surprise. He did his best on each hole, took every stroke seriously, and yet managed to have fun, to play and flirt and laugh off his own terrible score.

She respected that about him, the way he always did his best, yet accepted that a game was a game and hey, not everyone can win. Even with that temper she'd seen at work, he'd never be one of those guys who screamed at the referee over his kid's baseball game.

The afternoon's storm had left several inches of new snow on the ground, and on the way into Kelli's house, Jamie scooped up a handful and lobbed it at Curran.

It caught Curran square in the shoulder. She saw the devilish flash in his eyes as he wiped the wet snow from his leather jacket. He leaned down, picked up a clump of snow. Victoria tested the snow, packing it with the toe of her boot. Full of water, perfect for snowballs.

Curran formed a ball in his hands, eyeing Jamie. "You can either apologize, or suffer the consequences."

Jamie snorted. "Let's see what you've got, Oz-boy."

He tossed the snowball, catching Jamie in the head, and the fight was on. Victoria joined in, and she and Curran held their own against the other three, until, after a while, she simply couldn't resist the obvious target of Curran's back.

She shifted back behind him, forming a snowball. He didn't seem to notice she had left his side. When he caught Kelli in the leg with a ball, Victoria tossed her snowball at him, nailing him in the back of the neck.

Curran howled as the snowball burst. He brushed at the snow, shook it off, then whirled around. She couldn't have turned off her grin if she tried.

He stalked toward her. "I thought you were on my side."

"I'm a double-agent."

"You'll pay for that."

"You have to catch me first." With that she took off running. She heard Curran's laughter and the sound of his boots hitting the ground as he sprinted after her. She tore around the house and headed for the barn.

She weaved around, then took a wrong turn and shrieked when she found herself cornered between Curran and the big red feed mixer, with an outbuilding on one side and a bank of plowed snow against the fence on the other. She doubled back, tried to fake him out like a basketball player, dodging right, then whipping back to the left. He threw an arm around her waist and caught her, but tipped in the process, sending them both tumbling into the snow bank. She landed on her back, on top of him.

The snow must have been cold, but she didn't notice. He warmed her too efficiently. She felt his groin respond to the pressure of her body against his. He nuzzled her hair, and when his mouth pressed against the side of her neck, she gasped and shifted her hips against him.

Oh, hell, what was she doing? She drew a shaky breath, then rolled off him. He growled, but let her go.

Victoria sat up, hating the need she felt to move out of his arms, then glanced sideways at him. Desire and frustration warred for dominance in his expression. "I'm sorry, Curran. I know I'm being unfair to you."

He pushed up to lean his elbow on the packed snow, his dark gaze pinning her like a butterfly to a specimen board. "I won't lie to you. At this moment, I'd give everything I own to strip you out of those pants and wrap you around me."

The image sparked her own bone-deep craving to feel him inside her. She ran her tongue across her dry lips, painfully aware of the way his gaze locked onto her mouth.

He shifted toward her and raised his gloved hand to her mouth, tracing a path along her lower lip with his finger. "It isn't so much your rules I have a problem with. What is unfair, Victoria, is expecting me to abide by those rules with no explanation."

He leaned closer, as if he meant to kiss her, then shook himself and pulled back. "You might try telling me why you won't let me love you sometime."

Her heart ached to unload, to share the deepest, darkest, worst part of herself. She couldn't do it. She didn't dare. He'd realize how wrong he'd been about the goodness in her. And Kelli. If Kelli found out, she'd lose her friend. How could another mother understand her willingness to give up her child?

Curran hung his head and got up from the snow bank. He took her hand, helped her to her feet and led her back to the house.

She had to tell him. It was the one thing still hanging between them. She had to, somehow, because it suddenly dawned on her that if she didn't, the strain of her secret might push him away regardless.

Where would she find the courage?

* * * *

Later that night, Curran stroked Victoria's hair as she sat beside him on the couch in Kelli's great room, watching a romantic movie. Exactly what he needed right now, when the only thing he wanted was a little romance of his own with the woman whose scent tingled in his lungs with every breath he took. The only thing worse than sitting through a "date" movie and itching with anticipation over the loving to come later, was sitting through the same movie, knowing the romantic atmosphere would end at his lady's front door.

Still, cuddling with her beat the hell out of the alternative. He found lately he missed her every moment they spent apart, and he dreaded being alone.

Halfway through the movie, he noticed Jamie and Kelli get up and leave the room. They'd been rather quiet since Kelli put her son to bed earlier. The tension between them grew all evening, and got so bad he could practically see it hanging in the air now.

After they left, Victoria shifted in his arms and looked at him. "Wonder what's wrong with them?"

"I don't know. Maybe Kel isn't ready for him to leave tomorrow."

Victoria raised an eyebrow at him. "That was a short trip."

"He has meetings Monday morning. Weekends are only so long, you know."

She nodded and laid her head on his chest, turning her attention back to the movie. Over the TV sound, Curran strained to hear what was going on in the front room, but whatever they were discussing, they did it quietly.

At least until he heard the door open and close. A few moments later, Kelli cried out softly. Victoria bolted upright and he vaulted over the back of the couch and ran into the living room.

Kelli sat slumped on the sofa, her head in her hands. Her shoulders shook. Curran sat beside her as Victoria knelt on the floor before her.

Curran rubbed his sister's shoulder. "Kelli? What happened?"

She sat up, wiped at her tear-streaked face with her sleeve. "I'm okay."

"The hell you are." Protectiveness expanded in his chest. "What did he do?"

Kelli shook her head. "Nothing, Curran. That's exactly the problem."

He'd tried to tell her not to take Jamie too seriously. He knew she'd get hurt, dammit.

Victoria said, "He'll be back, Kel."

"No, he won't." Kelli sniffed and Curran reached onto the coffee table for a tissue to give her. She wiped her nose. "I can't take it anymore. I can't take him needing me one minute and needing space and time the next. I can't keep watching him walk away, never knowing if that's the end of it."

"Kel, I warned you." He tried to say it gently, knowing it would sting regardless. "You can't change Jamie, no one can."

His sister threw her hands in the air in frustration. "That's just it. Jamie doesn't need to change so much as he needs to let go. He's got himself locked in this shallow, emotionless box he's afraid to release himself from. I can't take it. He knows I love him, but I told him until he's ready to love me back, I don't want him to come back. Going round in circles with him is tearing me apart."

Curran and Victoria stayed with Kelli until she unwound. He seriously considered making a visit to Jamie's hotel room and pounding some sense into him, but realized it would do more harm than good.

For being an evening of fun and games, it was chock full of frustrations. The worst was yet to come. He still had to drive Victoria back to her place, then walk away, alone.

* * * *

After Curran dropped Victoria off at home, she had time to feed Sassy before the doorbell rang. She glanced out the window. Curran's truck still sat in the driveway.

He prowled into the house when she opened the door, like some wild thing on the hunt. He took her hand, led her to the couch in the great room, then sat, tugging her down beside him. His green eyes were hard, his jaw set.

A chill rippled down her spine. She wasn't going to like this. "I thought you went home."

His eyes narrowed slightly. "I couldn't. I won't get any sleep anyway. Victoria, I am losing my mind over you, and you're still keeping secrets from me. Something else happened to you, aside from all that with Nate, something that is directly impacting our relationship, and I have had enough. I am not leaving until you explain it to me."

Victoria tried to swallow but couldn't get her throat to work. She was finally seeing for herself the side of Curran that cut a swath through the business world and stitched it together in his own image. The sheer power flowing from him stole her breath. A part of her found it amazing that he didn't frighten her. Instead, the strength and determination radiating from him set her hormones humming.

Hormones that were overridden by the desperate desire not to have this conversation. What if her actions disgusted him? What if he thought her pitiful and weak and wanted nothing more to do with her?

He bracketed her face with his hands, his gaze holding hers captive. Her time for pondering *what if* had run out. "Tell me, Victoria. I can handle anything but the questions and the silence."

She wasn't sure her voice would work. She sucked in a breath, then passed beyond the point of no return. "I told you there was no such thing as safe sex, other than no sex."

He released her, running his hand through his hair. "Don't dance around, woman. Get to the point. Did he pass a disease on to you or something?" The warmth under the sharp edge in his voice encouraged her to continue.

"I got pregnant."

His back stiffened. Okay, he clearly hadn't expected that as a possible answer. She felt herself cresting the top of the roller coaster's first big drop. It was all downhill from here. God help her.

"You weren't using protection?" He didn't sound accusatory. More confused than anything.

"He hated condoms. I was on the pill, but I went through a round of antibiotics with no birth control backup, and it failed."

He held himself apart from her, still as stone. His jaw ticked and his narrowed eyes bored into hers. "What did you do, Victoria?"

She folded her arms around herself. She felt herself plummeting down the drop, speeding into the double loop. "There was no way I could support a baby. Hell, I can't support myself half the time."

"Did you abort it?"

"I couldn't. He wanted me to, but it wasn't the baby's fault it got stuck with me." When she answered, he blew out a breath and slumped against the couch.

"You gave it up for adoption, then."

"I found a wonderful couple in Ohio. They adopted my son at birth."

She couldn't remember ever being more grateful than when he reached for her, pulled her into his warm, protective arms. She'd never felt emotionally closer to another person in her life. Silence cocooned them for a while as he held her, his fingers combing through her hair.

Her heart weighed at least a ton less. She no longer carried her secrets alone, any of them. "I can't believe I told you that."

"I'm glad you did."

She shifted away from him until she could meet his gaze. "Do you understand? I mean, it seems like the easy way out, but it had to be that way."

He silenced her with a kiss, a slow, gentle caress that sent warmth spreading into every limb, to the tips of her fingers and toes. When his mouth left hers, he said, "Victoria, I can't begin to imagine how difficult it was to give up a child."

"Then you see why I can't take that chance again?"

Hurt glowed in his eyes. "Do you honestly believe you'd be in the same position with me? Dear God, I can think of nothing more wonderful than having a child with you. I would take care of you both for the rest of your lives."

And there it was. The one thing she both expected and dreaded. The roller-coaster of her heart skidded past the safe stop and plunged off a cliff. He'd support a child. He'd even support her. No marriage. No love. She would be tied to him forever by their mutual creation. Could she watch him go on to other relationships, perhaps even a wife, while parenting a child with him? No. She could never take that chance.

"How old would he be now?"

"He turned two on November fifteenth."

"Is it an open adoption? Have you seen him at all?"

Victoria shook her head. "They offered to keep me in his life, but they are his parents. Besides, I've always feared I would look at him and see Nate staring back at me." She winced. She should have kept that part of it to herself. What an evil, horrible thing to think about the child that had grown inside her.

She hazarded a glance at Curran, but found no trace of condemnation in his eyes. He drew his fingertips along her cheek. "I see Kelli struggle with that sometimes when Rob is being a terror. I know she wonders if he might have violent tendencies when he gets older, because of Jonas."

He kissed her again, then settled against the back of the couch and wrapped his arms around her. She sank against his chest, listening to the steady beat of his heart. She was glad he told her how Kelli felt about Rob sometimes. Maybe she would understand, or at least not judge her harshly enough to lose their friendship.

After a moment, Curran chuckled softly. "You amaze me, Victoria."

His words caught her off guard, left her brain a little fuzzy. She amazed him? "Why?"

"Everything you've been through, you've handled without anyone there to shore you up. You have to be the strongest person I've ever known."

"I wouldn't say that. I survived, that's all."

He shifted and nudged her chin up with his finger, urging her to look at him. "Don't shrug off compliments, honey."

In her experience, compliments were only given if they were the backhanded sort. With Curran, she was beginning to learn what real ones were like. "Okay. Thank you."

He hugged her close. "You're very welcome."

Chapter Thirteen

Curran ran his fingers through Victoria's silky hair as he held her, processing everything she'd just told him about giving up her child.

His heart ached for her, for the pain she lived with. At the same time, he admired the way she faced her problems head on and handled them. Small wonder, though, that sex wasn't high on her to-do list. That she let him touch her at all was a bit of a minor miracle. "Tell me something."

"Anything."

"Were you pregnant at the time he hurt you?"

"Yes, about six months. I nearly lost the baby." A shiver rippled across her shoulders, and he held her tighter, kissed the top of her head. Memories came back to him, of the call from Kelli, crying, begging him to come get her and Rob. The terror in Rob's eyes as the memory of his parents' fighting haunted him. Kelli pleaded with him to let Jonas go to jail rather than to his grave. He'd known then, if the man had laid a finger on his nephew, he'd have killed him.

As much fury as he felt for Nate Fielder at this moment, the man was lucky to already be dead.

"How did the adoption work without his permission?"

Victoria sat up and looked at him, her earlier guarded expression replaced by openness. "I didn't need his permission. Nate was an attorney. He drew up the papers severing his parental rights as soon as he realized I was serious about bringing the baby into the world. He wanted to be sure if I kept it, I would have no claim on him for support."

"Lousy son of a bitch."

"Yeah, he was that. And, knowing his mother, I can tell you, the title fits." A shadow flitted through her eyes, and she bit her lower lip. "Well, since I've bared every shred of ugliness in my soul—"

"Hey, quit that." He placed his palm against her cheek, holding her gaze with his own. "What you did for your son was not ugly. Far from it."

She looked away, nodded, went back to biting her lip. As he opened his mouth to ask what she was thinking, she said, "Why did you retire?"

Now there was a question he'd no desire to deal with. But after everything she'd told him, how could he say he didn't want to talk about it? It would be a figurative slap in the face. "You may not like the answer."

She broke into a gentle smile. "I didn't figure you'd like my answers, either. But we can't change what we've done to make things more attractive, can we?" She took his hand in hers. "You walked away from a life people envy. Why?"

The morning came back to him crystal-clear. The tabloids hit the shelves, splashed with photos of Amanda and her other lover. The office phones rang off the hook with media folk wanting his comments. He never gave them. Instead he walked into his office bathroom and stared at himself in the mirror. If he'd turned sideways, he was sure he would have disappeared entirely, he'd grown so two-dimensional. "I hated who I had become."

He cursed and cleared his throat, then continued, knowing his words would obliterate the man she thought he was. "I spent years creating this image of myself to show to the world. As much as I liked to complain about women dating me just to get the media coverage, I did exactly the same thing. It wasn't by chance I managed to date the hottest women in the market."

Dredging all this up, speaking of it, made him edgy. He left the couch, paced away.

Behind him, Victoria said, "I thought you couldn't stand the media. You were horribly cranky the day I interviewed you."

She told me everything. She did it, so can I. He shoved his hands in his pockets, forced out the words. "Of course. How better to capture the media's attention that to let them know I couldn't stand them?"

He turned to face her. "Jamie's called me a shark for years, but I don't think even he knows how deep that aspect of my personality goes. Everything was plotted. The women, the parties, the interviews."

Victoria's brow knitted. "Why?"

"I wanted to be famous. I wanted to be important, ever since I was a kid. I wanted to be respected and admired and sought after. I craved it, I needed it." He shrugged. "So I created it."

She stood, the naturally sultry way she moved momentarily distracting him. She walked to him, but she wrapped her arms around herself. There for him, yet giving him the space he needed to breathe. It nearly buckled his knees, the way she instinctively knew what he needed most from her.

"So, you had everything you wanted. What changed?"

"I was living with Amanda Dannen."

"She cheated on you."

He rubbed his forehead. "The news broke wide, everyone knew about it. It seriously pissed me off, until I suddenly realized the only reason it mattered to me was because it put a black mark on my image that I hadn't anticipated first. I felt nothing. I was completely numb inside. That's when I realized there was nothing of me left except the part I crafted for the world to admire."

He took a step closer to her, needing the warmth of her. "I didn't know who I was any more. I hated the thing I had become."

"So you walked away."

"Yes."

"And have you found yourself again?"

"I like to think so. The old self rears its ugly head from time to time."

She smiled. "Yeah, I've seen him. He stood on my porch and said some pretty rotten things one day."

His throat constricted. "Yet you forgave him."

Victoria shook her head, placed her hands on his shoulders. "No. He's still a bastard. But I forgave you, and that's all that matters."

She stepped into his arms then, and he buried his face in her hair, holding her to him, wanting never to let go.

If he'd ever felt more vulnerable in his life, he couldn't recall it. Her gentle acceptance humbled him, filled his heart till he thought it would overflow. Somehow, standing here, with Victoria in his arms, he couldn't imagine another bad thing ever happening to either of them. From here on out, life would be perfect, in a way he'd never plotted or dreamed.

* * * *

Two weeks later, Curran stood in his sister's great room, using a rented helium tank to fill multicolored balloons.

Robby danced from one end of the kitchen all the way through the great room and back again. "Is it time yet, Mom?"

Kelli put her hand on her hip and raised an eyebrow at her impatient son. "Look at the clock. What does it say?"

He stared at the digital clock on the microwave. "Six-oh-eight."

"What time does the party start?"

"Seven-oh-oh." He hung his head and trudged into the living room.

Curran tried not to laugh. Poor kid. Time tended to stand still at that age, when awaiting one's own birthday party.

The doorbell rang. He heard Rob pound across the floor to the door, then, "Jamie!"

He looked at his sister. Her skin paled and the ice cream scoop dropped from her hand, clattering on the tile countertop. He'd spoken to Jamie once since his last trip, and in the interest of friendship, he'd studiously avoided discussion of Kelli. He doubted his sister had heard a single word from his friend in that time.

She walked into the front room. Curran tied off the balloon in his hands and followed, though whether as a cheerleader or a defender, he had no idea.

He looked over his sister's shoulder at Jamie, crouched by the door next to Rob, a huge, shiny green package at his feet. Rob looked up at Kelli, grinned, then bobbed his head in response to Jamie. He threw his arms around Jamie's neck, and the hug Jamie gave him in response bothered Curran. *Mate, he needs a father, not a fun friend who comes and goes as he pleases.*

Jamie stood. "Now, why don't you go hang out for a few minutes until your party starts, so I can talk to your mom?"

"Okay. Can I open my present now?"

"Sure. In the other room, though, if you don't mind." Jamie's gaze met his, and he added, "Maybe you can take your Uncle Curran with you."

Robby whooped and picked up the package, balancing it carefully in his little arms as he took off toward his bedroom.

Curran crossed his arms over his chest and leaned against the wall. "And maybe Uncle Curran can keep an eye on you and make sure you don't leave my sister in tears again."

He stared his friend down until Kelli laid a hand on his arm. "It's okay. I can handle this. Don't you have a few more balloons to do?"

He looked at his baby sister, so much stronger than she'd been a few years ago. Strong, determined, and plenty old enough to manage her own romantic business. He went back into the great room, back to work on Rob's decorations. Yeah, so Kelli was a grownup. That didn't mean he couldn't keep an ear open for trouble.

Kelli spoke first. "I thought I made myself pretty clear last time about your comings and goings, Jamie." Her voice sounded hard, firm. Good girl.

"You did," Jamie said. "But I had already promised Robby I'd be here when he turned six. Besides, I really needed to talk to you."

"So talk."

Curran started blowing up another balloon, but halted when he realized he couldn't hear over the sound of the helium tank.

"Kelli, I've been thinking, pretty much constantly since you told me to take a hike. I know I've kind of jerked you around, and I'm deeply sorry."

Curran relaxed a bit. Okay, he apologized. Good.

"It's fine, Jamie."

"It's not fine, dammit. Listen, it broke my heart when Alexa died, and I never, ever wanted to feel anything that intense again."

They were silent for a moment. Curran silently cheered his best friend on. *Come on, Jamie, if you're trying to make up, keep at it. You can do it.*

Jamie spoke. "What scared me to death, sweetheart, was realizing that as much as I loved her, the feelings I have for you are an entirely different order of magnitude. As terrifying as it is to love you so much, the thought of losing you is a whole lot worse."

"Jamie, are you sure?" Kelli said. "I can't take any more back and forth with you."

"I've never been more sure of anything in my life. Will you marry me?"

Curran grinned. Very nice. As long as he was on his knee at the time, damn near perfect.

"What about Robby?" Kelli said.

From down the hallway, his nephew shouted, "Rob says yes!"

That's your cue, Kel. Don't blow it.

"Yes. Oh, Jamie, yes!"

Curran silently applauded, listening to the laughter, the joy coming from the living room. Soon enough, it would be his turn. He hoped he did at least as decent a job as Jamie.

* * * *

Victoria hated being late for anything, but missing part of Rob's birthday party made her feel awful. She glanced at the clock on the dashboard. Ten after seven, and she was still a few minutes from the canyon turnoff.

She picked up the cell phone and called Kelli's house. Jamie answered, catching her off guard. Hadn't Kelli said it was over between them? "Hey, Jamie, it's Victoria."

"Hi, Vic. Curran's handling the piñata. Want me to get him for you?" He sounded chipper. Must've worked things out with Kelli. Definitely time for some girl talk.

"No, I just called to say I'm on my way. I had an apartment to see, but I'm almost at the exit, and, oh, shoot, Robby's present is still on the kitchen counter. I'll have to stop home, then I'll be over. Fifteen minutes or so."

"I'll tell him. Drive safe."

Dang, being late bothered her. It was worth it, though. If she'd waited until tomorrow, the adorable one-bedroom in elderly Mrs. Sanchez's basement would have already been taken. She actually liked it, she'd be allowed to keep her rat, and the rent was exactly the meager amount she could afford. She'd gladly paid the deposit.

She didn't like the idea of moving to Taylorsville, so far from Curran. But she couldn't stop the Campbells from returning in three weeks to reclaim their home, and everything closer in her price range was so awful even Sassy wouldn't be comfortable.

How was she going to tell Curran she'd rented a place? When the subject came up a few days ago, he had wanted to go apartment hunting with her. She couldn't let him come. One look at the first dive on her list today and he'd have bought her a condo or something. She fingered the pearl strand at her throat. He gave great presents, but letting him help with housing would make her feel like a kept mistress. Only without the sex.

She looked at the clock again. So, now she was fifteen minutes late. Shoot. She hoped the robot building set she bought Robby would buy her forgiveness. She pulled into the drive and parked in front of the garage, her eyes adjusting to the darkness when she jogged to the front porch.

Too dark. The porch light came on automatically when the sun went down. She wondered if there were extra light bulbs in the house or if she'd have to make a run to the store later.

She paused long enough to identify the house key by the moonlight filtering through the gathering clouds, then stepped onto the porch and slipped the key in the lock.

Her skin prickled. Something wasn't quite right, and it was more than the inherent spookiness of unexpected darkness. She turned the key, and the hairs on her nape rose as she caught movement from the corner of her eye. Her heart jumped into triple-time, and she opened the door. She rushed in, whirled around, shoved the door to close it—

The door stopped, swung inward again. A man stepped over the threshold.

She couldn't move, couldn't breathe. Her heart surged into a desperate racing. She'd left a light on over the stove in the kitchen, and in the feeble light that bled into the living room, she recognized the man who slowly pushed the door closed behind him.

Same surfer-blond hair, same bulky, body-builder physique, made even larger by the black bomber jacket he wore.

Greg Fielder. Nate's younger brother.

The last time she saw him, he'd lunged at her after Nate's sentencing, screaming filthy words at her. The family attorneys had to physically restrain him. She fought the fuzziness invading her brain, the nearly overwhelming sensation of fainting when she realized what he held in his right hand.

A gun.

She stared at him, her mind flying. She still had her keys, she knew the layout of the house.

He grinned and took a step toward her and she bolted for the kitchen. She raced through the kitchen into the great room, threw open the lock and tore out through the French doors to the backyard. Somewhere behind her, he cursed. She all but flew around the house to the right, out to the driveway. She ripped off her glove, identifying the car key by feel as she ran. She pulled open the vehicle door—

A crushing pain exploded in the back of her head. The world disappeared in a swirl of blackness.

* * * *

Curran glanced at his watch, then shoved his hands in his pockets and turned his attention to the light snowfall beyond Kelli's living room window.

Nearly eight. Victoria was an hour late. She had been on the freeway just down the canyon when she called. Finishing the drive and stopping off at home for the gift accounted for about twenty minutes, at most. Where in the hell was she?

The tension in his gut twisted, sparking a craving for a cigarette. Dammit, he was never going to quit if he gave in every time he was stressed about something. He mentally shoved at the need for nicotine, then scrubbed his hands through his hair and turned away from the window.

He picked up the phone he'd left on the piano, dialing her cell. It kicked into voice mail. Not a big surprise. Cell connections in the mountains were always touch and go. She could be two minutes from the house and the call might not go through.

He tried the number to the Campbells' house. Five rings, then it too went to voice mail. With a curse, he dropped his phone in his pocket then stalked into the kitchen.

Kelli paused in dishing up ice cream and looked at him, her brow knitted, concern in her eyes. He shook his head, then pasted a grin on his face and started handing out ice cream to Rob's little mates.

Rob himself was engaged in a discussion of ski technique with Jamie and the surprise birthday guest, Ian Garrett, a member of the U.S. Ski Team. Ian's father was the electrician when Curran's house was built, and he'd skied with Ian a couple of times since they met. Curran listened for a while until Rob said, "Well, I watched your last race on TV, Mr. Garrett, and I think you should have turned harder on that first gate. I bet that's where you lost."

Ian looked very thoughtful. "You know, dude, you might be right. I'll have to work on that. Thanks for the coaching."

"No problem. I'm full of good ideas." Robby shrugged and headed for the ice-cream serving station.

Ian's shoulders shook with a stifled laugh, and Jamie chuckled, looking up at Curran. "If Rob still has all the 'good ideas' when he grows up, let's put him in charge of the company."

Curran willed himself to smile. "Good idea." He held a hand out to Ian as the skier stood. "Thanks for coming, mate. You made Rob's day."

Ian grinned. "Hey, glad to do it, Curran. I can't believe how much that little guy knows about the slopes. He'll end up on the team himself if he keeps it up."

"That's his dream." Curran forced his feet to stay put, suppressing the urge to pace as he watched Ian say goodbye to Rob and the half-dozen other kindergarteners. A little later, Curran helped wipe faces and hands when everyone finished devouring cake and ice cream. He assisted in finding shoes and coats as mothers came to collect their children.

Finally, Curran stood in the kitchen with Jamie as Kelli herded Rob down the hall to take a bath. The vise around his heart cranked tighter, and butterflies took up residence in his stomach. Where was she?

Jamie crossed his arms over his chest. "You're worried."

"Hell, yes, I'm worried. It isn't like her not to call."

"Have you called her?"

"Can't reach her at home or on her cell." A chill traveled down his spine. "Something's wrong. I've a very bad feeling about this."

"What are you going to do?"

"I'm going to find her." Curran turned on his heel and strode into the living room, grabbing his coat off the couch. He thrust his arms into the sleeves, checking his pocket for the truck keys.

From behind him, Jamie said, "Wait up. I'll go with you."

He turned, glanced at his friend. "No, stay with Kelli. I'll call when I know anything."

Jamie nodded, and Curran stalked out of the house into the worsening storm.

He drove down the lane. God, he didn't have the slightest idea where to begin looking for her. She had to have been in an accident. What else could have kept her away, kept her from calling?

The truck headlights illuminated a dark blue sedan parked on the lane's narrow shoulder. Stupid place to park, especially when the plows would likely hit it coming through in the morning. He glanced at the Campbells' house as he passed, then hit the brake, the truck skidding a few feet before the antilock brakes kicked in. He reversed until he could see through the trees. Something pale sat in front of the brick home. He pulled into the curved driveway.

The white SUV, the pale object he'd seen between the spruces, sat before the garage. He stopped the truck beside it and climbed out.

The house was nearly dark, save a light coming from one of the back rooms. The kitchen maybe. He stepped onto the porch and rang the bell, then knocked on the door. Nothing. He knocked and rang again, then strained to hear any sound, any movement within the house.

Nothing.

"Victoria!" He left the porch, went out on the path to the driveway and looked back at the house, staring at the dark windows. The strangest sensation of being watched trickled down his spine and he shivered. He'd have sworn he saw movement in one of the main floor bedroom windows. A cold sweat broke on his skin.

He turned away, passed the SUV, then stopped when a small lump on the concrete caught his eye. He walked between the SUV and his truck, crouched down to look at the ground. The snow was starting to pile up, but even under the thin covering of flakes, the moment he touched the object, he knew what he'd found.

Victoria's keys.

His stomach churned, his blood froze in his veins. She was in trouble, in that house, if he could believe his gut instinct, and after the years he'd spent relying on it, he had to.

The image of the sedan parked on the side of the lane rose in his mind. A car he didn't recognize, between this house and his own. The feeling of being watched…dear God. Someone was in the house. She must have stumbled on them when she stopped off for Rob's gift.

Think, Shaw, think.

He was ill-equipped to mount a rescue, and if whoever had her was watching, the best thing he could do for her would be to play it casual. He stood, walked around to the driver's side of the truck, climbed in. He backed away from the house, then pulled onto the lane. The second he was beyond sight of the house, he picked up his cell phone. A hundred yards down the lane, the signal spiked high enough to be sure a call would go through.

He stopped the truck, rubbed his damp, shaking hands on his jeans, then dialed 9-1-1.

Chapter Fourteen

"Wake up, bitch."

Victoria couldn't see. The world was dark and out of focus. She shook her head to clear it and hissed at the burst of pain behind her left ear.

She blinked hard, raised her hand—no, she couldn't. Her shoulders ached. Slowly she identified where she was. One of the bedrooms. She lay on her right side, facing the door. Okay, that would make it one of the rooms on the front of the house, facing the lane.

She ran a quick mental inventory. Head painful. Arms damned uncomfortable. Tied behind her. She shivered. Feet, okay. Shifting told her they were bound at the ankles.

Something in the corner moved. A knife of terror slashed down her spine. Gradually her vision cleared, and in the slight glow coming into the room from down the hall, she saw the hulking man come toward her.

Greg. God help her. Nate was the angel of the family in comparison. He smelled of gun oil and some spicy aftershave. He leaned over her.

"You're awake."

She couldn't swallow, her throat was too dry. "How did you find me?"

He swore at her. "Easy. I sent a letter to your old address, asked for address service on it, and the post office sent your updated address to me. Cost me, like, a buck or so."

"You can't do that."

"Stupid, of course you can." He grinned down at her, looking so very proud of himself. "I gave you more credit. Thought for sure they'd give me a forward to a post office box. But you're as dumb as Nate always said you were."

Her meek, downtrodden self nodded its head at that, but she shoved it back down. "Silly me. I never expected anyone named Fielder to show up on my doorstep."

He grasped the collar of her sweatshirt, yanked her up a foot from the bed, and growled in her face. "If you hadn't gotten my brother killed, I wouldn't have a reason to show up, now would I?"

He dropped her. Her shoulder and head simultaneously spiked pain, sending stars through her vision. She waited, breathed slowly, trying not to throw up. He just stood there, staring down at her. She had to keep him talking. His silence scared her. At least if he talked, she might figure out a way to escape.

"You sent a letter to get my address...wait—" Pieces clicked into place in her head and her stomach clenched. "You sent those letters? The package with the toys?"

He snorted. "Like the prison was gonna let notes to you leave Nate's cell?"

This was getting worse by the second. "He dictated them to you?"

"They were based on his calls to me. I thought I'd help him out a little."

Oh, God. Nate hadn't written them. Nate probably hadn't even known it was happening.

Greg was the pampered baby of the family. She never knew exactly what sort of trouble he got into, but from hearing snippets of Nate's conversations with his mother, she surmised the family paid out enormous amounts of money over the years to smooth out Greg's troubles, to victims, to cops. She didn't know what Greg was capable of, but at the moment, getting out of this alive didn't seem all that likely.

He was talking. She made herself tune in to his words. "You really should have mourned for him. It would have been better for you. But when Mother saw that you were out partying, she was seriously pissed. Playing around like you're some star or something, trying to be better than you are."

Partying? Confusion added another twist to the fear churning in her stomach. "What are you talking about? When did your mom see me?" She worked her wrists, but they wouldn't loosen much. Tape. He'd used tape, not rope. How could she wriggle out of tape?

Greg reached into his jacket, pulled out a folded newspaper and waved it two inches from her face. Even in this pathetic light, she could see what it was. Not a newspaper. A tabloid. The tabloid.

"Shoulda left your hair blonde. You were prettier. So what I want to know is how a stupid little skank like you managed to get hot with that Shaw guy. Guess he likes 'em brainless and obedient, just like Nate, huh?" He dropped the tabloid on the nightstand beside the bed.

She choked on a cry. Curran. She'd give anything to see him one more time.

She sucked in a breath when Greg crouched by the bed, his face on a level with hers. He grinned and her soul shrank from him, but she willed her voice to be steady when she spoke. "What do you want, Greg?"

"I want Nate's kid."

Ice formed in her belly. "What?"

"You heard me."

"What on earth are you going to do with a child?"

"Not me, stupid whore. Mother. She's been on drugs just to keep her sanity since Nate died. Keeps saying she doesn't want to live. I figure, if she has her grandchild, something of Nate that she can love, she'll be okay."

Somewhere, outside, someone called her name.

Greg bolted up, then hurried to the side of the bed and looked out the slight opening in the curtain. After a moment, she heard, faintly, an engine. Someone had come to the house. Curran! He'd be worried because she missed the party. How late was it? Being knocked out completely whacked her internal clock. It felt like two in the morning, but maybe it was earlier.

Greg cursed, then jogged around to her side of the bed again. "We're running short on time now. Tell me where the babysitter lives. We need to get the kid and get moving."

"You can't have him."

His lip curled and he spat on the floor. "Oh, you think?"

"I don't have him to give you. He was adopted."

He backhanded her across the cheek. Her face stung. "Don't lie to me, whore. You're not the type to give up your kid."

"How the hell would you know what 'type' I am?" She flinched when his hand pulled back, but kept talking. "I'm not lying. Look around the house, Greg. There isn't a single thing for a toddler." Would he grow desperate enough to kill her? She tried to think, to formulate a plan. Nothing came to mind.

Greg lowered his hand and pursed his lips, thinking. "You know who adopted him."

She didn't answer, but he stepped down to her feet. He tucked the gun into the back of his waistband then reached into his jacket pocket. He pulled out a knife, flicked the blade open. She held her breath as he cut through the duct tape binding her ankles, waiting for the blade to slip.

He efficiently freed her, then flipped the knife closed and hauled her to her feet.

Feet that were dead asleep and wouldn't support her. She sagged against him. He held her upper arms, keeping her on her feet until she balanced her own weight. The feeling rushing back to her toes hurt, but it helped her sharpen her attention on her surroundings.

He grabbed his gun, and yanked her out of the room by her right arm. She dragged her feet as much as she dared. Curran would call the sheriff, wouldn't he? How long would it take them to get here? Unless Curran didn't realize she was in trouble. In that case, she was on her own.

"Where are you taking me?" she said.

He pulled her down the hall. "We're gonna take a road trip to get the kid, then just for kicks, we're going home. You owe my mother an apology. Hell, I'll take you to the cemetery and you can apologize to Nate while you're at it."

Her pulse raced. She made herself breathe more slowly, evenly. He'd take her home, huh? Now she knew what a mouse felt like when a housecat went hunting to bring offerings to its humans. "What then?"

His laughter raised gooseflesh on her arms. He'd kill her. Curran. She'd never get the chance to tell him she loved him.

Greg hauled her into the living room, snagged her purse from the floor where she'd dropped it, then pulled her out the front door, into the light snowfall.

He glanced at her purse. "Which pocket do you keep the keys in?"

The keys! He wanted to take the SUV. "I had the keys when I took off before. I must have dropped them when you caught me."

He let out a string of expletives and yanked her arm hard as he dropped to the ground by the SUV, pulling her down beside him. He looked under the vehicle, hauled her up with him, walked around. No keys.

The sound of approaching vehicles made her heart trip with hope. Greg's head snapped up at the noise, and he hustled her back into the house and slammed the door as three sheriff's department vehicles pulled in front of the house. The red and blue lights flashed through the darkness in the living room.

She craned her neck to see out the sidelight. "Why aren't there sirens?"

Greg pushed her against the wall behind the door. "So I wouldn't hear them coming, you brainless bitch."

"What now?"

"Shut up and let me think." He pressed her to the floor in the corner, then he paced a few steps in each direction.

He obviously hadn't planned on police presence. Okay, this was good. He couldn't shoot her now. He'd need her as a hostage. He wouldn't get out of the house without her. She shifted sideways to make her hands more comfortable, and settled to wait, praying she was right. Praying for her life.

* * * *

Curran waited in his truck, parked on the road shoulder, until the sheriff's department vehicles and paramedics whipped past him. He pulled the truck around and followed the authorities back to the Campbells' house.

He turned off the truck and jumped out, only to be stopped as he neared the line of police cars by a young, clean-shaven deputy.

"Sir, you need to stay back."

He leveled a hard look at the officer. "I don't intend to disrupt your work, but the woman I'm going to marry is being held in that house, so anything that goes on here, I'm entitled to know."

The deputy nodded. "I understand, sir, and once we know exactly what the situation is and what we're dealing with, I'll make sure you're informed." He pointed past Curran. "Is that your truck? We have backup units en route, you'll need to move it."

Curran crossed his arms over his chest. "I'm not leaving."

"I'm not asking you to. Just back your truck in between those trees over there. You'll be able to observe but you won't be in our way."

Curran stormed away and moved the truck off the wide driveway and onto the patch of snow-covered lawn, ignoring the tree branches scraping the side of the truck. He drummed his fingers against the steering wheel, watching as the deputies milled around. Minutes passed. Someone called out on a loudspeaker, telling those in the house that they were surrounded, and instructing them to pick up the phone, that the deputies wished to speak to them.

More vehicles arrived, including an additional paramedic van. Exiting one of the county trucks was the sheriff. A gray-haired bear of a man, Curran recognized him from his last re-election campaign.

A knock on the passenger window of the truck startled him, sending his already quickened pulse into orbit. He hit the button to unlock the passenger door and Jamie climbed into the truck. Curran growled at him. "Took you long enough."

"Hey, I figured they didn't need any more cars down here, so I walked." Jamie's face was heavily etched with concern. "What's going on so far?"

"Hell if I know." The need to move, to do something, grew too strong. Curran opened his door. "I'm damned well going to find out, though."

He heard Jamie scramble out of the truck, following him as he strode straight for the sheriff. Another deputy stepped into his path. "Sir, you're too close. Back off."

Curran held his ground, but otherwise ignored the man in front of him. "Sheriff Tanner!"

The sheriff heard him, and Curran waited where he was until the man finished his conversation and walked over to him. The deputy left as Curran introduced himself, then said, "Sheriff, I need to know what is happening, because it appears the answer to that is nothing."

Jamie groaned beside him, muttering something about his failure to be polite.

Sheriff Tanner met his gaze evenly. "Mr. Shaw, there are certain procedures to be followed in a hostage situation."

Curran's temper surged to the surface. "I don't want procedure, dammit. I should be giving you a layout of the house. Aren't your people supposed to storm in there and rescue her? And make no mistake, when you go in, I'm coming along."

The sheriff frowned beneath his gray and brown mustache, laid a heavy hand on Curran's shoulder. "Look, son, I understand how you feel, I really do. But this is not some big action movie, and you're not a hero. If we can get this guy to release Miss Linden by talking to him, we'll do it. I won't lie to you, it may take hours. If we see that isn't going to work, then when we do make a move, you are staying put. You got that?"

"And if I don't?"

Sheriff Tanner's brows raised and his chest puffed out, making him more imposing. "How much good would you be to her if you got shot? Or thrown in jail for interfering with an officer? Do you get my drift, son?"

Curran nodded and the sheriff turned back to the situation at hand. Curran cursed and rubbed his forehead. It wasn't in his nature to wait for other people to handle things. When something needed doing, he jumped in and did it. Victoria was in serious trouble, and there was nothing he could do about it.

Jamie clapped him on the shoulder. "Come on, Curran. You heard the sheriff—this could be a long wait. Let's go back to the truck, bud."

They sat in the cab in silence. The cold seeped into Curran's bones, but if he turned on the engine for the heater, he wouldn't hear what was going on. So he listened, and watched, and froze.

The woman I'm going to marry is being held in that house. The words twisted his heart. He couldn't put his finger on exactly when it happened, but he knew precisely when he'd realized it. Last week, when they went horseback riding, they'd paused at the top of the mountain to take in the breathtaking view of mountains and sky stretching into the distance. Victoria laughed, breaking the silence, and in that moment, in the joy radiating from her, the truth occurred to him.

He loved her.

The understanding satisfied him as much as it shocked him. He'd had his share of relationships, but it was never serious. Well, Amanda had been sort of serious, enough to move in with him. For the most part, though, women decorated his arm and shared his life for a little while, until they tired of one another. Love was never a part of it.

He hadn't exactly come from a family history of solid, life-long relationships, so he didn't have a lot to draw on. But the feeling was there. Warmth and happiness and belonging and comfort, centered at his heart, radiating out to every cell of his body.

He'd always heard, if you have to ask if it's love, it isn't.

Curran didn't have to ask. He knew.

The possibility of pain had struck him with his next breath. What if she didn't love him in return? His love could be a deal-maker or breaker, depending on when he revealed it. Until he was more sure of her feelings, his own would stay locked in his heart. So he hadn't told her.

Orders barked over the loudspeaker yanked him into the moment. What if he never got the chance to tell her? He pulled the tiny box from his coat pocket, popped the lid up. He'd carted the ring around for two days now. A band of platinum. A white marquis diamond as full of flash and fire as her eyes. Matching rubies, her birthstone, flanked the center stone.

He might never get the chance to see it on her finger. To see her draped across his bed wearing nothing but the ring marking her as his.

Curran dropped his head against the seat, squeezed his eyes closed, and breathed deep, trying to keep his anguish locked away. He had to maintain his composure. He'd be useless to her if—no, when, *when* she was released, if he let his heartache and fear get the best of him.

Jamie stirred on the bench seat, and a flutter of gratefulness passed through him. His friend had a knack for knowing how to give support, and at the same time, leave him in peace with his thoughts.

Curran clamped down on the stress-induced craving for a cigarette shivering inside him. The physical need had left him ages ago, but the psychological addiction still haunted him. He carried an 'emergency' pack in the glove compartment, and as his crutch called to him, he gritted his teeth, internally fighting the battle.

The situation with Victoria was completely beyond his control, but dammit, if nothing else, he could at least control his addiction.

* * * *

Victoria scooted up against the wall in the shadowed entry of the house, a few feet from the front door, folding her legs under her. Every muscle screamed with the effort to get her frame off her hands, restrained firmly behind her.

Greg towered over her. "What are you doing?"

"My hands are going numb, I'm just trying to get comfortable."

He leaned down further, until his mouth neared her ear. "Your comfort is the least of my problems, so hold still."

He was trying to sound cool, she knew, but in the light flooding into the house from the police cars, she saw sweat beading on his forehead, dripping down his cheeks. He paced three steps away, three steps back, his hands trembling. His index finger rested on the trigger. One slip, and she could end up bleeding.

"You could let me go, Greg. I'm not worth this," she pleaded, desperately searching for the hot button that would make him release her. "I ruined Nate's life, okay, I admit it, and I'm sorry. Your mother will understand that you can't get the baby. Just let me go before you go to prison too, like Nate." As the words left her mouth, she winced, hoping he didn't decide she was the source of all his misery and shoot her.

"No, here's what I'm gonna do." Desperation made his voice harsh. He yanked her to her feet, turned her so her back was against his chest. "Yeah, you're tall. The only good thing about you, those long legs of yours. They can't take me out without shooting you, too, and they won't take that chance."

"Where are we going? We don't have my keys, remember?"

Her face burned as he hit her cheek with the butt of the gun, scraping her. The warmth of her own blood on her cheek made her want to scream, but hysteria would only make her more likely to end up dead, so she clamped down on the urge to fall apart.

"My car is parked down the street a ways, but they'll try to get me from behind. Oh, hell, this'll be easy. I just threaten to blow your brains out unless they give me the keys to one of the cop cars. Climb in, drive away, get the kid...yeah, piece of cake."

Greg pulled her against him, his arm around her waist, opened the door with two fingers of his gun hand. As the door swung inward, he screamed, "Anybody so much as breathes, the bitch is dead!"

She flinched as the barrel of the gun pressed hard against her right temple. "What if this doesn't work, Greg?"

"Then you die. Showtime," he said, nudging her knee with his. "Move."

* * * *

Curran's heart slammed to a stop when the house door opened. He bolted from the truck, rushed the line of deputies standing against their cars, weapons drawn. One pushed him back, and Jamie grabbed his arms as Victoria emerged from the house, a burly blond guy behind her. The guy had his arm locked around her waist—

And he held a gun to her head.

Fury and fear drove spikes through his heart. Curran surged against Jamie's grip, breaking free for a moment before a Park City officer on site as backup shoved against his chest, sending him back a few steps.

Jamie grabbed him again, hard, pulling his arms behind him. "You're not helping her this way, Curran. Chill out, bud."

His gut knotted at the sight of red streaks trailing down her cheek. "Oh my God, she's bleeding."

Terror stood out starkly on her features, but even from here, the alertness in her eyes gave him hope. She was glancing around, assessing her situation.

And he, with all the money at his disposal, with his power, with his fame, with his ability to turn the world on end to suit himself, could do absolutely nothing for her.

The helplessness, the anger at his impotence gushed through him like water through a bursting dam. None of it mattered. Nothing he spent his life working towards meant a damn thing. The one truly important thing in his life was a finger-squeeze away from lost.

And he stood there, watching.

* * * *

The bright lights made her eyes water. Victoria blinked hard a few times, then focused on the ground at the edges of the lights, trying to see beyond them. Figures. Cops. A lot of them. She'd seen standoffs in the movies. Surely every one of those officers stood with their weapon trained on Greg. Trained on her, really. She made a great shield.

"Throw me the keys to that sedan, officers, and we'll be on our way." Greg managed to sound cocky, though the waver in his voice blew some of the effect. His breathing grew more labored, his arm squeezed against her stomach. He was scared.

There had to be something she could do. If he got her into a car, if they drove away, she knew they wouldn't get where he wanted to go. If they were stopped in the car, well, the baby was for his mother, but Greg wanted vengeance on *her*. If he thought he was going down, there was no doubt in her mind, he'd take her with him.

An officer started forward, keys dangling from his fingers. "I'll give the keys to you."

"Back off!" he shouted, his voice harsh in her ear. "I said throw the fucking keys!"

Greg's sweat and her own blood trickled down her skin. Her stomach churned and rolled. There had to be a way out of this. What could she do? They couldn't take him down with her body shielding him...

When the officer took another step forward, Greg swung the gun away from her temple and shot the deputy in the leg. The man screamed and dropped to the ground. As Greg shifted the gun further to the right, yelling at the cops to get back, Victoria grasped the opportunity to act. She dropped, a dead weight slumping against Greg's arm.

His grip broke and shots rang through the air as Victoria tumbled forward into the snow.

Chapter Fifteen

Noise exploded around her. Gunshots. Shouts.

Cold. Why did snow have to be so cold? With her hands bound behind her, Victoria couldn't push herself up, let alone wipe the flakes from where they burned cold against her skin.

People surrounded her, a sea of black boots and brown uniform pants. Hands grasped her arms, and for a moment, panic ripped through her, but the grip was far more gentle than Greg's had been. Something tugged at her wrists, then her hands shifted apart.

Sheer joy at being alive rushed through her, filled her. The crowd walked her away from the house as she brought her hands in front of her. Pain shot down from her shoulders, but the stretching ache in her hands and wrists as she flexed and turned them felt wonderful.

She looked at the faces around her, one female, the others male, all with shining badges pinned to their chests. She heaved a sigh of relief. The cavalry had come.

She looked back, over the shoulder of an officer. Greg lay in the snow, three officers looking over him, paramedics kneeling to work on him. The snow grew redder as she watched. Blood. Greg's blood. Was it wrong to feel better about that?

Everyone seemed to be talking at once, and she tried to pick out individual questions. Why was her brain moving so slowly? She nodded her head. Yes, she was okay. She felt cocooned, insulated somehow, separate from the bedlam surrounding her. She vaguely remembered feeling this way before. Oh, yes. After Nate left that night, when she'd called the ambulance. She'd been so calm, so removed from everything.

She needed to get warm— "No, I don't want to go to the hospital." She needed a blanket— "I really am fine, I swear." She needed—

"Victoria."

Curran. She honed in on his voice as he pushed past the officers surrounding her, focused on his face, on his amazing, incredible, handsome face, and how in the world had she ever thought him only mildly attractive?

Then her vision clouded. Tears fell from her eyes. A cry filled with all her fears, her need, her love for him tore from her throat.

Her strength flooded out of her as she threw her arms around his neck. Against the warmth of his chest, safe in the tight circle of his arms, she let go and wept.

She's safe. Curran held her as she shuddered against him, sobs wracking her entire frame. Tears obliterated his vision, coursed down his cheeks. She lived and breathed, and he owed God a lifetime worth of good behavior in exchange. He ran his hand up her back, caressed her hair, until he touched a matted spot near her ear and she whimpered in pain.

The son of a bitch had hurt her. A fierce appetite for vengeance, a hunger to tear the guy apart coiled in Curran's gut. The desire to help Victoria swamped his own need, banking his anger. Loathe as he was to separate himself even a hair's width from her, he had to see to her injuries. "Victoria, honey, let me look at you."

He tried to set her back from him, so he could examine her, but she tightened her arms around his neck.

"Please," her smoky voice broke. "Don't let go of me."

His heart ached for her. "Never, honey, never. But you're hurt. Let me see."

She squeezed him again, then relaxed enough for him to ease her back. The skin across her right cheekbone was scraped, bloodied and oozing, beginning to purple. He gently grasped her chin, turned her head to the side. Blood caked her hair behind her left ear and down her pale neck.

Too pale. She trembled in his hands, jacking his protective instinct sky high. He looked past her, focused on the paramedic who stood nearby, holding a blanket. He nodded, and the man draped the blanket over her shoulders. Curran released her long enough to wrap the wool around her, then curved his arm about her waist.

The paramedic examined the cut on her cheek and said, "If you'll come with me, ma'am, we can get you fixed up." She nodded, and Curran walked with her toward the ambulance. She stumbled once, and his heart followed suit. He swept her into his arms and carried her the rest of the way, grateful for the opportunity to hold her.

Victoria felt the tiniest bit more stable, linked to reality by Curran's touch. She swiped at her damp eyes and sat in the ambulance, allowing the paramedics to clean her injuries. Every moment out of Curran's arms was torture, but she couldn't exactly sit on his lap while the EMT bandaged her cheek.

The other paramedic tsked when he cleaned the hair behind her ear enough to look at the wound. "We'll need to take you to the hospital for this one, ma'am. It's a small cut, but it'll still need a couple of stitches."

Curran leaned in to look at the wound and she tightened her grip on his hand. "I don't want to go to the hospital. It takes forever, and if it's stopped bleeding, what does it matter? I don't care if it scars."

"Ma'am, we can't force you to go, but we strongly recommend it," the paramedic said. "It's more than a question of scarring. There's also infection to consider."

A strange, happy look crossed Curran's face, and he ran his thumb along her jaw, then withdrew his hand from hers. "Give me a moment. I have a solution in the truck."

She clamped down on her desperation as he jogged toward the big red pickup. He leaned in through the passenger side and rummaged in the glove compartment for a moment, then returned, his long strides swallowing the snow-blanketed ground.

Curran raised his hand and showed the small tube of liquid stitches to the paramedics. One of them laughed and the other said, "Well, that's definitely an option."

Victoria's brow furrowed. "You're going to glue my cut?"

Curran grinned and nudged her knees, urging her to turn to the right. She shifted, giving him better access to her injury.

"Trust me, honey." She felt pressure as he held the injured skin together, then a cold wetness trickled against her scalp.

"Last fall, Robby took a tumble in the barn and gashed his arm. The thought of stitches terrified him, so the ER doc glued it." He leaned closer, his warm scent comforting her. His breath played against her scalp as he blew softly, helping the glue set.

She sat quietly under his ministrations, everything around them fading. She loved him, with every particle of her being, and he was here for her, had been the whole time. She'd never told him she loved him, never dared lay herself that far on the line.

None of her insecurities mattered now. She wanted him to know, even if this wasn't meant to work out and they went their separate ways after she moved into her new place. Brushing so close to death gave her a new perspective on her life, and she'd never forgive herself if she didn't tell him how she felt.

As Curran declared the glue dry, a deputy approached. "Miss Linden, can you answer a few questions for me?"

"Yes."

"Did you know your assailant?"

"Yes." She looked up at the officer, comforted and encouraged by his gentle smile. The authorities had always been good to her. "His name is Greg Fielder." Curran drew a sharp breath, and she glanced at him. Her heart tripped at the dark anger in his eyes. She focused on the deputy. "I'd feel a whole lot better if you tell me he's dead."

The deputy nodded, as if he understood her need. "Yes, ma'am, he is. Can you tell me what he wanted?"

"His brother went to prison in California for assaulting me, and was killed by another inmate several weeks ago. Greg wanted payback because I testified. In his mind, it was my fault Nate died."

She told him what had happened, from how Greg had surprised her on the porch to the moment she dropped against his arm. The deputy noted her injuries, then closed his book. "You've obviously had a long evening, Miss Linden, so I won't keep you further, except to ask if you know how to reach Mr. and Mrs. Campbell."

She nodded, looking back at the house. "They were in Hong Kong when I spoke to them last. They'll be home in a few weeks. Mr. Campbell's cell number is programmed into my phone, and that's probably in my purse or maybe in the SUV, I really don't remember."

The deputy wrote the information in his book. "We'll look for your phone. If you could come to the station in the next couple of days to sign a statement, that'd be great. How are you feeling?"

"If you're asking if I feel the need to go to the hospital, the answer is no."

The deputy glanced at the paramedic hovering nearby, who shook his head. "She's a lucky lady, came out of this one pretty well."

"Do you have someplace to stay for the next couple of days?" the deputy asked.

The words were so close to those spoken to her in the hospital by Danielle, the abuse center counselor. *Do you have anywhere to go? Can you go home?* Her mother made it clear that home was no longer an option. She'd gotten what she deserved for living with a man who hadn't married her.

Curran's thumb caressed the back of her hand. She turned her gaze to him. She opened her mouth to ask, to beg if necessary, but he spoke first. "I've got her, deputy. She's coming home with me."

The deputy nodded, smiled and walked away. Victoria didn't trust her voice to work. He volunteered to take care of her. Even if he didn't love her, it was more than anyone had ever done for her. She simply stood and stepped into Curran's embrace.

* * * *

"What about Sassy?" Victoria asked as she settled her clothing into the drawers in one of the extra bedrooms.

Curran forced his gaze away, trying to quell the need to see those shirts and underthings in the drawer in his own room. She was fragile and exhausted right now. He wouldn't put that sort of pressure on her. "Jamie took her base cage over to Kelli's. Rob is more than happy to take care of her for a couple of days."

She nodded, then gathered a small stack of clothing she'd left atop the chest and sighed, looking longingly through the open door of her private bathroom. "I'd give anything for a hot shower."

He shook his head. "You can't get the glue on your head wet. However, I did run a bath for you in the master suite. The tub has jets. I thought it would relax you."

Her smile infused him with joy. "Thank you."

He guided her down the hall to his room, showed her into the bathroom, then pressed in the lock on her side of the door. She watched him and said, "You don't have to lock it, Curran."

He ran a hand through his hair and chuckled. "Oh, but I do. You can't relax if you don't feel completely safe."

A look of confusion deepened the amber of her eyes. "I am safe with you."

Her words humbled him. "Thank you. Take your time, honey." He withdrew and closed the door behind him.

Curran sat on the edge of the bed, then picked up his coat from where it lay half over the bedside. He dug into the pocket, withdrew the ring box. He slid the ring out, then tossed the box and the coat across the room, missing the chair he'd aimed for.

He turned the ring, mesmerized by the brilliance of the stones in the soft lamplight. The ring fit over the first knuckle of his pinky, and he left it there, scrubbing his other hand against the side of his face.

Everything had changed tonight. He had changed.

He had to ask her.

* * * *

Victoria stood at the sink and turned her head, carefully cleaning the rest of the blood from her hair, taking care to avoid the cut responsible for the mess. Satisfied that she'd gotten all the gore, she sank into the huge, deep, blue tub, instantly grateful for the gift of a hot soak. She ran the jets for a while to loosen up her knotted back, then turned them off and let the water soothe her until it grew lukewarm. She didn't realize how far her muscles had weakened until she tried to stand up. It took her three attempts before she felt secure enough to actually step out of the tub.

She dried off with a thick white towel. Wow, it was warm. She'd always wondered about people who afforded such luxuries as warming towel racks. The heat of the cotton against her skin made her reconsider. Perhaps the rack should be reclassified as a necessity.

Normally she slept in the nude, but parading around in front of Curran buck-naked wasn't a great idea. She pulled on a pair of flannel pants and a button-front pajama shirt that didn't match. She brushed her teeth, then threw her dirty clothes into the laundry hamper. She jolted to a stop before she closed the lid, realizing what she'd just done. The intimacy of tossing her clothing in with his spread a tingle through her. She couldn't help it. She felt more at home here than anywhere since her childhood. As if she belonged.

She left the clothing and turned the door handle, popping the lock open. She stepped out into his room and found it empty. The master suite was huge, bigger than most apartments she'd lived in. The hardwood in the hallway stopped at the door, with thick ivory wriggle-your-toes-in-it carpeting covering the bedroom floor. The carved mahogany headboard behind the king-size bed set off the navy, probably down-filled, comforter.

Victoria rubbed her eyes and sighed. Who was she kidding? She liked his world, but she didn't belong in it. He was the finest man she'd ever met, and he treated her like gold.

She loved him. But it would never last.

He didn't love her. He'd had ample opportunities to say something, and he hadn't. What other conclusion could she draw?

"Victoria." She turned as he entered the room. She'd heard water running earlier, while she soaked. His damp, tousled hair told her he'd showered. A bright white T-shirt hugged his muscular chest, black sweat pants covered the rest of his fine form.

His eyes swept across her from head to toe, heating her skin before his gaze met hers. "Have a good soak?"

"Wonderful."

He approached her slowly, a whirlwind of emotion in his eyes. "I, uh, I know you're exhausted, but I have some things to say, and they really can't wait."

Ominous sounding words. She wasn't in the right frame of mind to consider what he meant, what he planned to say, before he actually said it. She sat on the edge of the bed, because it was the closest piece of furniture. He paused a moment, staring at the bed. Then he shook his head and sat beside her.

He took her hand, rubbing his thumb over her knuckles. "My timing is awful. But I've been waiting for the perfect moment, and after tonight, all I can think of is how much time I've wasted."

He cupped her chin and leaned toward her. He kissed her, a tender touch that brought fresh tears to her eyes. He eased back, traced her jaw with his fingertip. "I love you, Victoria. You are the most amazing, real, incredible woman I've ever known. You're worth more to me than everything I've spent my life pursuing. I like the man I've become with you, and I never want to go back to the man I was without you." He brought her hand up to his mouth, kissed her fingers. "Marry me. Please."

A dream. That explained it. But a glorious one she never wanted to wake from. She took his face in her hands and kissed him to be sure he was real and she was awake. When her voice finally worked, she managed to say, "I love you, Curran. You are the first man I ever loved, and you will be the last."

Her words visibly choked him up. He blinked and swallowed hard, a half-smile crossing his lips. "Is that a yes?"

"Yes!"

He lifted her left hand, and she watched as, his hands trembling, he slid a delicate, perfect ring onto her third finger. He stared at it for a moment, ran his finger along its edge, then drew her into his arms.

They held each other for a long time, until a yawn forced its way out of her. He loosened his hold on her, leaned back to look at her. Ugh, what a way to ruin a perfect moment. She smiled and shrugged. "Sorry. It isn't the company."

He laughed softly. "I know, you've had a hell of a day, but I was impatient."

"You're forgiven."

She went to stand, but stopped when he wrapped his fingers around her forearm. A serious look crossed his face, and she waited, her heart beginning to pound.

"Victoria, it's grown more and more difficult to sleep alone over the time you've been in my life. After tonight...I'm not trying to pressure you, but I need to feel you in my arms. I swear, I'll keep my hands to myself. I just know I won't sleep at all with you down the hall."

* * * *

Curran turned back the covers for her and watched her settle herself on the left side of the bed, trying to shake the image lodged in his brain of her naked save the ring. It was a powerful vision to say the least, but tonight was not the night for it. Tonight she needed comfort and cuddling, not some desperate, sex-starved monster attacking her. As much as he wanted to fully make her his, the fact she wore his ring would have to be enough.

He took the right side of the bed. He'd have been happy just knowing she lay near him, but as he pulled the comforter over them, she scooted across the no-man's land in the center of the bed to lie at his left side. He shifted his arm around her, and she snuggled close, tucking her head under his chin, draping her arm across his chest.

His traitorous body perked up, but he concentrated on the incredible comfort of her warmth along his side. He stroked her hair with his left hand, careful to avoid her wound. His right hand stroked her arm. He took a deep breath to steady his pounding heart, then let it out slowly so it didn't sound like a disgruntled sigh. She was giving him everything he could ask of her, and meeting her needs took a far higher priority than his own.

Victoria knew she couldn't possibly fall asleep like this, with his fingertips caressing her arm through her flannel sleeve, his other hand toying with her hair.

He loved her. He wanted to marry her. Tonight he stood beside her, supported her, gave her everything she needed, and asked for nothing in return, except that she marry him. Even that was a gift for her.

And what had she given, except her consent? He'd laid himself on the line for her and she'd offered nothing of herself, not really. She'd said she loved him, but it wasn't enough. Part of her still held back.

"Curran...how do you feel about a fast wedding?"

He stilled. "My love, you say the word and I'll have us in Vegas and married before sunrise."

That willingness to dive in headfirst was what she desperately wanted to hear. And now, she needed to face her fears head on. She needed to commit herself to him, to bind herself to him. To trust him completely, with her entire being. She knew Curran would never back out after putting the ring on her finger. In his mind, that was as solid as saying *I do*. The most definitive way she could seal the deal was with herself.

She trailed her fingers across his chest, a thrill zipping through her at the hitch in his breathing. She continued, tracing down the center of his abdomen to his waistband and back up, across the firm muscles of his stomach. His arm tensed around her, but otherwise he lay motionless, letting her touch him. Irritated at the barrier of cotton between her hand and his skin, she grasped his shirt at his waist and pulled up. His right hand curved around her wrist.

She boosted herself up on her elbow, gazed down into his eyes. The depth of desire in them startled her. Her own craving for him flared hot in her belly. "Please, Curran. I need this. I need to touch you."

"I don't want to do anything you'll regret. Are you sure?"

She nodded and he slid his hand up her arm to her nape, urging her mouth down to his. She kissed him, tasted him, while she finished pulling his shirt up, baring his chest. She splayed her fingers against his heated skin, feeling his heart leap against her touch. She shifted down along his body, then pressed her lips to his chest. He gasped, and her pulse throbbed, reveling in the scent of his freshly scrubbed skin. She planted a trail of kisses along every band of hard muscle on his chest, his abdomen.

The longer she touched him, the more the ache inside her grew. She wanted him, wanted to feel him inside her. Still, the yearning for him grew sweeter as it intensified. She wanted this to last.

She rose over him, throwing the covers back, then straddled his hips. The hardness of his erection sent bright, hot need spiraling to her core. She pulled his shirt higher. He shifted to allow her to lift the cotton over his head, off his arms. He brought his arms down, resting his hands on her hips.

As she adjusted her legs closer to his sides, she slid her hips forward. He groaned and bucked against her once, then stilled himself and closed his eyes, breathing hard, his fingers flexing against her waist.

She didn't want his hands still, she wanted them on her, caressing her. She leaned down, ran her tongue across his lips then kissed him deeply. She sat up again, began unbuttoning her shirt.

He stared at her fingers as she worked, his gaze dark and hot. She reached the final button and a moment's uncertainty made her shiver. The intensity in his eyes fueled her determination. She shrugged the flannel from her shoulders.

He swallowed hard, shifting under her again. His hands tensed, grasping her hips, holding her against him.

He was waiting for permission, she realized. He was letting her set the pace, giving her full control.

She knew how much Curran disliked being the passive one, letting others be in charge. Yet, in this most intimate of negotiations, he gave her the lead. Her heart swelled with the love of him, recognizing his love for her. Even if she wanted to stop now, he'd abide by her wishes.

Stopping was the last thing she wanted to do. "Touch me, Curran. Please."

She didn't have to ask him twice. He lifted his hands, touched his fingertips to her collarbone, drew them lightly down over her breasts, across her ribs and stomach, leaving her skin alert and tingling. He caressed her, driving the throbbing inside her to a faster tempo.

It was safe to be in control, to be calling the shots, but Victoria recognized she had one hurdle to jump in order to fully give herself to him. She had to let him take charge. The only man she ever submitted to had used his power to hurt her. She had to trust Curran. She'd never be entirely over the past until she gave the control to him.

She lay against him, skin to skin, kissed him thoroughly, then wrapped her arms around his neck. She knew what she wanted to do, what she needed to do. How did she communicate that to him?

He stroked along her spine, pressed his lips to her shoulder, then gently shifted her onto her back. He rose up on his elbow, touched her face. "Do you want this, Victoria?"

She breathed the word *yes*, and his mouth covered hers as he took the power and control from her in a fluid, seamless shifting.

Curran's pulse pounded as he pulled back to look at her. He traced her features with his fingertips, losing himself in her trusting gaze. Victoria's willingness to let him love her humbled him, his heart so full of feeling for her it hurt. To his knowledge, he'd never disappointed his lovers, but this was the only time it ever really mattered. Knowing Victoria, knowing how difficult this decision must be for her, he was determined to make this the best experience he could. To somehow show her, in every touch, how very much he loved her.

He concentrated on kissing her, letting his fingers play across her skin. He dipped his head, followed the same path across her creamy flesh with his mouth, with his tongue. He lavished attention on her neck, her breasts, her abdomen, until her breath came fast and shallow, until she clutched at his shoulders, digging into his skin with her short nails. Only then did he slip his hand beneath the waist of her pajama pants.

Her lack of panties nearly undid him, as he caressed her hips, then reached lower. A moan thrummed deep in her throat, and she went completely still, barely breathing as he touched her. Concern flooded him. Was she struggling with her decision to let him make love to her?

Curran raised his head to look at her, relieved to see passion in her eyes rather than distress. "All good?"

"Oh, yeah," she said softly. "Very, very good."

He grinned, realizing her stillness came from focusing on his touch. He kissed her, then sat up. She lifted her hips as he tugged her pajamas off, quickly shedding his own.

He stretched out beside her, returned to touching her. He explored every inch of her, with his fingertips, with his mouth. She was perfectly real, from her lovely breasts to the pale, narrow marks networked across her skin from carrying a child. She'd carry his child one day. For now, she was all he needed. And she was his.

His own excitement and joy increased as he discovered her, learned the places, the touches that made her gasp, made her arch against him, made her cry out.

When he was sure neither of them could hold out any longer, he reached across the bed to the nightstand for one of the packets in the drawer.

Victoria watched him, the stark need etched on his face shooting a hot thrill through her veins, all the way to her toes. She feathered her fingers into his hair as he sheathed himself and nudged her legs open with his. He poised over her. She touched his face, his chest, relishing the desire in his eyes, the heat that echoed her own.

And then, as her gaze held his, he slowly joined them together. Her body stretched and gave, allowing him to fill her. He moved carefully at first, and she felt her soul twining with his as the rhythm built. The passion, the brilliant melding of emotion and physical craving grew so great she couldn't bear it. She closed her eyes and clung to him. He held her as they drove each other higher, as every part of her seemed to swirl downward, drawn like light to a collapsed star, until everything pulled together in such exquisite sharpness she couldn't breathe.

She went over the edge, and the release rolled through her in wave after wave, sending everything fluttering back to its proper place inside her. Curran shuddered as she clenched around him. With one last thrust, he met her in sheer bliss. He collapsed against her. She wrapped her arms and legs around him, relishing his weight, feeling completely whole and absolutely loved for the first time in her life.

After a moment he stirred, shifted his weight off to her side, pulling her close to him. He deposited the gentlest of kisses on her forehead, her temple, her chin, her mouth. He looked into her eyes. "I love you."

Happy tears sprang into her eyes and she smiled up at him. "I love you, too."

He wiped the tears from her cheeks, then threaded his fingers through her hair and smiled. "You realize, of course, that you're stuck with me now, my soon-to-be-Mrs. Shaw."

She laughed and hugged him. "Mr. Shaw, I wouldn't have it any other way."

Epilogue

The Salt Lake International Airport was bustling on the tenth of May. Curran sat drumming his fingers against his thigh, watching passengers lining up to board, others disembarking from planes and hurrying down the corridor.

Mum would surely cry. Hell, he'd probably cry, just to have survived the flight.

He glanced at his phone display. He had about fifteen minutes until boarding call, and the sedatives the physician had given him were starting to kick in. If they'd timed it right, and his body responded properly to the medication, he should be relaxed enough to get on the plane, then conk out for a few hours. He had tablets to get him home to Oz and back again, hopefully without his usual panic attack surfacing.

It was all hopeful thinking at this point. It wasn't the first time he'd tried medication over the years, but nothing before had worked well enough to get him on the plane.

His tapping fingers stilled when Victoria captured them with hers. She wrapped her arm around his shoulders and kissed him on the cheek. "Feeling loopy yet, sweetie?"

"A little." He looked into her bright eyes, filled with love for him, and sighed. "What if I can't do this?"

"That's a possibility. The doc said sometimes situational panic attacks are too strong to control with anything short of general anesthesia."

"So if I still can't board that plane—"

"Then we say, hey, we tried, and we send our wedding picture with Kelli." She stroked his face. "Curran, it'll be all right."

He lifted her hand, kissed her knuckles. "And you won't think I am a hopeless wuss?"

"She won't," said Jamie from the seat opposite his. "But I will."

"You know, mate, I do have the power to fire you."

Jamie folded his newspaper and leveled a look at him. "I fully expect you to at least demote me when you move company headquarters to Salt Lake. Which, by the way, I hope you hurry up and do. Kelli won't marry me until we can stay in Park City, and I can't do that until you move my office."

Kelli approached with Rob in tow. "Sorry, my love, this boy is not going to school in Los Angeles."

"There are private schools."

Rob hopped onto the seat next to Jamie. "But I like my school."

Jamie grinned at the boy and ruffled his hair. "I know you do, bud. Don't worry. Uncle Curry and I will iron this whole thing out while you're on summer break." He raised an eyebrow at Curran. "Yes?"

Curran broke into a smile. "Yeah, as soon as we get back from Australia, we'll get to work."

The boarding call for their flight's first class passengers sounded over the loudspeaker. Curran's heartbeat doubled and his mouth went dry. He met Victoria's gaze, a glimmer of worry behind her smile. He stood up with her and the world tilted slightly. Together, they walked toward the attendant, Victoria's arm supporting him around his waist. She handed their boarding passes to the smiling young woman, who welcomed them aboard.

They stepped into the skyway. The jet itself was only a few yards' walk through this tube. His lungs constricted. Victoria stopped and turned to him, placed her hand against his cheek. "Curran, breathe. Come on, yoga breaths, with me."

She breathed slowly, deeply, and Curran focused on her, blocking everything else out of his mind. He followed her, drew air with her, until his head cleared a little, and his heartbeat no longer felt like a jackhammer.

Somehow, he got through the rest of the skyway and found himself settled in his aisle seat. Victoria stowed their carry-ons and sat beside the window. When they eventually flew over the ocean, she'd close the little shade over the portal so he couldn't see out. If he couldn't see the ocean, he could pretend he was still safe over dry land.

As Jamie, Kelli and Rob settled into their seats across the aisle, Victoria bracketed his face with her hands and kissed him hard. She eased back and looked into his eyes. "You're going to be okay, Curran. You can do this."

He nodded and snuggled her close to him, breathing her perfect scent deep into his lungs. Yeah, the medication was making a difference. But the biggest difference of all was right here, in his arms. She faced her deepest fears, he could damn well face his. And with Victoria by his side, he could do anything.

His mum was going to love meeting his bride.

About The Author

Lucy Francis grew up with characters living in her head, clamoring for attention. Whether those characters were elves, knights, aliens or earthlings, she listened and wrote their tales, which always included love. She still listens, plays matchmaker, and scribbles the resulting stories. Lucy has lived all over the United States, but calls Utah home. She lives with her husband, five children, and a pet menagerie that once included nine different species. She loves horses, fixing broken things, Irish dancing and tending the urban forest she planted in her front yard.

Visit Lucy Francis at:

www.lucyfrancis.net

www.facebook.com/lucyfrancisauthor

Twitter: @LucysKissyBooks

Here is a sneak preview of

Finding Refuge

By Lucy Francis

Coming May, 2012

Chapter One

Travis Holt sat in his truck, eyes closed, fingers clenched around the steering wheel. Melancholy seeped out of the prison inside him and he brutally shoved it back into place. Lunch hadn't helped his mood any, and he still had several hours of work left for today. He didn't have the time to feel anything.

A gentle breeze wafted through the half-lowered window, brushing over his face and ruffling his hair. He drew a deep breath of air touched with the scent of warming earth. The smell of spring that was so late in coming this year. He missed the way things used to be, when spring arrived on schedule in March, and summer was in full bloom by the time the end of May rolled around. June was always hot when he was a kid, but the last several years in Utah had seen snow in the mountains and cold, wet weather in Salt Lake valley until the middle of June.

He hated it. Just one more frustrating thing in his life that he couldn't control. The misery squeezed him hard, and he opened his eyes and fought back: turning on the truck, cranking up the stereo, heading for the next stop in his packed Monday list of crap he had to do. Thinking about the past didn't do him any good at all. Neither did the present, really, but at least if he stayed rooted in the here and now, living moment by moment, the knowledge that he was a failure didn't swamp him completely.

He sang with the rock anthem pounding through the speakers, distracting himself from the weight of his life. Because the awful truth nagging at the edges of his thoughts was that he'd reached the limit of what he could carry. One more thing dropped on top would push him under. He'd drown. If he didn't acknowledge that fact, he'd make it through every day, no matter what hit him.

Travis pulled into the driveway of the sprawling, French Country-style mansion sitting high on the Mount Olympus foothills. His client had spent a hell of a lot of money for a spectacular view lot, and Travis believed the man truly got what he paid for, with the primarily glass rear of the new house facing the valley. As he exited his truck, he noted the vehicles of the plumbing and electrical subcontractors parked on the drive. He crossed the path through the newly landscaped yard to the covered front porch.

His parents would have preferred he live in a home like this, preferably near them in Federal Heights. But he'd never give up his little chalet in Midway. The mountain town gave him room to clear his head. Living there, even with the daily commute, kept him sane.

Travis walked into the high-ceilinged, stone-paved foyer. Plastic sheeting covered the floor, protecting it from dirty workboots. Martin Delgado, the job supervisor, stood beyond the foyer in the open, airy sitting room, talking on his cell phone. Travis waved, and Delgado quickly ended his call.

"Hiya, boss," Delgado said, clipping his phone onto his belt.

"Are we on schedule?"

Delgado snorted. "Of course, man, you think I'd let you down?"

Travis smiled. "Good, because I'm talking to Mr. Jasper five times a day, and if this place goes into overtime, I may strangle him before he ever gets the keys."

"I feel for you. It's almost done. Rachel's putting up the fixtures and plates and Harley is just about done with the finish plumbing."

"Okay. I'm going to have a look around so I can tell Jasper I was here in person, and everything's fine."

Delgado laughed and reached for his phone when it beeped. "You do that, Travis. I'm glad I'm not you."

Yeah. Being me is even less fun that it looks. Travis went up the wide, lavishly milled, curving stairs, meaning to give the house a look from the top floor down. His intentions flew out the nearest window when he walked into the master suite and found himself staring up at the most perfectly curved rear-end he'd ever seen poured into faded denim. Sweetly rounded below a narrow waist, it was the sort of ass that women were forever trying to work off even though men begged for more.

He refocused, shaking off the buzz of appreciation zipping straight to his groin, and forced himself to take in the whole picture. The woman stood too far up for safety on a six-foot ladder, facing the opposite wall. She twisted a light bulb into the pewter fixture on the coved ten-foot ceiling. His gaze wandered up to dark brown, wavy hair. Pulled into a ponytail at the nape of her neck, the waves cascaded down the length of her red t-shirt, swaying at the top of her hips. He'd expected to find Rachel Garrett, his electrician. This tiny, curvy thing was definitely not Rachel.

"Who are you?" he asked.

She didn't respond. He stepped forward. "Are you here with Rachel?" He reached out and tapped the heel of her red tennis shoe. "Hello?"

She jumped at his touch, turning toward him as she took a hasty step down.

Her foot missed the ladder rung.

Travis reacted instantly, catching her as she fell, stepping back so she didn't hit the ladder.

A surge of fire blew through his system on the heels of the adrenaline rush, the heat pulsing through his chest as he held her, as his mind identified where he ended and she began. One arm held her around her waist, the other wrapped across her legs below her hips. For a moment, she stayed where she'd landed, half over his right shoulder, then she straightened. That position brought her breasts to eye-level.

Her t-shirt, caught between them, molded against her, making it damn near impossible for Travis to swallow.

Heart pounding, Travis forced his gaze upward, meeting her dark brown eyes. The confusion in them threw ice water on his hormones. Small hands pressed against his shoulders and he loosened his hold on her, trying to ignore his physical interest as she slid down his frame to the floor.

She backed away a step, her gaze on her feet, her cheeks dusted pink, and pulled earbuds from her ears. The music blared through them. Ah. She hadn't heard him.

"Hey, sorry I startled you," he said. The rest of his words died in his throat when her gaze lifted and she smiled. A sweet, welcoming smile that lit up her entire self. It slid down inside him, stunning him and leaving a trail of light. No one he'd ever known had a smile like that.

"It's okay. Thanks for catching me before I hurt myself." She hitched her thumb over her shoulder at the ladder. "Guess I should have taken the 'do not stand on this step' warning seriously, huh?" Her voice was low, with a slight whiskey-rasp.

It was a punch to the gut after anticipating that she'd sound like a little girl to match her small size. She couldn't be more than, what, five-two? A grin spread across his face, he couldn't help it. "Pretty sure the warning is there for a reason. Are you here with Rachel?"

"Yeah, I'm visiting her, and *attempting* to help." She shrugged. Her smile faded and the part of Travis that had revived inside because of her smile died again, too. It stung. How could he fix that?

"You were doing great, I messed you up." He held out a hand. "I'm Travis Holt."

Her handshake was surprisingly firm. "Andri Miller."

"Andri? Interesting name."

"Short for Andromeda. I know, I know, my mother is Greek, so I come by it honestly," she added hastily as his smile widened.

"No, it's a beautiful name." The sweet blush colored her cheeks again and his stomach flip-flopped.

Her gaze shifted to the right and she said, "You about got me killed, sending me up on a ladder like that."

Travis turned to see his electrician walk in. Rachel Garrett, dark red hair looped through a baseball cap, looked Andri over. "You appear unscathed."

Andri pointed at Travis. "Thanks to the hero."

A sharp jolt of pleasure hit him. He'd love to play the successful hero again, anytime. He bit down on the thought that her need for a hero was his fault. He refused to let his failings shadow her words.

Rachel stood beside him, tall enough to meet him eye to eye. "Yep, that's Travis. He spends his copious spare time rescuing damsels in distress." She nudged him with her shoulder, and that contact from his lifelong friend snapped him out of the magnetic pull emanating from Andri.

Shaken by his reaction, he steeled himself and glanced at his watch. "Unfortunately, speaking of spare time, I have none. Rach, you'll be finished today?"

"Yes. Another half-hour maybe, and we're out of here."

"Just what I wanted to hear, thank you." He nodded at Andri. "Nice meeting you."

She smiled as she said goodbye, but he yanked his gaze away from her. That smile was kryptonite, best avoided since he couldn't hope to fight the way she drew him without even trying.

He did a high-speed check of the rest of the mansion, pausing only to confer briefly with Delgado. The plumber had already finished and gone. Inspection complete, he beat a hasty retreat to the truck.

Andri. He'd known Rachel forever and never run into this friend of hers before. She'd said she was just visiting Rach, so chances were that he'd probably never see her again. And while that realization pained him, it also relieved him.

There were two kinds of women. Those who played, and those who didn't. Andromeda Miller was decidedly one who didn't. She sent off waves of home and hearth and 'till death do us part' vibes. Absolutely off-limits, and he knew precisely why—stability was the one thing he needed, the one thing he wanted. The one thing he didn't deserve.

It was also a hell of a catch-22. If she wasn't what he thought...well, he'd paid the price for mistaking a player for a stayer before, with his ex. And if she really was what he read her to be, a good girl…damn, he couldn't go there. He'd only end up failing her somehow, like he failed everyone else, and in the process, she'd learn to hate him. He knew if he ever saw that light in her eyes replaced with hatred, it would utterly destroy him.

One more thing added to the pile. No. He simply wouldn't allow himself to go there. Period. No matter how much he wanted to cling to the lifeline her smile had thrown him.

Praise for *The Silence of the Volcano*

Almudena Konrad's powerful memoir not only defines a very personal legacy of courage and love but gives us a life-affirming tale. *The Silence of the Volcano* is an amazingly honest work, an interwoven tapestry of personal and professional experiences, and a tale of fortitude, full of tenderness and gentle humor. This is a fascinating, moving and vigorous book.

— Carlota Caulfield, author of *A Mapmaker's Diary.*

This powerful memoir takes you deep into the heart of one woman's struggles and triumphs as she navigates a landscape of adversity and self-discovery to find the fiery determination to conquer obstacles that once seemed insurmountable. This is a story of unearthing the courage to defy societal expectations, breaking free from stifling conventions, and embracing one's true self. Prepare to be inspired and moved.

—Kirsten T. Saxton, author of *The Passionate Fictions of Eliza Haywood.*

With unabashed candor, Almudena shares a life of courage, survival, loss, strength, and love. Her narrative voice captivates readers with its blend of gentleness and emotional depth. Almudena's determination to forge a life uniquely her own amidst challenges is inspiring to all who journey with her.

—Susan Wang, Computer Science Professor.

A moving story of struggle, perseverance, and determination. Beautifully written! Uplifting and powerful!

—*The San Francisco Girls Book Club.*

FIRST EDITION

Designed by David Prendergast

Hardback ISBN 979-8-9893068-0-0

eBook ISBN 979-8-9893068-1-7

Paperback ISBN 979-8-9893068-2-4

TheSilenceOfTheVolcano.com